THE GRUDGE

KAZ ELLIOTT

For David - without whom this book might not have been written.

Thank you for your continued support and encouragement.

ACKNOWLEDGEMENTS

I would like to thank Nicky Moore for her continued support and encouragement. In addition Carol Matthews, Christine Angilletta, Mand Ellis, Jacqueline Phillips, Tracie Beck, Lisa Canning and everyone else who has sent me their good wishes over the past few months throughout this incredible journey– thank you for believing in me. Also, a big thank you to my favourite Welshman for lending me your name (you know who you are!)

I would also like to thank my partner, David, for his patience and time prior to publication. It was gROYt!

Finally, I would like to say a very special 'Thank You' to the lovely Jenny Cullinan.

You were my very first customer, and your incredible support and feedback is so appreciated.

kazelliott4@gmail.com

PROLOGUE

"Say goodbye to your wife and child, Max, and remember – you could have prevented this. You could have done as you were told and just paid up but you decided to gamble with their lives. I just hope you can live with your fucking conscience, Max, I really do"

As he said the words, Tommy was reminded of the reason he was doing all this; the reason behind all the hatred he felt for Max Reid and he began to cry silently, memories of that terrible day flooding his conscious mind.

As he pulled back the safety catch, a red mist descended over Tommy McLaughlin. In his mind's eye, Max Reid was on his knees in front of him begging not just for the lives of his wife and child, but also for his own life to be spared. Tommy fantasised that he was the man in control, in charge of the situation. He got to decide whether the bastard lived or died. Well, today was the day that he was going to make Max Reid wish that he *was* dead.

Tommy took the phone from his ear and held it up in mid-air. Then he fired the gun twice in rapid succession. The sound of gunfire reverberated around the room - an ear-splitting sound that echoed off the high ceiling - causing Tommy to drop the phone. It landed on the coffee table, bounced off it and ended up on the floor. Tommy put down the gun, placing both hands over his ears. The noise in this enclosed environment had almost deafened him.

Max heard the gunshot, rapidly followed by a second shot - a 'double tap' execution. Letting the receiver fall from his hand he collapsed onto the floor, his mouth falling open in a silent scream. Suddenly every thought, every emotion he had been battling to keep in check, came to the fore – concentrating his mind on the terrible, gut-wrenching truth. It was more than he could bear. The bastard had killed them – killed them both.

With a devastating sense of finality Max Reid knew that it was all over. Jenna was dead; their unborn child was dead, both of them murdered in cold blood and he had done nothing to save them. He had gambled with their lives and he had lost.

Max felt that he might actually stop breathing right then and there, such was his pain. He had lost his reason for living, the reason he got up every morning. Jenna had been his life's blood. He had worshipped her. Their child hadn't even taken his first breath and now he was gone from him forever.

He would never get to meet his first child. Never know the joy of fatherhood. Never hold his wife in his arms again.

At that moment, Max Reid did not want to go on living, and Tommy McLaughlin had his revenge.

CHAPTER ONE

Eileen Kelly had had enough! She stomped to the bottom of the stairs, one hand on her hip, the other clutching a tea towel, and vented her frustration at the top of her lungs. "Jenna, would you get your arse out of that fucking bed? I'm sick to the back teeth of callin' you, girl. Your breakfast's goin' cold here!"

Jenna Kelly rolled over and pulled the duvet over her head. She was sick too – sick of this place, sick of her life and most of all – sick of hearing the sound of her Mother's coarse language and screeching voice bawling up at her every morning. Jesus! What she wouldn't give for a place of her own. It was ten thirty on a Saturday morning, and Jenna Kelly couldn't see a single reason to be out of bed.

Eileen sat down heavily at the formica-topped kitchen table and poured herself another cup of tea from the pot. Sighing, she lit a cigarette and drew deeply on it. It was the same every Saturday. Jenna would be hung over from last night's partying and no doubt in a foul mood; Eileen would put her breakfast in front of her, and she would push it away. Eileen had long since given up hoping for a peaceful life, especially with that lazy mare and her tantrums.

Eileen Kelly had been born in the East End almost thirty four years ago to an Irish dock worker, Joseph Kelly, and his downtrodden wife, Sara. Life had been tough growing up - really tough. They barely had enough to make ends meet most days and had to survive on their wits. Clothing was

11

always hand-me-downs, or whatever their Mother could afford from the local second-hand stall and dinner invariably consisted of mutton stew and chunks of stale bread or corned beef and mashed potatoes. Even that wasn't consistent. Eileen and her three brothers Aidan, Joey and Danny had gone to bed many times with nothing in their bellies but the growling of hunger pangs and the knowledge that breakfast time wouldn't bring any respite.

Strict Roman Catholics, Mr and Mrs Joseph Kelly attended Mass regularly and taught their off-spring to fear the Lord. The priest was forever calling in of a Sunday evening, regaling them all with tales of hell-fire and damnation. Sara Kelly made him welcome with a place by the wood stove. After all, it didn't do to upset Father O'Malley, him having a direct line to The Almighty and all! Often she would dish out a smaller portion of stew for herself and the children in order that Father O'Malley could be properly catered for. The children dreaded him calling around, knowing that his visit would mean endless quizzes on their knowledge of the Good Book and Hail Mary's before bed.

At sixteen Eileen had left school with no qualifications and had found herself a job in the corner shop, working for Big Georgie Hamilton and his wife, Dorothy – or Dottie as she preferred to be called. They were nice people to work for and had taken the young girl under their wing, always ready with a mug of steaming hot tea on a cold winter's morning when Eileen arrived at six-thirty to help with the newspaper deliveries. The wages weren't much but, after paying her keep, Eileen still had a couple of quid to herself. She saved what little she could in a jar, which she kept under her bed, and promised herself that she would buy her family something nice for Christmas this year.

She would often take the jar and empty the entire contents out onto her eiderdown, before counting it and returning it to the hiding place under the old, iron bedstead. She would feel a warm glow as she counted, dreaming of the things she would buy her Mother and Father, and of the looks of delight on her brother's faces when they opened her presents to them. Eileen loved her family very much, even if her parents were a bit too strict at times. She knew it was only because they wanted to protect her from sin. At least, that's what they told her.

Eileen was a good girl, an obedient daughter. She worked hard but apart from her shifts in the little shop she saw very little of the outside world. Her Mother often needed her to help out at home with the younger ones, and by the time they were all bathed and fed of an evening Eileen had very little time left to enjoy anything she might want to do. Eileen liked to read whenever she had the chance. She loved books and devoured them with fervent interest, preferring historical novels and romance. Her Mother frowned upon the latter, calling them 'the devil's own doing' so Eileen kept her romance books at the back of the little shelf on her bedroom wall, hidden from view by an encyclopaedia Britannica and a copy of The Good Book.

One cold January afternoon Eileen had been stacking the shelves with tins of beans and corned beef when Old Mary came hobbling into the shop. Old Mary lived down the street from Eileen and they often saw each other in passing, stopping to chat a little on the way. Eileen liked Old Mary very much, thought her kind and amusing.

On this particular day Old Mary looked tired and, being a helpful sort, Eileen offered to carry home the shopping bags for her as she was almost finished her shift. Old Mary accepted the offer gratefully and, as they made their way along the narrow streets back home, they chatted about this and that, laughing at each other's tales.

Eileen talked about her three younger brothers and the scrapes they got themselves into and Old Mary would howl with laughter as Eileen described in detail how their father had caught them shinning up next door's apple trees and had shouted at them so loud they had almost fallen out of the branches in fright. The three of them had been taken upstairs that evening and given the belt.

Eileen remembered their howls of pain as Joseph Kelly administered his own brand of hell onto their backsides. They hadn't been able to sit down properly for a week afterwards, and had promised faithfully to never again climb next door's trees. A few days later they were caught climbing the trees in the park and when Joseph reminded them of their promise they argued that the only promise they had made to him concerned their next door neighbour's trees, and therefore they hadn't broken their word. Joseph Kelly gave all three of them an extra wallop across the arse that afternoon for their damned cheek – and they never climbed another tree.

Eileen carried the heavy shopping bag into Old Mary's kitchen and put them onto the wooden kitchen table. She loved this house, with its smell of bacon and eggs lingering in the faded wallpaper, and the kettle always boiling on the little gas cooker. She accepted an offer of a cup of tea and the two sat, warming their hands on the steaming hot mugs, as the evening drew in and the street lamps lit up the narrow, terraced street outside.

"I've been meaning to ask you, Eileen, how do you fancy coming over to my sister's house with me on Saturday evening? I promised her I'd pay her a visit and to be honest, love, I can't face the journey on my own. My legs ain't what they used to be and I worry about fallin' in the road" Old Mary smiled at her from the rim of her mug. "You could come with me for a couple of hours - help me out like, and my sister's got a daughter about the same age as you. You never know, you two might hit it off, like – become friends. What d'you say, love?"

Eileen considered this for a few moments. She had to admit she would love the chance to get out of the house for a few hours, and Old Mary was good company even if she was nigh on seventy. Who knows? She might like her sister too and make a new pal to hang about with at the weekend. She nodded enthusiastically. "I'd like that very much, Mary, thank you for asking me; I will need to ask my parents of course, but I can't see why they'd refuse"

Smiling now, she thanked Old Mary for the tea and promised to ask her Mother as soon as she got home and let her know the answer on her way home from work tomorrow.

It was an excited Eileen Kelly that lay her head down to sleep that night. She was *invited* somewhere! She was going to visit, and she couldn't wait for Saturday to come.

CHAPTER TWO

That was how it had started. Old Mary had taken Eileen to visit her younger sister, Joanie, and her seventeen year old daughter, Margaret. The two younger girls had hit it off almost from the start and spent hours upstairs in the little two up, two down terraced house, swapping clothes and trying on Margaret's wigs and fur coats. It was a scream and the two girls could often be heard falling about with laughter as the two older women sat below chatting over a glass of sherry.

Eileen's parents didn't mind if she went visiting with Old Mary. After all, she was a church goer and a good Catholic. They couldn't see any reason why their eldest child shouldn't have a little innocent fun.

Often they would stroll home together as it started going dark and Old Mary would say "Oh, be a good girl now, Eileen, and come and help me over the step". Eileen knew what this meant – she wanted her to stay for a nightcap, although Eileen couldn't touch the sherry herself- her being only sixteen. If her parents caught a whiff of alcohol on her breath that would be the end of her Saturday visits to Joanie's house, and Eileen couldn't bear the thought of never going there again so whenever Old Mary offered her a sip she would shake her head and laugh " Now, Mary, you know I'm not going to drink it, so why would you offer it?" to which Old Mary would reply "Aye, but if I didn't offer ye any you'd be goin' about telling folk what a tight-arse I am, and I couldn't have that, now could I?" Then she would laugh loudly and pour herself a generous measure of sherry 'for medicinal purposes'.

Eileen would sit by the fire sipping a glass of lemonade and keep the old woman company until the clock struck eleven then she would bid her goodnight and make her way across the street and up the stairs to her bed.

Eileen loved Old Mary. She was hilarious when she had had a few drinks and would have Eileen in stitches with tales of the things she got up to in her younger years. Eileen would squeal with laughter whenever Old Mary started on about her ex-husband Albie. "He was a bad bastard" she would start. "Always did think with what he had *down there*, that one" she'd say, nodding at her own crotch as she spoke. "Trouble is – he didn't have two bloody brain-cells in *that* either!" Eileen chose not to point out that, actually, nobody had any brain cells in their gonads - instead she just held her ribs and howled laughing at the old woman's obvious disappointment.

One such night, as Old Mary sat reminiscing, Eileen asked her why she had never had children. Old Mary had stared back at Eileen with tired, rheumy eyes and an intense sadness came over her.

"I 'ad a daughter once" she faltered, the memory obviously still painful. "My Alice" she smiled up at Eileen now and a tear formed at the corner of her eye. "God took her when she was sleepin', love. She was almost two years old she was, when He took her away from me. He decided in His wisdom that she didn't belong down here with us, and He took her for one of His angels". Old Mary took a swig of her sherry and sniffed away the tears. "She would've been fifty three now. She was a Spring baby, born in May, an' all the flowers were out when she was born....they was out when she was buried too, love, only I didn't want to look at 'em then. Too much sadness in me 'eart, see"?

Eileen did see, and she felt heart-sorry for the old woman in front of her. How tragic to have lost her only child in that way. Eileen felt the tears threatening her own eyes now and, not wanting to embarrass her companion, she averted her gaze and pretended to be studying the faded printed pattern on Old Mary's curtains.

One Saturday evening, at Joanie's house, Margaret had suggested that they both went out for a drink to the local pub. It wasn't far and they only need stay an hour. Eileen had been unsure. "Suppose my Dad finds out? He'd kill me if he caught me out drinking" she sat on the edge of the double bed in Margaret's room watching as her best friend applied rouge to her cheeks and lips.

"Aww, come on will you, Eileen, you're old before your time, girl!" she had playfully ribbed her friend and Eileen had laughed along with her, but still she was terrified at the thought of being seen in a public house.

"Tell you what then! Let's get the bus into town and we can find a little pub down some quiet back street -somewhere your Dad isn't likely to find out about. What d'you say to that then, Eileen, will you come?"

Eileen knew there was no getting out of it. If she refused to go it might seem to her friend that she was being a snob, a 'goody-two-shoes', and she didn't want to run the risk of offending Margaret. So, with a deep breath and a giggle for good measure, she agreed to accompany her into town for a drink. After all, what harm could it do?

"Just the one, mind" she smiled now as she stood watching her friend apply another coat of lipstick. Eileen thought Margaret was the most beautiful girl she had ever seen. With long, blonde hair, wide blue eyes and the kind of figure Eileen could only dream about she could easily have her pick of the boys. Eileen, on the other hand, shared none of her friend's attributes. She had a rather plain sort of face, her nose was covered in freckles and her hair was a mousey brown mess. Eileen hated her hair. As soon as she was old enough she vowed to have it dyed a decent colour, because the one that God had seen fit to burden her with was non-descript and boring! Pulling on her coat now she ran after Margaret down the stairs and the two girls popped their heads around the living-room door to say goodbye.

Old Mary and Joanie were having a heated argument about the best way to make good gravy and their voices were so loud that they didn't hear the girls. Joanie and Mary had always been the same – they had argued their way through life from the day they spoke their first words. Both in their seventies, they continued to find things to argue about, even though the subject matter was the same as it had been twenty years ago. It was always about cooking, and who was the better at it. Of course, Old Mary thought she had the title, but her sister was having none of it. In the end they invariably ended up pissed and falling about laughing, the argument soon forgotten. Such was the relationship between the two sisters.

*

Eileen and Margaret found a little pub called The Blue Bell, out of the way of prying eyes, and had settled themselves at a table in the far corner of the bar with a glass of Babycham each. The pub was cosy if a little outdated, and the barmaid was warm and friendly. Eileen had never tasted anything alcoholic before, save the wine at Holy Communion, and God Himself knew you didn't get anywhere near enough of the stuff to get drunk on.

 Eileen thought that Father O'Malley must secretly be watering it down because it seemed to get thinner each week. It had always seemed odd to her that Father O'Malley seemed to be permanently too hot. His cheeks were always bright red from the heat – even in winter! Eileen wished she knew his secret because she could never get warm herself. She felt a glow settle on her as she sipped her drink. She was enjoying the taste of her new-found freedom, even if it was for only an hour.

The two girls sat chatting about this and that and giggling as they discreetly studied the people in the bar, trying to guess what each person did for a living.

"I reckon him over there is a truant officer" Margaret hid her mirth now behind her hand as she saw Eileen follow her gaze to where a man in his thirties, stiff collared and ram-rod straight, stood sipping a half pint of mild at the far end of the bar. "I reckon he lurks around street corners and pounces on the children who haven't gone to school that day".

"Well, I'll soon let you know, Margaret, because our Aiden has been bunking off school again, and when my father finds out his arse will be red-raw for a month, and no mistake!" Eileen rolled her eyes up to the ceiling as she spoke. They laughed merrily at the images in their minds of Aiden squealing in pain as his backside felt his father's belt.

Just then the bar door flew open and a group of young men came pushing and shoving each other through the doorway, shouting loudly to one another and laughing raucously as they made their way over to the bar. The icy cold January wind came in with them and a few of the regulars could be heard complaining that 'some people were born in a barn' before one of them got up to close the outer door, muttering under his breath.

The two girls shivered now as the door was flung open a second time and the last of the group came falling through it, all wild-eyed and red-haired. This really was a cold winter and no mistake!

Eileen couldn't take her eyes off the latecomer. He had to be the most gorgeous specimen she had ever laid eyes on. Not that she had had much experience in meeting with the opposite sex. She felt herself blushing as her eyes drank him in – all six feet of him – as he ordered a pint at the bar and shouted across to one or two of the others. My, he was a sight to behold! Margaret, seeing her friend's expression, kicked her under the table.

"OUCH!" Eileen protested loudly as her friend's foot connected with her shin-bone. "What the heck was that for?"

"You know very well what, Eileen Kelly! Now put your eyeballs back in their sockets, it's high time we were going"

Eileen scowled at her friend good-naturedly. She knew that if they didn't make a move now they'd likely miss the bus back and then she really would be in trouble. Taking one last look at the handsome young man standing with his friends at the bar, she sighed inwardly and wished for darker hair and bigger breasts.

The Saturday night visits to The Blue Bell continued on a weekly basis throughout the rest of January and February, each time the two girls setting off earlier and earlier, until one night they had managed to down three glasses of Babycham each before stumbling giddily to the bus stop to make their way home.

The group of young men they had seen in the bar on their first visit hadn't been in again, and Eileen had to admit to herself she was disappointed not to see the red-haired one in particular. Not that she'd stand a chance with him! Not with Margaret there anyhow.

On that particular occasion Eileen was feeling nervous despite the amount of alcohol she had drunk because she knew that she was going to have to sneak straight upstairs as soon as she arrived home. If her father got a look at her he would know immediately that she had been drinking. Why on earth couldn't she have stopped at two drinks?

As they stood waiting for the bus they heard a group of men making their way toward the pub they had just fallen out of and they watched the gang as they drew closer. Eileen immediately spotted the tall, red-haired young man that she had seen in the pub on that first night. She felt her stomach somersault as she caught sight of him, his head thrown back as he laughed at something one of his friends had said, and she wished with all her heart that she were her friend Margaret instead of this plain, mousey-haired overweight nobody. He wouldn't look at her twice, a man like him. She felt suddenly self-conscious, acutely aware of her own shortcomings as the group drew level. How she wanted to just disappear into thin air on the spot! She fidgeted with her coat and turned her face away.

"Well...if it isn't the two lovelies from The Blue Bell, lads" Eileen's heart lurched as the object of her desire stopped in front of them and smiled at her showing even, white teeth. "You're nay going home, are ye?" he cajoled in a broad Glaswegian accent. Margaret, sensing an opportunity, smiled seductively and replied "Why, is there a reason to stay, then?" Eileen felt the first pangs of jealousy now as her best friend appeared confident in front of this Adonis.

"Well, that depends on you two lovely girls, doesn't it now? Will you join us for a wee dram?" he smiled at Margaret and Eileen in turn now and they looked at each other for confirmation before Eileen blurted out:-

"We...we have to be home soon, th..thank you for asking" she felt her cheeks burn with embarrassment as her friend glared at her, clearly annoyed at the childish response. Eileen Kelly hated herself more than Margaret ever could at that moment. She wished the ground would open and swallow her up.

"What she means is – we have to meet someone across the other side of town. Isn't that right Eileen?"

"Um...yes. Yes, that's right, we are. I mean, we do" Eileen prayed for the bus to arrive now as this gorgeous stranger in front of her held her gaze for a few seconds too long. She felt as though she were floating on air as their eyes locked and it was all Margaret could do to pull her friend away.

"The bus is here, we'll be seeing you" she steered Eileen towards the edge of the pavement as the young man started to walk away, his friends calling out at him to hurry up as it was his round.

"Yes, I hope so" he called. Margaret smiled now, a big, wide flirtatious smile. She could tell he fancied her from the second she saw him making his way over to where they were standing. All the boys fancied Margaret.

"I think your wee friend there is an absolute knockout" he shouted as he nodded at Eileen's back. Margaret stood staring at him for a few seconds. She felt certain she must have misheard him. Surely he didn't fancy *Eileen*! Not when he could have *her*! Realising her mistake, she pushed Eileen onto the bus and paid for the tickets.

Eileen hadn't heard the comment, let alone realised it was aimed at her. She noticed that her friend was unusually quiet on the bus ride home and asked her several times what was wrong. Margaret, who had never in her life been second best to anyone, least of all a mousey-haired plain Jane like Eileen, was miffed to say the least. It didn't occur to her that, up until that moment, they had been best friends. It never occurred to her that she was being spiteful and jealous of her friend. She seethed with fury at the imagined slight she felt and ignored Eileen all the way back home.

Eileen had managed to get upstairs without her father catching sight of her and had stumbled into bed, grateful for the safety and warmth of her eiderdown, and still perturbed as to why Margaret had been in such a funny humour on the way back. Perhaps it was her 'time of the month' she thought. Yes, that would be it, she felt sure.

It never occurred to Eileen to think badly of her best friend, or anyone in fact. Eileen was a good girl, a good daughter and a good friend. One day, God willing, she would make some man a good wife, and two or three children a good Mother. It was really all she wanted out of life. A home of her own, a husband and a family.

Eileen fell asleep dreaming that she was wearing a beautiful, white lace wedding dress and walking on her Father's arm down the aisle toward her intended husband – his red hair combed back neatly and his eyes full of love for her.

It seemed, however, that fate had other plans for young Eileen Kelly.

CHAPTER THREE

Eileen had arranged to go to The Blue Bell with Margaret on Easter Saturday and had saved enough to buy a new, blue dress to wear. She had hardly been able to contain her excitement as she carefully folded the dress and put it into a carrier bag to take over to Old Mary's. When Sara Kelly had asked what was in the bag Eileen had told her Mother a lie for the first time in her young life and said it was some material that she had picked up cheap at the market for Old Mary to make some kitchen curtains. Not being given to nosiness Sara Kelly had accepted the explanation without question or asking to see into the bag. Eileen had been sure she was blushing bright red but her Mother had waved her off cheerily and told her to be sure to be home by eleven.

Once she and Old Mary were safely on the bus over to Joanie's, Eileen confessed her duplicity to her friend, fearing that she would be punished in some way for telling lies to her Mother. Old Mary, sensing that the young girl was impressionable, had smiled gently and told her "Just go to Confession tomorrow, girl, and tell Father O'Malley all about it; he can't tell anyone so your secret's safe and besides – he has enough dirty little secrets of his own if the rumours are to be believed!"

Eileen didn't ask Old Mary exactly what those rumours were. She didn't feel it was her place to and besides that she could hardly confess her sins to a priest if he was a sinner himself now, could she?

When they arrived at Joanie's she discovered that Margaret had already left without her. Joanie sensed the girl's obvious disappointment at this change of plan and tried to smooth things over.

"She wanted to wait, love, but she was meeting a friend from her old school first, and she wanted to set off in plenty of time so that you two could have your evening out together. She said she'll meet you in the usual place, love, around seven-thirty" Joanie put an arm around Eileen's shoulder now. "Pop up and use Margaret's room to get ready if you like, love; you're more than welcome to use any of her stuff, I'm sure she won't mind".

Eileen nodded politely and skipped up the stairs, her mood lighter now. Margaret hadn't let her down after all - she was just going to meet her there!

*

Arriving at The Blue Bell, Eileen nervously pushed open the Bar door and peered into the smoke-filled room to see if she could spot her friend. The place was packed out and the jukebox was belting out a rock and roll classic as Eileen made her way over to the corner table where she and Margaret usually sat. There was an elderly couple sat at the table, obviously enjoying a Saturday evening together in their local pub. They were chatting to another couple who sat at the next table and Eileen waited politely until a break in the conversation before asking the old lady:-

"Excuse me. I was wondering whether you'd seen my friend in here, we come in together every Saturday evening"

The old lady, clearly hard of hearing, leaned across the little table and cupped her ear. "You what, love? What did you say? What did she say, Alf?" Her husband shook his head, pointing to his hearing aid and then at the jukebox.

"Sorry, love, you'll 'ave to speak up a bit, only I can't hear a bleedin' thing above this racket" He smiled at his wife and she waved her hand at him in mock annoyance.

"Honestly, Alf, you wanna get a new battery in that bleedin' thing". She roared with laughter now and Eileen realised that she was probably three sheets to the wind.

"N..never mind" she muttered and made her way back the way she'd come; perhaps Margaret had arrived by now.

"These bleedin' youngsters of today, the way they just push in on yer conversation and then, before you 'ave chance to answer 'em proper, they're off again. Ain't got no bleedin' manners any of 'em!" the old lady shouted to her husband, before knocking back the last of her gin and pushing the glass across the table. "Ere, get us another, will you Alfie" she grinned, before sliding off her chair and landing in a heap under the table - much to Alfie's dismay.

Eileen was just about to leave the pub. Margaret was nowhere in sight and she was not about to buy a drink. A young girl alone, drinking alcohol in a public bar? That would never do!

Just then she felt a tap on her shoulder and she turned, a wide smile on her lips now, expecting to see Margaret standing behind her. Thank God her friend had turned up, she thought.

"About time, too!" she laughed. The smile was quickly replaced with a look of complete surprise as she rounded on the laughing face of Jimmy Wilson, the red-haired young man she had been secretly keeping an eye out for over the past two months. Now he was standing right there in front of her, large as life, and Eileen nearly died of embarrassment as she stood, eyes wide, staring at him like a rabbit in the headlights.

"Yer wee friend no' shown up then, darlin'? He smiled at her now – a broad, confident smile that made Eileen's stomach lurch. She thought he surely must have the nicest green eyes she had ever seen. They seemed to twinkle in the subdued lighting of the bar and Eileen stared into them, totally unable to speak for a few seconds.

Realising that she had been staring at him like a love-struck idiot she blushed and shook her head. "No, we were supposed to meet here at seven-thirty but she hasn't arrived. *Yet*"

Jimmy Wilson knew a good thing when he saw one and this one was ripe for the picking. He had never found it too difficult to pull the birds. All he had to do was flash that killer smile, buy them a couple of shorts and whisper a few sweet-nothings into their ears and he was home and dry. He decided there and then, as he watched Eileen Kelly struggling to make conversation, that she was his for the taking. If he had anything to do with it she'd be dropping her knickers to him before last orders round the back of the pub, and Jimmy Wilson always got the girl.

A couple of hours later, after plying her with vodka (and on the pretence of keeping her company until her friend showed up) Jimmy was shoving his cock into Eileen Kelly against the back wall of The Blue Bell public house, and Eileen had gone home on the last bus blissfully unaware that she would soon be carrying a belly full of arms and legs. Jimmy Wilson had finished fucking her, zipped up his trousers and moved on to his next unsuspecting victim.

CHAPTER FOUR

When Eileen missed her second period she had realised her predicament with sickening clarity. She had been truly terrified of telling her Mother, knowing that once she did her Mother would let on to her Father and she would be out on her ear. A staunch Roman Catholic, Joseph Kelly had warned her for as long as she could remember "Come home pregnant, my girl, and you'll be looking for a new home by sunset" He meant every word too. Joseph was not a man given to making idle threats and, daughter or not, if she shamed him she would be out.

Eileen had managed to conceal her condition from her parents with looser-fitting clothes, but Old Mary was a different kettle of fish. Three months into her pregnancy Eileen had been walking home from an errand and had spotted the old woman scrubbing her doorstep on her hands and knees. Feeling sorry for her friend she had gone over and, taking the scrubbing brush from her hand, had insisted on doing the rest of the step. It was as she was standing up that Eileen came over faint and would have fallen into the road had it not been for Old Mary grabbing her arm. Ushering her inside she had ordered her to sit by the fire and had gone hobbling into the kitchen on tired, old legs. Returning with two mugs of steaming hot tea she pushed one into Eileen's cold fingers before taking her seat opposite.

Old Mary watched Eileen over the top of her mug. She could see the girl was terrified, and as pale as a ghost. She decided to broach the subject as gently as she could.

"You're lookin' a bit pale, love, you feelin' alright then?" she ventured. Eileen nodded her head, a bit too enthusiastically for Mary's liking and in that moment she knew she had been right in her suspicions. "How far along are you then, love? Do your Mum and Dad know you're havin' their grandchild then?"

Eileen stared, wide-eyed, at the old woman opposite and knew she could no more lie to her friend than she could disown the infant in her belly. "I....erm..." she faltered, before bursting into tears. "I'm about three months" she admitted. "My parents don't suspect a thing! If they knew they'd throw me out on the spot, I can't go to them" she sniffed as Old Mary passed her a clean, white handkerchief on which to blow her nose.

"The Father isn't about, I take it?" she inquired gently. Eileen burst into tears. The truth was she had been taken in by the man, had trusted him, and since he had had his way with her she hadn't set eyes on him again. Old Mary guessed as much. She had no wish to judge the girl, God knows she hadn't led a blameless life herself, she wasn't about to make the poor little girl feel any worse than she clearly did already.

Getting out of the armchair she scuttled across to where Eileen was sitting and, plonking herself down heavily on the arm of the chair, she took the weeping girl in her arms and held her as three months of fear and worry came pouring out. Rocking her to and fro, Old Mary whispered soothing words to the young girl who had come to mean so much to her over the months. She couldn't ever replace her Alice, no-one could, but in some small way Eileen Kelly had filled the void left in Old Mary's empty life since that bastard God had taken her beloved daughter from her.

CHAPTER FIVE

Six Months Later

On Christmas Eve, Eileen had seen the opportunity to take a bath in front of the fire whilst everyone else was out at Midnight Mass. It was becoming harder and harder to move comfortably, or find clothing that disguised her ever-increasing belly. She badly needed relief from the tight corset she had been wearing for the past six months. Old Mary had given her the corset, telling her to pull it tight and she would be able to conceal the pregnancy for the time being. Of course, Old Mary had assumed that sooner or later the girl would have to bite the bullet and tell her parents the truth of her situation. That day didn't arrive and Eileen had continued to wear the corset even though she could barely breathe at meal-times.

Eileen was excused from going to Church because she told her Mother that she had her 'time of the month' and felt unwell. Sara Kelly had allowed her daughter to remain at home as long as she gave her word she would spend the evening studying her bible. Eileen had readily agreed – anything for a bit of peace. Once they were out of the way she had filled the bath with hot water – boiling kettle after kettle for almost an hour - and had stripped off in the sparsely furnished living room. Un-doing the corset had been a difficult process, her belly now so big it strained at the whalebones and bent the garment out of shape. Finally free of its constraints she had breathed heavily for a few moments before draping her dress and underwear over the fire-guard and sinking gratefully into the soothing water – her guilty secret kicking in her belly as she submerged herself in the luxurious warmth.

She had been laying back, her head resting on the rim of the old tin bath when she heard the front door opening. They were back! She must have drifted off to sleep as the warm water soothed her aching body. How long had she been there, lying in the water which was now lukewarm? Her pulse was racing now, her heart hammering in her chest as she tried desperately to find a way to conceal her condition from her Mother and Father

Jumping up, she tried to clamber out of the bath, the heaviness of her unborn child making her slow and cumbersome. In her haste she lost her footing and fell over the edge of the tin bath, landing heavily on her knees just as the living room door flew open and the cold December air rushed into the room bringing with it the inevitable finality of discovery.

The youngest of her brothers, Danny, had raced in from the cold with his cheeks frost-bitten and rosy and caught sight of her as she tried to conceal her pregnant belly with a towel, his big brown eyes wide in disbelief. At nine years old Danny knew enough about the birds and the bees to realise that his beloved sister had been with a man and had brought home the evidence to boot!

"MA! MA! Our Eileen's going to have a baby!" he shouted at the top of his lungs, his hand still gripping the door handle as his young mind struggled to take in the sight before him – his sister, fat and pregnant and totally naked. Eileen, feeling like a prized cow at a cattle market, scrambled to her feet and tried in vain to retrieve her dress, still warming on the guard, before the rest of her family bore witness to her shame.

Her Mother's mouth dropped open as she rounded the door and caught sight of her daughter, the rest of her brood trying with all their might to push past her to see for themselves what all the fuss was about.

"My God, girl, what have you done? What have you gone and done?" Sara Kelly rushed toward Eileen and slapped her daughter full force across her face. Eileen burst into tears, seeing now with stunning clarity that this would be one Christmas she wasn't going to be spending with her family under this roof.

When Joseph Kelly walked into the room his only daughter was on her knees on the floor, her water's having broken over the threadbare carpet, screaming in fear. Whether it was fear of the impending birth or the fear of her Father she didn't know. She just knew that this night would stay with her forever.

*

Jenna Kelly was born on Christmas Day at 4.15 in the morning at the local hospital. Hearing the screams from outside the house, Old Mary had guessed what had happened and had rung for an ambulance to come quickly, fearing for the safety of the young girl and her child. She knew there would be murders going on in the house opposite and she had stood watching and waiting until the ambulance finally arrived to take Eileen to the Maternity Hospital. She didn't call the police. She knew better. No matter what – you *never* called the Old Bill, not if you didn't want your house burned to the ground in the night whilst you slept!

Eileen had had a relatively easy labour, just four hours. The midwife reckoned she was one of the lucky ones –according to her some of the babies she had delivered had kept their Mother's in labour for two days or more! Eileen didn't feel very lucky at all - in fact she thought that this must surely be the worst day of her life. An un-married Mother at seventeen, no sign of her baby's Father and now she was homeless too. Merry fucking Christmas!

Joseph Kelly had stuck to his principles and refused to speak to his daughter again. He had told her in no uncertain terms that she would not be welcome back into his house, and that as far as he was concerned he no longer had a daughter. She was dead to him, and dead to the rest of her family. Eileen had looked at him in total disbelief that he could say such a wicked thing to his own blood. He didn't ask to see the child, neither did her Mother. Eileen had never felt so utterly alone in all her of her young life.

On Boxing Day afternoon a cab pulled up outside the Maternity hospital and Old Mary climbed heavily from the back seat, using a walking stick now to support her tired, old legs. She found Eileen asleep in her bed, her baby daughter lying awake in her crib just staring with unfocused eyes at the strip lights above her little head.

Old Mary sat quietly by Eileen's bedside and decided there and then to take the girl and her child in, to give her a home – if she wanted it – for as long as she wanted it. The girl was like a daughter to her and she wouldn't turn her back on the poor mite now, in her hour of need.

Old Mary took Eileen's hand as the girl opened her eyes to the only visitor she had seen since giving birth and squeezed it tightly in her own.

"Looks like it's just the three of us then, love, from now on. What d'you say then?"

CHAPTER SIX

Eileen cradled the beautiful, auburn-haired child to her breast. At seventeen she had no experience of babies yet she seemed to know instinctively just how to love this little mite, and love her she did. Her baby daughter might be the product of a quickie at the back of The Blue Bell public house – a night that Eileen had tried hard to forget – but she would never suffer a moment's pain because of it. Eileen would see to it that her child was loved. Always!

She finished feeding the child and, placing her gently into her crib, she allowed herself to sink back onto the crisp, white hospital pillows. She was grateful to have a bed right now; a warm bed, three hot meals a day and a beautiful baby daughter to cherish. She felt blessed, even in those dire circumstances, she felt truly blessed.

She let her mind wander back to the night in March when her Jenna had been conceived.......

Eileen had seen Jimmy Wilson as her knight-in-shining-armour on that Easter Saturday night. She had been stood up by her friend and had felt utterly rejected. She suspected that Margaret had been lying when she had claimed to be meeting an old school friend and had, in fact, been meeting a boyfriend. This suspicion fuelled Eileen's feelings of inadequacy and she had accepted the offer of a drink from Jimmy more as a way of reasserting her own worth than anything else. After all, why shouldn't she have a drink with a man in a bar? She was seventeen, eighteen next year, and she knew most of the regulars by sight, if not by name. She had smiled eagerly as he pulled out a stool at the bar for her and had felt proud to be with him as he ordered their drinks, clearly a man of the world in Eileen's eyes.

*

A couple of hours later and Eileen was feeling decidedly worse for wear. The clear alcoholic drink that Jimmy had bought her was having a bad effect on her. He had told her it was just a single shot of vodka with some lemonade, but in fact there were three shots in each glass and Eileen had unwittingly drunk three of them. Jimmy kept standing up, on the pretence of looking for Eileen's friend, but on one such occasion he had caught the eye of one of his pals and they had exchanged knowing smirks. Clearly, Jimmy had a reputation amongst his friends as a ladies' man.

"I...I don't feel very well, Jimmy. I think I need to go to the ladies' room" Eileen was slurring her words now as the three triple vodkas hit her. She made to stand up but Jimmy caught her arm and pulled her back down. "Hang on a wee minute, an' I'll walk you out for some fresh air" he grinned at her now, flashing even, white teeth. Downing his scotch in one, he stood and offered Eileen his arm. She took it gratefully and Jimmy steered her toward the bar door. "Jus' round here, Eileen, there's a wee pathway that leads to the back of the pub - no-one can see you there"

Eileen, in her drunken stupor, allowed herself to be steered towards the backyard of the pub where empty beer barrels were stacked up against the wall. She stumbled as her foot caught one of the barrels and she let out a cry. "Hey, be careful, we don't want ye comin' te any harm, do we?"

Jimmy had placed a protective arm around her now and Eileen felt safe in his company. No one could harm her, not whilst Jimmy Wilson was there to protect her.

CHAPTER SEVEN

Eileen closed her eyes now as the awful memories of what had taken place behind The Blue Bell public house came flooding back. Jenna moaned softly in her sleep and Eileen knew she wouldn't wake for an hour or more. She allowed her mind to take her back to last Easter Saturday, a night she had tried so hard to forget. Now, though, with the result of that very night lying in a little crib at the side of her bed, she could no longer ignore the way in which her daughter had been conceived. She heaved a sigh as she recalled how she had allowed Jimmy Wilson to walk her around the back of the pub, believing that he was someone she could trust; someone she was safe with.

Eileen had been grateful for the opportunity to get some fresh air, away from prying eyes. She was horrified at how drunk she was and the thought of anyone seeing her in that state made her all the more determined to hide around the back of the pub until the effects had worn off. After all, Jimmy had assured her, ten or fifteen minutes in the fresh air and she would be as right as rain. Of course, Jimmy was banking on this young woman feeling anything but. Once outside in the cold, March wind as it whipped at her face and blew her hair into her eyes, Eileen felt decidedly worse for wear. She turned to Jimmy for support. "I feel faint, Jimmy, I think I'm going to be sick" she urged.

Jimmy, sensing that his opportunity had come, pushed Eileen up against the wall and, unbuttoning her coat, he pushed up against her and began kissing her on the neck and ears, all the while whispering that everything was alright; she was alright with him. Eileen sensed that something was amiss as Jimmy started unbuttoning her new blue dress. The small, pearl buttons fastened all the way down from the neckline to the waist. It was one of the things she had most liked about the dress when she had first seen it hanging up on the market stall some weeks ago. Jimmy began pulling the buttons apart now, slowly at first then more eagerly, as Eileen struggled to keep them closed.

"Jimmy, no, I... I can't!" she tried to push his hand away as it sought her breast. "Come on, love, you know you want it! You've been givin' me the fuckin' glad-eye all evenin'" Jimmy persisted now - grabbing hold of Eileen's left breast and squeezing it hard. Eileen gasped as he forced her bra down and cold, grasping fingers met her warm, naked skin.

Eileen Kelly had never in her life let a boy see her naked. She was a virgin and proud of the fact. Yet here she was, at the back of The Blue Bell pub, drunk out of her mind and Jimmy Wilson was flicking her nipple and rolling it between his thumb and forefinger.

Far from being aroused, Eileen became terrified and tried in vain to push Jimmy away. "Stop it, stop it would you?" she cried out as he grabbed hold of the front of her dress and yanked it open, the beautiful pearl buttons snapping off in all directions leaving her bra and midriff exposed. Whether it was the sight of Eileen's firm, young breasts straining against the flimsy, cotton brassiere or the sudden appearance of her naked skin below she would never know, but at that moment things turned nasty - very nasty indeed.

Eileen felt the tears sliding now from beneath her closed eyelids as she lay on her hospital bed and re-lived every terrifying, sordid moment. She could hardly bear to remember it, so ashamed was she of the things that had happened to her at the hands of Jimmy Wilson as she had lain there, drunk and terrified, on the cold, hard ground.

Jimmy had raped her that night. She screwed up her face in agony as the words formed in her mind. *'He raped me'* Great, wracking sobs escaped now from Eileen's chest and she buried her face into the pillow so as not to wake her baby daughter.

Her child would never know the way in which she had been conceived. Eileen would make sure that the filthy bastard who fathered her would never spend one second in his daughter's company. The poor little mite was not to blame for her no-good father.

Eileen let nine months of pent-up anger and humiliation, shame and fear come pouring out now, her body shaking violently as she tried to stifle the sound of her own suffering in-case her baby should wake from her slumber.

Almost two hours later Old Mary found Eileen Kelly curled up into the foetal positon, hugging one of her pillows to her belly, and sobbing uncontrollably, looking every bit like the homeless, young girl she was.

"You're comin' 'ome with me, girl, that's what you're doin', you're comin' 'ome with me and you're bringin' that little girl along too, an' I'll not 'ear a word to the contrary neither" she bent over the girl as she lay shivering on top of the bed and she wrapped two arms around her and held her close as the girl continued to sob quietly into her breast.

That had been seventeen years ago. Old Mary had passed away just four years later and left everything to Eileen Kelly – 'who became like a daughter to me' – in her will. Eileen inherited not only the modest little terraced house across the street from her blood family, but also the better part of twenty-six thousand pounds.

Eileen had almost fallen off the chair in the solicitor's office when he had read out that part of the will. "Are...are you sure that's correct, Mr. Swainson, Sir? Only, I don't mean to be rude, like, but Old Mary never 'ad two 'alfpennies to rub together as far as I knew. Oh, she 'ad a war widow's pension o'course, but nothing like this much. You sure you read that right, Mr. Swainson?"

Arnold Swainson had peered over the top of his *pince-nez* and smiled warmly at the benefactor of Mary Evans' estate, such as it was. He had been Mrs. Evans' solicitor for almost fifty two years and had known her as a young woman, just married to her young man in the Royal Navy. When their only child had been pronounced dead from cot death syndrome three years later, Arnold Swainson had feared for Mrs. Evans' sanity, but with the proper care and strong tranquillisers the following summer had seen a slight improvement and, although they didn't go on to have more children, they seemed happy enough. Until, that is, Mr. Evans had been caught with his pants down, quite literally, in the back bedroom of one of the couple's friends, Maureen Jackson.

Mary had gone around the back way to see her friend one morning, believing her husband to be away at sea. She often liked to pop in for a cup of tea and a chin-wag when her Albie was away. It was what kept her going.   Maureen's husband, Joe, was also in the Royal Navy but served on a different ship so on the rare occasions they both came home on leave at the same time the four would get together and have a good old knees up down the local.   Mary and Maureen had become close over the past few years. The trouble was Maureen had become a whole lot closer to Albie Evans than she had to his wife, and when Mary had popped her head around the back door on that fateful spring morning, she couldn't possibly have known that her Albie was popping something of his own into Maureen Jackson.

"Coo-eee, you there, Maur?" Mary walked through into the neat lounge with its chintz sofas and porcelain figurines and, not seeing her friend, became concerned that something untoward had happened to her. After all, her back door had been wide open! She must be upstairs. Maureen would never have gone out and left her back door open.

The sight that met Mary Evans as she pushed open the bedroom door was enough to render her speechless for a few moments. Her Albie, her *husband*, had his cock shoved firmly into Maureen Jackson's mouth, and she was sucking it back and forth for all she was worth. Albie hadn't heard his wife entering the room, such was his sense of bliss; Maureen, however, saw her best friend out of the corner of her eye and promptly snapped her jaws closed onto poor Albie's member, which subsequently shrunk to the size of his thumb as his wife clobbered him around the head all the while screaming at him "You dirty, stinking, two-timing bastard.

47

You filthy, womanising piece of shit!" Maureen had fled, naked, and locked herself in the bathroom until she thought her friend had managed to knock Albie out of the back door, down the ginnel and into their back kitchen. Only then did she unlock the bathroom door and peep out. At which point Mary Evans had punched her square between the eyes, knocking her back into the bathroom – her particulars laid bare for the entire world to see. Mary screeched "I'd kick you in your muff, you dirty ol' cow, but I'd be frightened of losin' me fuckin' foot!" and with that Mary's friendship with Maureen was over.

*

Eileen thought back over the day that Old Mary had come to her in the hospital and held her tightly as she had cried for what seemed like an eternity. Then, once Eileen had been given the all-clear from the duty doctor, she had come to collect them both in a cab, and take them home.

Eileen and her baby girl moved into the house across the street from where Eileen had grown up; the house she had often visited - never guessing that one day the woman that everyone called Old Mary would become her surrogate Mother.

Old Mary had made it clear to Eileen that she had a place here with her for as long as she wanted it, and that nothing would change that. Eileen, for her part, kept the house clean as a new pin, and cooked the evening meal for them both. Jenna thrived and grew into a bonny toddler in no time, always a happy child she was the apple of Old Mary's eye. The woman she now regarded as her Mother. Old Mary had been more of a Mother to her than her real Mother across the street had since she had given birth and Eileen had vowed she would take care of her dear friend for as long as the old woman lived and breathed.

Eileen Kelly finally felt that she had come into her own as she walked to the bus-stop with a cheque for nearly twenty six thousand pounds in her handbag. She had vowed she'd use the money wisely, and invest it for the future. After all, she had Jenna to think of, and God Himself knew how costly raising a child could be. She might just treat herself to a new hair colour though. After all, a couple of quid couldn't hurt, could it?

She decided to stop at a little café and purchased a coffee and a doughnut before choosing a table in the window, where she sat in a daydream watching the rest of the world go by. She would never be able to say 'Thank You' to the wonderful woman who had been like a mother to her from the moment she had walked over the step of the old woman's house, and her happiness was tinged with sadness as she thought of Mary Evans and wished with all her heart that she was here now.

CHAPTER EIGHT

Eileen poured herself a cup of stewed tea from the pot as her daughter made her way downstairs. She had been feeling tired lately, and it didn't help when Jenna did nothing around the house

Jenna was a lazy mare and no mistake! She saw housework as something other people did, and expected her Mother to wait on her hand and foot. Eileen rarely complained though. She was grateful for the roof over her head and having a child to love. Jenna, on the other hand, complained about everything from the food her Mother put on the table to the state of the furniture and the price of make-up.

Eileen could never understand why it was that Jenna couldn't seem to hold down a job for longer than five minutes. Every couple of months Jenna would start a new job and within a fortnight she was back on the dole. Jenna spent money like water and Eileen was constantly putting her hand in her purse to supplement her daughter's lifestyle.

At seventeen Jenna Kelly was a beauty. Blessed with her father's auburn hair and gorgeous, emerald green eyes she knew she was a looker. Jenna wouldn't look twice at any man unless he earned a big wedge and drove the latest car. She was going places, and she would remind her mother of it on a regular basis.

Sitting down heavily at the small, formica-topped table Jenna stared down at the plate of bacon and eggs in front of her. It looked disgusting! Why the hell couldn't her mother buy something decent for breakfast, like croissants for instance? It never ceased to amaze her how people ate that muck, all full of grease and cholesterol.

"I'm not eating THAT!" she spat. Pushing the plate away she picked up the cold cup of tea and, taking a sip, she wrinkled her nose and demanded a fresh cup. Eileen put the kettle on. There was little point arguing with her daughter when she was in one of her strops.

"I was thinking of popping to the market today, love. D'you fancy coming with me?" Eileen put a fresh cup of tea in front of her daughter and waited for her response. She hadn't spent much time with her only child lately; Jenna always seemed to have plans of her own. She hoped that, today – just for once - she had managed to put the idea to her before she had time to plan anything else. She missed spending time with her only child.

Jenna sipped the scalding liquid and eyed her Mother slyly. She needed some new make-up and this might provide the perfect opportunity for her to get some – *gratis* - from her Mother. She also needed a dress for Saturday night. There was a new club opening up in town and Jenna fully intended to be there on the opening night. It was rumoured that some serious faces were going to be there, and she fancied herself as the girlfriend of one of them. After all, they had the kudos, the money and the flash cars. What self-respecting girl wouldn't want a bit of that for herself?

After eating two rounds of toast and drinking a second cup of tea Jenna agreed, much to Eileen's delight, to go with her to the market, as long as she promised to treat her to some make-up. The dress could wait until they were at the market – Jenna knew how to play her Mother. Once she

51

started demanding some money for a new dress in a packed Market, Eileen would be embarrassed as her daughter's voice got louder and louder. She'd give in and buy it to keep the peace. Oh yes, Jenna Kelly knew *exactly* how to get what she wanted!

Eileen smoothed down her long, mousey brown hair and applied lipstick, judging herself in the mirror as she did so. She was looking older these days, she decided. It was high time she had a new hair-do, and as for her clothes — well most of them had been hanging in the wardrobe since not long after Jenna was born. Eileen had gone without since giving birth to her only child; the way she saw it a Mother's duty was to put her child first, even if it meant mending and making do herself. Eileen couldn't remember the last time she had bought a new dress or treated herself to a cut and blow-dry at the hairdressers.

Picking up her old, imitation leather handbag she checked to ensure she had her purse and house keys then, once she was satisfied, she pulled on her green wool coat, a bargain from the local charity shop. It was a nice coat, but one of the buttons was missing and it had seen better days. Eileen sighed as Jenna came bounding down the stairs, freshly washed hair tumbling around her shoulders and a face made up to perfection. Eileen couldn't see why her daughter needed make-up at all, such was her natural beauty.

They made their way to the stop at the end of the street and caught the bus to the Roman Road Market. Jenna loved the market stalls with their brightly coloured, cheap outfits. True — she felt she deserved to wear only the very best designer gear — but her budget wouldn't allow for it so she made herself happy with the latest fashions from the market- stallholders and told herself that, one day, she would walk around this place in Gucci and Ralph Lauren; Jimmy Choo and Manolo Blahnik on her feet. Eileen was happy just knowing her shoes didn't have holes in them.

Two hours later Jenna Kelly arrived home carrying a bag containing a new red mini-dress, a new pair of black stilettos and a make-up bag full of new foundation, lip-gloss and mascara. She felt very pleased with herself. It hadn't taken much effort to get the money out of her Mother, she just waited until one of their neighbours spotted them and popped over to say hello. Jenna knew full well that her Mother would rather die than have anyone think she wasn't providing for her child, and that she would feel a certain amount of pride at being able to treat her daughter to a new outfit as her neighbour looked on.

Oh yes, Jenna Kelly knew *exactly* how to play the game where her Mother was concerned. Jenna Kelly was going places. As far away from her Mother and that shit-hole she called home as fast as her latest boyfriend could take her!

CHAPTER NINE

It was Saturday night and Jenna Kelly was dressed to the nines. She sashayed past the doormen, wafting cheap perfume and wearing her most seductive smile. The doormen all knew Jenna, she was a regular in the clubs, and most of them had tried it on with her at one time. Not that any of them ever got anywhere. Jenna had promised herself she would save herself for her wedding night, for her husband, and she had stayed true to herself.

The Starlight Club was spectacularly glamourous, all mirrors and crystal chandeliers. Jenna took in the lush, black leather couches, the low glass tables, the subdued lighting and the well-heeled clientele and made her mind up there and then that one day she would own a club like this. One day it would be her name above the door; it would be her doing the hiring and firing and her raking in the profits. By hook or by crook, Jenna Kelly was going places, and this was as good a place to start as any.

Making her way over to the cocktail bar she ordered a Martini and, while she waited for her drink, lit herself a cigarette. Drawing deeply on it, she blew out the smoke slowly and smiled as the barman placed her cocktail onto a black, monogrammed coaster. She was out to make an impression tonight, and she could see that already the club was beginning to fill up. One or two faces were entertaining friends in darkened corners, no doubt mixing business with pleasure, and she eyed them discreetly through the mirrors on the back of the bar. The deejay was playing all the latest dance tunes and the dancefloor was heaving with young, wide-eyed

54

girls trying to catch the eye of a good-looking young man, whilst they just stood in packs eyeing up the talent on display and trying to figure out which one they should approach at 2 a.m. for a slow dance, knowing that if a girl accepted an invitation to smooch at that late hour, with a guy who hadn't even offered to buy her a drink all evening, then a shag was practically a dead cert. Jenna Kelly was never going to be one of those air-headed bimbos, desperate for a bit of attention. She had her eye on the main chance, and she was going to wait until the right opportunity presented itself. She casually sipped her Martini as she watched the club fill up to capacity.

Just then a roar of applause broke out and Jenna turned to see a handsome, well-built man she had never seen before make his way across the room to a group of men in the far corner, all suited and booted in their finest for the opening night. As he reached them they each held out a hand to shake his, smiling warmly. Clearly the owner of the club, he exuded charm and confidence, and he responded warmly – shaking each man's hand and exchanging a few words to each one before moving on to the next.

Jenna watched as the men, all known around the East End as club owners, drug dealers and big-money earners kowtowed to this man; clearly they held him in high regard. She stood with her back to the bar and drank him in. He was around six feet tall, with dark blond hair and a confident smile. Jenna sensed the man's charisma, even from this far away, and she could only watch he took his seat and the rest of the group followed suit.

She wanted to meet him. All she had to do was figure out a way of getting his attention without making it too obvious. Picking up her drink she walked slowly across the crowded room, making a bee-line for a small table which was positioned directly opposite the group of men. Perfect!

Sitting down on one of the high stools she crossed her legs seductively and tossed her auburn curls back, sipping her drink as she surveyed the group discreetly out of the corner of her eye. They didn't seem to have noticed her and she wondered how she was going to make the club owner's acquaintance. Taking out her pack of cigarettes she pulled one from the pack and fumbled in her clutch bag for her lighter. Funny - she was certain she had it a few moments ago. Perhaps she has left it on the bar. She stepped down from the stool and, picking up her drink, she was about to make her way back across to the bar when she sensed a presence behind her.

Turning, she found herself gazing into the bluest eyes she had ever seen, and a smile so dazzling it almost took her breath away.

"Allow me" he offered and she smiled at him as he flicked the lighter and held it out. She leaned ever-so-slightly towards him and, smiling again, she lit her cigarette from the flame. The man waited until she had taken the light and then snapped the very expensive-looking gold lighter shut.

"Thank you, Mr?....." she paused. She could see laughter lines around the corners of his eyes and estimated him to be about thirty-five. He held her gaze for a full five seconds before answering.

"Max. Max Reid, and it's my pleasure" he beamed. "Can I get you another drink?"

Jenna couldn't believe her luck. He must have spotted her as she walked across to the table, although she could have sworn he hadn't so much as glanced in her direction once.

"Thank you – Jenna Kelly" Jenna held out her hand and Max took it, but instead of shaking it as she expected he lifted it to his lips and kissed her fingers very, very lightly. As soon as his lips made contact with her skin she felt her insides turn to jelly. This man was charm personified and she was feeling decidedly charmed! In fact, she was quite taken with him.

Placing his hand on the small of her back he gently steered her towards the bar. The barman, seeing his boss approaching, made his way to the end of the bar and smiled broadly. "Yes Sir? What can I get for you?"

Max ordered another Martini for Jenna and bourbon on the rocks for himself. Chinking his glass to hers he said "Cheers" before taking a large swig of his drink. Jenna followed suit and found herself eyeing Max over the top of her glass as she sipped her Martini. He was attractive and immaculately groomed. She caught the scent of a very expensive cologne; took in the beautifully cut suit and the silk tie. This man knew how to impress.

"Are you the owner of this place?"

"I am, yes, do you like it?" he smiled

"It's wonderful" she enthused "Absolutely beautiful, you must be very proud"

Max laughed. "I don't know about proud, Jenna, but I'm certainly a few grand lighter since I finished paying for it.   Tell me – are you here alone this evening?"

Jenna suddenly felt embarrassed. She didn't want to lie, but then she didn't want him thinking that she was the kind of girl who made a habit of trawling night-clubs looking for men either. In the end she decided to tell a half-truth. She explained that she had been hoping that a few of her friends would be here tonight as they were not in the local pub. She said that she had just arrived and had been looking for them when he had come over to light her cigarette. Well, it almost the truth. She hadn't expected her friends to be in here, but she had cast an eye over the crowd just in-case.

"I hadn't planned on staying long, if I couldn't find them" she added, conscious now of a warm glow spreading over her as the Martinis worked their magic

"Well, Jenna, I've a proposition for you!" he smiled at her then – a slow, mischievous smile, and she felt nervous as she wondered what he was about to suggest. She needn't have worried. Max finished his drink before continuing.

"Why not join me for supper? That is – unless you've eaten already? I hear the restaurant here is very good" he joked.

Jenna had to admit she felt hungry. In her haste to get out of the house she had skipped tea and now she was regretting it, the effects of the two Martinis she had drunk making her feel slightly giddy.

"That's settled then!" he beamed, and they left the bar and made their way up the stunning, lit stairway to the upper floor restaurant where the waiters were busy serving wine and fetching dessert or coffee to the late evening diners. The whole place oozed class and Jenna felt like a princess as Max took her hand and guided her up the last of the stairs.

The tables were set apart at discreet intervals and covered in crisp, white tablecloths with ornate silver candelabra in the centre of each table. The soft glow of the candlelight added to the overall ambience and Jenna couldn't fail to be impressed as the Head Waiter appeared out of nowhere and greeted his boss warmly, before showing them to an intimate table in the far corner of the room and expertly lighting the three candles on their table. Clicking his fingers at the wine waiter, he wished them both a very pleasant evening, adding that should they require something that was not on the menu he felt sure that it would not be a problem.

The wine waiter rushed over to the table and offered them both a wine menu. Max watched the girl opposite him as she studied the menu hard. He suspected that she knew nothing about wine, given her age, and to save her from embarrassment he ordered a bottle of Cristal champagne and gave the menus back to the waiter.

Once they were both settled, and sipping on the deliciously chilled Cristal from cut-glass crystal glasses, Jenna found herself feeling more relaxed. Max ordered them both a melon boat starter with scallops to follow. He watched her discreetly as she ate, taking in the long, auburn hair and the thick, black eyelashes – her eyes were truly mesmerising and it was all he could do not to stare. She looked up suddenly and caught him watching her. Blushing slightly she smiled and said brightly "This is wonderful, Max, really wonderful. Thank you for the invitation"

Max raised his glass in response and they chatted about this and that until the meal was over. Ordering them both Irish coffees he lit a cigarette and passed it across the table to her. She took it and thought how very sophisticated this man was. He knew all the right things to say, all the right things to do. She felt a little out of her depth.

It was gone two o'clock by the time they had finished their coffees and Max ushered her downstairs, stopping on the way to thank the Head Waiter and say goodnight to a few stragglers who were making their way out of the club.

Addressing the Head Doorman he ordered his car be brought around the front and, a few minutes later, Jenna found herself sitting in a top-of-the-range, chauffeur-driven Mercedes. As she sank back gratefully into the soft, cream leather seats she waited for Max to join her. Opening the door on the other side, Max climbed in beside her but the car didn't move.

"Just give me a few minutes" Max dismissed the chauffeur and he climbed out of the car, clicking the door closed behind him. Billy Andrews knew his boss' routine by heart. He knew that in ten minutes he'd be driving the young lady home and Max Reid would make his mind up later whether he wanted to see the girl again.

Max Reid was cautious about women. He'd learned the hard way when his ex-wife had taken him to the cleaners after the divorce. Married less than two years, the marriage had failed after Joanne complained that Max didn't spend enough time at home and had started an affair with her fitness coach. Max, for his part, couldn't blame his wife. He knew he'd neglected her and he knew it would cost him dearly, in more ways than one.

"Never again, Billy" he once exclaimed after a particularly nasty meeting at the solicitors. Joanne Reid had demanded far more than he had wanted to give and the divorce had been a bitter struggle. Thankfully there were no children to get caught up in the crossfire, but Max Reid had had his fingers burned badly. He was basically a decent man and had wanted his soon-to-be-ex-wife to have a comfortable life, so he had swallowed his knob and given her what she wanted in the end.

Max turned now to face Jenna, his face serious. He liked this girl, perhaps a little more than he should. After all, she was young enough to be his daughter. He knew he should just walk away, forget about her. But he was hooked.

"I'd like to see you again, Jenna, if you'd let me?" Max's voice was gentle yet strong at the same time. Jenna turned to answer him and his lips met hers. She hadn't expected it and gasped slightly, before allowing his mouth to cover hers, his tongue exploring - probing the inside of her mouth. She moved her tongue against his and felt herself becoming aroused. He placed his hand at the back of her head, entwining his fingers into her hair as they kissed. He was without doubt a skilful kisser and Jenna felt her heart beating faster as the kiss became more passionate.

Moaning gently, she leaned against him, her firm breasts pushing against his chest. She wanted this man. She wanted him so much. Suddenly she felt she might just forget about saving herself for marriage.

Suddenly, and without warning, Max pulled away from her. She was left gasping for breath as he simply unlocked the door and climbed out of the car. Why was he getting out? Had she done something wrong?

Max turned and leaned into the car. He kissed her on the cheek, thanked her for keeping him company and then bid her goodnight. Jenna couldn't believe it. One minute they had been locked in a passionate kiss and just as suddenly she was left sitting in the car, alone.

"Make sure she gets home, Billy, and then make your way back – there's a few people I need to see before calling it a night" Billy doffed his cap at his boss and climbed into the front seat of the car. "Where to, Miss?" he asked politely. Jenna turned to see Max walk back into the club without a backward glance. She felt utterly deflated. What could she possible have done wrong that he should simply dismiss her in this way? Well, she wouldn't see him again. No way was she going to allow him near her again after the humiliation she had just endured; he could go straight to hell as far as she was concerned. *Talk about rude*!

After giving Billy the address Jenna settled back in the seat and leaned her face against the glass window, watching the late-night revellers making their way home. Some were laughing loudly; others were acting the fool to impress their mates or their girlfriends. But all of them seemed to have one thing in common. They all seemed happy, and right now that hurt Jenna Kelly more than she ever thought possible. She let the tears fall and silently cursed Max Reid. If he thought he could treat her this way and get away with it he had another think coming. She would show him!

CHAPTER TEN

Jenna lay staring up at the ceiling, feeling angry and resentful. She had been awake since seven and the only thing in her mind was Max Reid and the way he had rejected her last night. She couldn't understand it. Everything had been going so well – the kiss between them had been electric! So, why had she found herself going home alone?

Downstairs, Eileen had the kettle on and was singing along softly to the radio as she tidied the kitchen. She felt good this morning, not as tired as she had done lately, and it was nearly Christmas. Eileen loved Christmas. She loved decorating the little house and putting up the tree in the corner, covered in twinkling fairy-lights; most of all she loved wrapping presents for her daughter and placing them beneath the tree ready for Christmas morning.

This year she had really splashed out on Jenna. After all – she only had one daughter – so she wanted to make her Christmas as special as she could. She didn't expect much from Jenna in the way of a gift. Jenna always made out that she didn't ever know what to buy for her Mother, and Eileen would smile and say it didn't matter, that she was happy just having Christmas together.

Just then the doorbell rang and Eileen tutted to herself. Who the hell could that be at this hour on a Sunday morning? Well, they'd better make it quick – she had a roast dinner to prepare.

"Good morning, Mrs. Kelly?" a small, bearded man in a smart black uniform and a chauffeurs cap, holding the biggest bouquet of flowers she had ever seen, stood smiling at Eileen. She stared back at him all the while wondering if this was a prank. Who the hell wore a chauffeur's cap anymore anyway?! And who the hell would send her flowers?

"Yes, I'm Eileen Kelly, and you are?" she stood now, her back ramrod straight, one hand on her hip.

"I have been asked to deliver these flowers to this address" he spoke warmly now, and Eileen noticed he was not from around these parts. Judging from his accent she thought he was from up North. "Oh! I see" Eileen took the huge bouquet from him and said "I don't understand. Who has sent me flowers?"

The man smiled again as he offered his apologies "I'm so sorry, Mrs Kelly, I should have explained properly. You see – the flowers are not for you, I'm afraid. They're for your daughter, Miss Jenna Kelly"

Eileen felt an overwhelming wave of disappointment as she took in what she was hearing. How ridiculous had she been to imagine for one second that such a beautiful bouquet could possibly be for her? Who on earth would be sending *her* flowers, for goodness' sake? She didn't know anyone, let alone have a boyfriend.

"Of course, yes, I didn't think...I mean, I knew who they were for, of course I did" she blushed now as she tried to close the door.

The bearded man took a step forward and, sticking his foot inside the door, he stopped Eileen from closing it.

"One more thing, please, Mrs Kelly, if I may?" Eileen opened the door a little and waited.

"If you would be so kind as to let Miss Kelly know that the car will be here to collect her at eight o'clock?"

Eileen had had enough of this fucker now. First he hands her a gigantic bouquet, filling her with all sorts of daft, wild ideas only to let her down with a bang. Now he's telling her that some bloke's going to be sending his fancy bloody driver round later this evening to pick up her daughter. *Her Jenna!*

"Er....just a minute, please, if you don't mind! Who do you work for? Who sent these flowers, and who thinks he is taking my daughter out this evening?"

"I work for Mr Max Reid, Mrs Kelly. Mr Reid sent the flowers, and - believe me - he will take good care of Miss Jenna. Mr Reid is a gentleman, Mrs Kelly. Good day!" With that he strode down the front path of the little terraced house and climbed into the front seat of the most beautiful car Eileen had ever seen.

"JENNA!! JENNA, GET DOWN THESE STAIRS, THIS INSTANT! D'YOU HEAR ME, GIRL? GET DOWN HERE NOW!" Eileen could hardly believe her ears. So, Max Reid was going to take good care of her daughter, was he? 'Over my fuckin' dead body' thought Eileen.

Stomping back into the kitchen she flung the bouquet into the bin. If some suave bastard thought he was going to have his way with her Jenna he'd got another think coming! The bloody cheek of him, sending his ruddy chauffeur round here with a bunch of bloody flowers indeed! Eileen was more than a bit peeved that they weren't for her.

"Over my fuckin' dead body will he be takin' you out, girl!" she exclaimed, just as Jenna came walking through the kitchen door.

CHAPTER ELEVEN

Jenna Kelly was on pins. She had almost died with excitement when her Mother had seen fit to inform her that "Mr Max FUCKIN' Reid seems to think he's takin' you out tonight; sendin' 'is bleedin' car round, he 'is, if you don't mind!"

Jenna didn't mind. She didn't mind at all as it happened. After retrieving the bouquet from the bin, and giving her Mother a look to kill, she had taken it upstairs and read the attached card:

Please have dinner with me. The car will collect you at 8p.m. Give me the chance to explain. Max x

Well, Jenna would give him the chance to explain himself, as he had asked so nicely. She would let him explain precisely why he had kissed her with such passion only to pull away and leave her feeling humiliated. Once he had finished grovelling she would tell him exactly where he could shove his fucking explanation! She would walk out and leave him just as he had done to her!

*

Jenna was pacing the bedroom floor at almost eight o'clock. She had been ready for over an hour and was beginning to grow impatient to see Max Reid again. She told herself that it was because she wanted revenge; that she wasn't the kind of girl to let a man make her feel so bad.

The car pulled up outside Eileen Kelly's little terraced house at precisely eight o'clock. Eileen sat in her armchair, a cigarette burning away as she fumed quietly to herself. Who the hell was this man, anyway? He must be minted if he could afford a ruddy chauffeur! She stood and made her way over to the window. Pulling back the net curtain she peered through the glass at the fancy Mercedes outside her home, and wondered what the neighbours would be saying as they watched her daughter climb into the back. Eileen wondered what it felt like to sit in the back of a car like that. She doubted she'd ever get the chance to find out.

Just then she heard Jenna come bouncing down the stairs. She wanted to warn her to be careful of this man, whoever he was. Eileen Kelly knew all about how men could trick you into trusting them. She knew only too well.

"Jenna, love, just tell me - where did you meet this Max Reid? And where's he takin' you tonight? You're only seventeen years old, love, you need to be..."

"Oh, for heaven's sake, Mum, give it a rest for once, can't you? I'm going out to dinner. I'm not going to an orgy! If you must know I met him at his club last Saturday, he owns The Starlight"

Realising that her Mother wouldn't know The Starlight Club from the bookies she rolled her eyes up to the ceiling, tossed her auburn hair and picked up her coat from the back of the chair. Honestly, sometimes she despaired of her Mother. Didn't *she* ever have a life when she was younger? She must have done, Jenna decided. After all, she'd had her, hadn't she?!

Dressed in a demure black dress and high heels, Jenna Kelly looked older than her years, and Eileen felt sick to her stomach as she watched her only child walk down the path to the waiting car, and God knows what else!

Billy Andrews was under strict instructions not to discuss his boss with Jenna Kelly under *any* circumstances. He got out of the car and, holding open the back door for her, he waited until Jenna was seated before clicking the door closed and climbing back into the driver's seat.

"Hello, where are you taking me...er..." Jenna realised she didn't even know the man's name.

"Billy, Miss Kelly, just call me Billy" he smiled now into the rear-view mirror at the young lady sitting in the back and – for the first time in fifteen years of working for the man – he wondered what the hell his boss was thinking of.

*

Pulling up at the entrance to the underground car-park, Billy swung the Mercedes left and down a long ramp before parking in a designated spot which was clearly marked: FOR RESIDENTS ONLY. Climbing out of the car he opened the door for Jenna and gestured towards the lift.

"This way, please, Miss Kelly" he smiled again and Jenna smiled back. She was enjoying the courtesy being shown to her by the chauffeur, and for a few seconds she imagined that he was her chauffeur – hired by her, paid by her. Yes – she liked that idea. She liked it very much. Jenna Kelly was going places. Of that much she was certain.

Jenna watching as Billy pressed the button for The Penthouse Suite. 'Wow' she thought 'Max Reid must be seriously rich to afford a place in this apartment block, and *The Penthouse Suite too!!'* She stood patiently waiting as the lift sped upwards for a few seconds before announcing its arrival at The Penthouse Suite with a 'ping'. The lift door opened and Jenna Kelly's mouth fell open. There, in front of her eyes, was the most fabulous apartment she had ever imagined in her wildest dreams. It was nothing short of spectacular. Standing across from her at the huge windows was Max Reid, dressed casually in dark trousers and a cream shirt. He turned to greet her as she stepped from the lift, Billy making a discreet exit.

"Jenna, thank you for agreeing to see me, it really is a pleasure. You look gorgeous" he smiled at her now and she could feel the butterflies in her stomach. "What would you like to drink?" Max gestured toward the well-stocked bar in the corner of the room and Jenna found herself smiling. He really was utterly charming.

"Thanks, I'd like a Martini please" Jenna suddenly felt grown-up as Max took her coat and kissed her on the cheek.

"It really is lovely to see you; I was hoping you'd come".

"Well, you asked nicely, so here I am".

"Yes, here you are, and very beautiful you look too, I might add".

Jenna felt herself blushing. She wasn't used to this kind of flattery. Most of the boys she had been on dates with had never even thought to pay her a compliment. They were just after the one thing, and Jenna had disappointed many an ardent young man by refusing to give out. The way she saw it she would only lose her virginity once, there were no second chances, and she was determined she would lose it to the right man.

CHAPTER TWELVE

Max had surprised Jenna by cooking them both a beautiful meal. She had to admit she was impressed by his culinary skills and had watched with fascination as he prepared the ingredients, chopping and dicing peppers, onions and garlic cloves. Jenna had never experienced anything like it and had savoured every mouthful as they ate.

The dining table was set into a corner of the room and was decked out in creams and golds, with ornate candelabra and beautiful Cala lilies as the centre-piece. Chrystal glasses were placed at the side of the two place settings, an ice bucket containing a bottle of Cristal champagne stood at the side of the table.

"Did you do all this yourself, Max?"

"Ah, I have a confession to make" he smiled at her now, his eyes twinkling in the candlelight "I'm afraid I had no part in all this, I have a housekeeper and she set the table for us. So, there you have it, my secret is out"

"It's lovely, really lovely" Jenna finished her meal and sipped on the ice-cold champagne as Max lit a cigarette.

"You said you wanted to explain, Max? It's just – I'm not used to being treated in that manner" Jenna was building up to walking out now. She would wait for his explanation and then she would let him know just how badly he had treated her. She would walk out on him, just like he had done on her. She was still angry about last night and she wasn't about to let him forget it. Nobody treated her like that and got away with it!

"I do want to explain, Jenna, but I think it would be easier if we were a little more comfortable. Let's take our drinks and sit on the sofa, shall we? Then I will tell you precisely why I walked away from you last night"

Jenna couldn't see the harm in finishing their drinks on the sofa, after all it was nearer to the lift – less distance for her to walk when she left him sitting there feeling rejected and humiliated. She picked up her glass and made her way over to one of the luxurious, black leather sofas. Sitting down, she felt herself sink into the upholstery and she felt the urge to kick off her shoes and curl her feet up. Max came and sat down next to her, not meeting her gaze.

"Would you like a smoke? Max pulled a cigarette from the pack and offered it to Jenna. She took it and he lit it before lighting one for himself. Jenna thought he suddenly looked nervous. Then she dismissed the notion. Why on earth would he be nervous with her? Max Reid wasn't the kind of man who got nervous. She waited as he got comfortable. This was going to be fun. What on earth did the great Max Reid think he could possible say to excuse the disgusting way he had treated her? She inhaled deeply on her cigarette and waited.

"The truth is, Jenna, I like you. I like you a lot. That's why I walked away" Max looked Jenna straight in the eye now as he went on "You see, I haven't been involved with anyone – not properly anyway – since the divorce, and I had planned on keeping it that way" He took a long drag on his cigarette before continuing. "Don't get me wrong, Jenna, there have been women" Max looked embarrassed now as he searched Jenna's expression for any hint of disapproval. He wanted to impress this girl, needed to for God's sake! He had thought of nothing else since last night and he felt he was making a total mess of trying to explain his feelings now.

Jenna sipped her drink and studied the man carefully. He seemed to be struggling with something. She couldn't decide whether that was because he was nervous or whether it was simply that he was buying time before coming up with the next one-liner. She decided it was probably the latter. The guy was full of shit and if he thought for one bloody minute that she was going to be sucked in again, well – he had another think coming!

"Do you have any fucking idea how you made me feel, Max? Do you?!" Jenna glared at him now, her emerald eyes flashing in the subdued light, her auburn curls bobbing up and down as she drove her point home. "You *left* me sitting there, in the back of your car, wondering what the hell I'd done wrong. One minute you were kissing me like I was the best thing that had ever happened to you and the next..."

"That's just what I've been trying to tell you, Jenna. Please....listen to me...."

"Fuck off, Max! If you think I'm falling for that rubbish you're mistaken. Let me tell you something, *Mister Max Reid*, no-one – NO-ONE – gets to treat me that way, okay?" Jenna stood up now and, slamming her glass down hard onto the smoked glass coffee table she turned to face Max.

"I'm going! Thanks for the free meal, and the champagne, but if you think that entitles you to any more of my company then you're sadly mistaken, so you can save your breath".

"Jenna! Wait, let me explain" Max was on his feet now as Jenna strode over to where her coat was hanging over the back of one of the dining chairs. Picking it up Jenna threw it over one arm and turned towards the lift.

Max Reid caught hold of her as she tried to make her way across the room. Taking hold of both her arms he pulled her towards him and kissed her on the mouth. Jenna tried to pull away but Max wrapped his arms around her and kissed her harder, his tongue pushing its way between her teeth until she responded by opening her lips slightly. Taking this as a green light, Max began to kiss her passionately, his breath coming in short gasps as his lips moved over her face, lightly caressing her nose, her cheeks, her eyelids. Jenna felt herself becoming aroused by him. She wanted to pull away but she felt powerless. He moaned as his lips made contact with her neck and he softly nibbled her ear lobe, all the while holding her close to his body. Jenna could smell the expensive cologne he wore. She could feel the hardness of his muscular body beneath the cream shirt; feel his hands on her body, caressing and holding her tight.

Suddenly, Jenna couldn't fight him any longer. She responded to his urgent kisses with ones of her own; their lips locked together as they savoured the taste of one another. She had wanted this. Deep down, she had wanted this. She hadn't thought that Max Reid wanted this, though. Now she knew differently. Now she knew that this man wanted her with all his being. She could feel his hardness through her dress as he pressed himself against her and she gasped with pleasure as his fingers slid inside her dress and found her nipple.

"Max, stop! Please, stop" she cried. She knew if she didn't stop him now they would end up in his bed, and much as she wanted him, she wasn't about to give away her virginity on their first night together.

"Jenna, I want you so much" he murmured in her ear now. "But I won't take advantage of you. I couldn't. I'm happy to wait until you're totally ready" Max Reid could hardly believe he was saying the words! When had he ever been happy to wait for any woman? This girl - this young girl - had gotten under his skin, and he was in over his head.

CHAPTER THIRTEEN

Three Months Later

Eileen Kelly was in a tizzy and no mistake! The flowers still hadn't arrived; the hairdresser had called to say she was held up in traffic and her daughter was throwing a major strop in the upstairs bedroom. Her head started to throb now and she poured herself another glass of champagne and washed down two paracetamol before rushing upstairs to where Jenna was pacing the floor in her underwear.

"Where the fuck is Sandra, Mum? She promised she'd be here at eleven o'clock - it's twenty five past already. At this rate I will still be sat here with my hair in bloody curlers at noon!

Eileen felt sorry for her daughter now. Clearly, Jenna was nervous and it showed. Picking up a champagne flute from the dresser she filled it and passed it to her, then sat down on the bed. If she could calm her down Sandra would be along soon enough, and if Jenna was worried that Max wouldn't wait well – he'd wait alright!

It had been only three months since the day that Eileen had watched her only daughter set off on her first date with Max Reid and now here she was about to marry him. At first Eileen had been totally against the match. She hated the idea of her Jenna being married to a man twice her age, and had made her feelings known in no uncertain manner. However, even Eileen couldn't fail to be charmed by Max Reid once she had met him and, seeing how well he treated Jenna, she couldn't object to him any longer. Besides, Jenna's mind was firmly made up.

"Max has proposed!" She had beamed as she showed off the stunning rock on her engagement finger. "And I've accepted, before you say another word, Mum. We're getting married in a month. Isn't it wonderful?"

"Oh, Jenna, you're not....are you?" Her Mother had looked down at her stomach, indicating that she thought Jenna was in the club. "Please tell me you're not pregnant, Jen"

"NO! I'm not bloody pregnant, Mum, and I'm insulted that you think that's the only reason Max has asked me to marry him! Actually, if you must know, we haven't had sex, so you can stop worrying now can't you?"

Eileen had been shocked to hear that her daughter was still a virgin. It was testament to the man she was marrying, proving that he really did love her if he was prepared to wait until they were married before sleeping with her. Eileen also admired her only child for sticking to her promise that she would be a virgin on her wedding night.

The doorbell rang and Eileen peered through the net curtains to see Sandra, the hairdresser from the local salon, hopping up and down on the step. As soon as Eileen opened the front door Sandra flew past her exclaiming "God, I need a pee, I've been stuck in traffic for nearly an hour...where's the bride-to-be?"

An hour later and Jenna Kelly stood in her wedding dress, hair and make-up all done, smiling at her Mother as she fussed over her, making sure the dress was done up properly and that her hair was perfect at the back.

"Oh, Jenna, you look like a princess!" Eileen had tears in her eyes now as she stood taking it all in. Jenna had chosen the most gorgeous, classic gown and the shape really flattered her slim figure. The flowers had arrived only ten minutes earlier and, as Jenna picked up her bouquet of Cala lilies (a reminder of her first date with Max), Eileen sniffed and downed another glass of bubbly before making her way downstairs and outside to the waiting limousine.

As Jenna had no Father to give her away, Eileen was travelling in the bridal car with her daughter. However, Jenna had drawn the line at her Mother walking her down the aisle, preferring instead to allow Max to choose an appropriate escort.

Max had called an old pal of his from his days in the building trade and the bloke had turned out to be quite a card. Jenna had gotten along well with Marcus Graham and had been only too happy to have him do the honours. After all, she didn't have any other male relatives. Someone had to give her away!

Arriving at the church some twenty minutes late, Jenna smiled warmly at the large crowd on onlookers as they wished her well and thought how wonderful it was that, in a short while, she was going to be Mrs Max Reid.

Max had taken one look at his bride and almost broken down, such was the love he felt for her. Only seventeen, she was the love of his life, and he vowed he would spend the rest of it making her happy. When he had proposed to her just four weeks ago he had felt so nervous he had almost thrown up in the bathroom before finally summoning up the courage to go down on one knee. Thankfully, Jenna had accepted straight away and had been ecstatic when he placed the five carat diamond ring on her finger.

He had managed to sort out the church in record time, thanks to a hefty donation to the church roof fund and the Minister had been only too happy to agree to marry them, despite his previous divorce, no questions asked. Max knew how to get what he wanted, and he wanted to marry Jenna Kelly. Nobody else had ever had the effect on him that she had. He absolutely adored her.

Jenna walked slowly now, one arm wrapped through the supporting arm of Marcus Graham, and smiled as she came face to face with her future husband. She wasn't sure whether she loved Max, but he made her happy and she certainly cared for him. She figured that would be enough to see them through, that love was something which probably grew between a couple as they spent more time together. Anyway, it didn't matter to her that she didn't feel all starry-eyed and romantic – that stuff was for kids, and she was a woman now.

Half an hour later, after signing the register and thanking the Minister, Max and Jenna stepped out of the church as man and wife, the spring sunshine casting its warm glow on the happy couple as the crowd of guests threw confetti. Jenna had wanted a big church wedding with all the trimmings and Max had spared no expense in getting it just right.

Three hundred guests packed out the church with some having to stand at the back as they watched Max Reid take his vows for a second time. Nobody had ever believed the man would take the plunge again after the way his first marriage had gone but they were all in agreement that young Jenna Kelly had been the best thing that had ever happened to him, judging by how wide his smile had been over the past three months.

The party afterwards went on until the early hours of the morning, everyone congratulating the happy couple and drinking the health of the new Mr and Mrs Max Reid. Max had been like a dog with two tails, proudly showing off his new bride and revelling in the camaraderie amongst his friends and business acquaintances. Jenna thought that she had never been as happy in her whole life as she was right now. The pile of wedding gifts was so high she joked that they'd be there for a week trying to take them home. She laughed merrily and danced with her new husband until almost three o'clock in the morning, until eventually the party started to wind down and Max suggested they make their way upstairs.

Max had booked the honeymoon suite for their first night as man and wife and no expense was spared decking the room out to impress his new bride. All around the suite were cut glass vases filled with Cala lilies and twinkling fairy lights hung around every window and adorned the four poster bed. Max wanted Jenna to have a wedding night to remember, and he had thought of everything.

Jenna gasped with delight as she took in all the flowers and candles, the fairy lights and the rose petals on the bed. She had never seen such a beautiful room – it took her breath away

"Oh, Max, darling, this is wonderful. It's like a fairy-tale!" she fell back onto the king-size, four poster bed and kicked off her shoes. "Let's have some champagne" She wanted to make this night last as long as possible.

"No, no more champagne, Jenna. I've waited three months to make love to you and I can't wait another minute longer. Come on let's go to bed, eh?"

Max began to undress and Jenna lay watching her new husband as he pulled off first his cravat, then his waistcoat and finally the gorgeous silk shirt. He looked handsome in this light, it flattered him. Jenna thought Max good looking but not devastatingly so. She had seen better looking men in the club, but Max had charisma and charm. He knew how to make her feel special, important. Jenna loved how he always knew just what to say, what to do in any given situation. She revelled in the kudos of being with him, the respect he commanded from everyone who came into his orbit. He was like a father figure to her and she felt she needed his strength and maturity. She would grow to love him in time, she felt certain of it.

*

Max lay on his back in the king-sized four poster bed - his arms wrapped around his new wife - and sighed contentedly. She was sleeping peacefully in his embrace, and he kissed the top of her head. Their love-making had been amazing – truly amazing – for him. He had taken things very slowly at first – Jenna was inexperienced after all – and he had been patient with her, whispering encouragements as they caressed, stroking her hair and telling her over and over how much he loved her.

He had been determined to make her first time memorable, something she would remember forever. His fingers found her wetness and skilfully brought her to orgasm before he gently penetrated her for the first time. Jenna gasped as her husband took her prized virginity, her fingers pressing into his shoulders, caressing his muscular body as he moved above her. As he continued to build a steady rhythm she was moaning softly beneath him, his every thrust becoming more urgent now as he neared climax. Her responses drove him almost to the point of no return and he had to slow his pace several time to prevent himself from coming too soon. He experienced the first rush of orgasm just as Jenna wrapped her legs around his back, her arms wound around his neck; he held onto her tightly as he came.

Max hadn't thought it possible to feel this much love for a woman. He had never in his life felt the way he did about Jenna. Just being inside her was everything he had dreamed of and more. Now she was truly his, body and soul. Max Reid was in love and it had consumed his every waking thought since the first moment he had met her.

*

Jenna slipped out of bed and, picking up her small clutch, she made her way to the bathroom. Closing the door quietly behind her she opened the sequinned bag and took out a pack of contraceptive pills. Filling a glass with water she popped a pill out of the foil and into her mouth, washing it down before replacing the pack in her clutch. Max had told her he wanted to start a family as soon as possible after they were married and she had gone along with the idea, but in the back of her mind she had no intention of having a baby just yet. In fact, if she were completely honest with herself, Jenna Reid didn't want children at all. Not now, not ever.

Slipping back between the sheets she curled up in her husband's arms and closed her eyes. Last night's love-making hadn't been all that she was expecting. Oh, Max had been patient, done all the right things, she couldn't deny that. Something was missing though. She hadn't *felt* the way she thought she would feel. It seemed to her that sex and emotion were two very different things. True – they'd had sex – but Jenna couldn't honestly say she had felt any real love for Max during the act. Perhaps it would come in time. She certainly hoped so, because she couldn't imagine being trapped in a lifetime of loveless sex.

For her, marrying Max Reid had been a means to an end. She had been determined from a very young age that she would never live the downtrodden life she had watched her Mother lead. No, she wasn't going to be a drudge for anyone, and as for kids – well, she would make sure there were no pitter-patters of tiny feet any time soon.

She had achieved the first part of her plan in making Max fall in love with her and now she was his wife. Jenna had her eye on The Starlight Club. She wanted Max to make her a partner in the business and if she had her way it wouldn't be long before she got her way about that too!

Yes, everything was going according to plan and Jenna Reid couldn't help but smile like the cat that got the cream as she reached down beneath the duvet and began fondling her new husband's cock.

CHAPTER FOURTEEN

Four Years Later

Jenna Reid was bursting with excitement. It was Christmas Eve and she could hardly sit still waiting for Max to come home. He had promised her the Christmas of all Christmases and Jenna had the idea that he would be fetching her gifts with him. She planned on ambushing him as he took off his over-coat to see whether she could spot any obvious clues.

Max only ever shopped in Harrods or Selfidges, Tiffany's or Garrards for her gifts at Christmas, but she hoped there might be one or two little gift bags from Fortnum & Mason's or Agent Provocateur. Jenna loved Christmas, but this one was even more special as it also happened to be her twenty-first birthday and Max was throwing a party for her at The Starlight Club.

Everyone who mattered would be there and Jenna hugged herself with delight as she pictured herself gratefully receiving all the wonderful, expensive gifts she knew they'd be bringing for her. Jenna loved gifts. She felt she *deserved* them. After all, she had made Max the happiest man in the world, hadn't she? It was only right that she should reap some of the rewards!

Max was feeling happy as he made his way home at around six-thirty. He planned on having a quick shower and shave and then he would be taking his beautiful wife out to dinner. The party was all set for tomorrow evening. Two hundred guests would be arriving at the club to help celebrate Jenna's twenty-first.

He knew she would be waiting in the hallway, eagerly eyeing what he might have brought home for her. Max smiled to himself. She would be disappointed if she thought her birthday gift this year came in a carrier bag. He planned to give her the biggest and best surprise that money could buy this year. She would be over the moon, he was certain of it.

Max's parents, James and Dorothea, were making their way to London from Hampshire for the Festive season. Max loved having his parents stay over at the apartment, although he sometimes got the impression that his wife resented them being there. Once, when he had questioned why she had such a long face during their stay, she had dismissed it as her just wanting to have him all to herself, and that she couldn't help feeling that way as, after all, they had not been married long and she still felt like she was on honeymoon.

Of course, Max had understood perfectly on that occasion, and had been secretly delighted to learn that his wife cherished their time alone so much.

Jenna had been careful to hide her true feelings after her husband had questioned her. She had lied to him easily, smiling sweetly as she gazed up into his trusting, blue eyes. The truth was she hated Max's parents being around.

James Reid had suffered a serious heart attack many years ago. The doctors had put it down to stress and too many nights burning the candle at both ends so, once he was released from hospital he had promised his wife, Dorothea, and the rest of the family that he'd take things easy from now on. True to his word he now made a point of being in bed by nine o'clock in the evening, avoided too much rich food and only drank on special occasions. Max had been terrified that he would lose his father that night, the only man he had ever truly admired and respected. It had been a very sobering experience for them all.

Shortly after his father was taken ill, Max Reid had found himself on the wrong side of the law and had served time in prison as a result of it. It was something that no-one liked to talk about, particularly in front of James Reid, because he had blamed himself for many years for his son's downfall.

It didn't matter what anybody said, James felt ultimately responsible for putting his own son behind bars. Max had just turned twenty-one when he was sent down for ten years and as he watched his only son being led away, James Reid truly believed that he would never smile or know a moment's peace ever again.

Max was released from prison after six and a half years with time off for good behaviour plus time spent on remand and with help from his parents he had started his own building firm, taking on renovations and property development contracts all over London. The work had come in thick and fast. Max Reid built himself a good reputation for being thorough and nearly always finished the work ahead of the deadline. Over the following three years he managed to carve out a decent living for himself.

It wasn't until he met an old friend from way back, however, that he Max became involved in the nightclub business. Marcus Graham and Max had been friends in school and when they bumped into one another quite by chance, Max had been delighted to see his old pal and they had spent many nights reminiscing over a bottle or two of Jack Daniels.

Marcus had explained to Max that had his eye on a very lucrative deal, and needed someone to invest with him. He explained that he wanted to buy a club in the East End, and that the current owners were looking for a quick sale as they wanted to emigrate. The club was called Jilly's, and whilst it wasn't doing too badly Marcus figured that with a fresh injection of cash, and a complete renovation, the place would be a good little earner for them both. Max and Marcus had shaken hands on the deal that night and things had moved at lightning speed after that.

The new club, renamed The Lounge Bar, opened three weeks before Christmas and the place had been packed to the rafters every night. People from all over the smoke were keen to make the acquaintance of the new owners, and it wasn't long before Max and Marcus had earned themselves the reputation of being diamond geezers – the kind of men you wanted to do business with. They were honest, fair-minded and open about their business dealings. They treated the staff well and paid them a good wage. They were respected by everyone who came into their orbit.

All in all, Max and Marcus could do no wrong and within two years they opened a second club, Annabel's, which catered for the kind of clientele who wanted their mistresses and their wives kept well apart! The club promised total anonymity for its members and it was a given right from the get-go that if anyone called the club to enquire as to the whereabouts of a particular club member the staff would claim not to know the individual and, no matter how many times the caller insisted that it was an emergency, the staff wouldn't budge an inch. The membership was pricey, compared to some of the other clubs around, but the members were happy to pay it because they were guaranteed a safe place in which to conduct their business, be that professional or personal.

That had been just over twelve years ago. Neither of them had considered even for a second that anything could possibly happen to spoil the charmed lives they were both leading. They were raking in the money hand over fist and the clubs were thriving. Max bought a new apartment in the West End and Marcus married Sally-Anne, his girlfriend of five years. The world really was their oyster, and the two friends would meet up regularly over dinner and congratulate themselves on their success.

Then suddenly, out of nowhere, disaster struck. Marcus' wife, Sally-Anne was diagnosed with breast cancer. She had been feeling unwell for a couple of months and one night, after taking a shower, she had noticed a lump in her right breast. Their G.P. took a biopsy, which was sent away for analysis. When, three weeks later, the grim-faced consultant gave Sally-Anne the news that the tumour was malignant, and particularly aggressive, she had collapsed into the arms of her distraught husband. They had travelled home in silence, numb with shock.

Within days Sally-Anne had been admitted onto a private ward at the Nuffield and undergone a mastectomy. Despite receiving reassurances from Marcus, Sally-Anne said that she felt less like a woman without her breast and refused to allow Marcus anywhere near her. She wouldn't even accept a cuddle from her husband.

Following the operation, Sally-Anne underwent an extensive course of chemotherapy which saw her hair fall out, and left her weak and despondent. Marcus had confided in Max that, at one point, he had feared he would lose her. She had been so low, following the chemotherapy, that Marcus worried his beloved wife might seek a way out of her misery once and for all. Terrified of what she might do in her desperation, Marcus wouldn't leave her side even to go out and buy a packet of fags. He'd send his housekeeper instead knowing that in her fragile mental state Sally-Anne could see his absence as an opportunity to swallow a handful of tranquilisers.

When Marcus told Max that he wanted to sell his share of the clubs, Max had understood immediately the strain his friend was under and suggested selling up altogether and splitting the profits fifty – fifty. That way, Marcus could take his share and use it to take proper care of his wife as she convalesced, and Max would use his half to start again, perhaps open another club somewhere. Marcus Graham needed all the help he could get at that moment in time.

"We've earned a good wedge from the clubs, mate, put your marriage first and spend all the time you can with Sal" Max had shaken his friend's hand and seen the fear in his eyes. Neither man spoke the words that they were both thinking – 'she might not have long left'.

*

Jenna Reid took her contraceptive pill with a slug of whiskey. She had forgotten to take it a few times since she and Max were married, resulting in a week or two of anxiety each time as she waited for her period to arrive. Max had suggested she see a doctor to find out why it was she was having trouble conceiving. Jenna had promptly burst into tears and Max had felt guilt when she suddenly began accusing him of not loving her.

"How can you say that, Max? Every month I pray that I'm pregnant and every month I have to face the fact that I've let you down – AGAIN! If you loved me you wouldn't put this kind of pressure on me all the time".

"Jenna, darling, please don't be upset. Of course I love you. You know I didn't mean anything by it, love. I just can't help wondering whether there's something wrong....y'know...." he trailed off.

"What? That I'm barren you mean? Is that what you mean, Max, that I'm barren? How COULD you?" she spat.

"No, I....I just meant...I just meant that perhaps if you saw a doctor he could rule it out. It's probably me..I've probably got a low sperm count or something. Forget I mentioned it, Jen, honestly. I didn't mean to upset you"

Jenna had smirked to herself as Max continued to place the blame for their childlessness on himself. If he wanted to believe he had a low sperm count who was she to argue? After all – he hadn't managed to produce any children with his first wife had he? Chances are it he *did* have a low sperm count. The contraceptive pill she took each day was just an extra precaution. Max didn't know what was good for him. If he had his way he'd soon have Jenna producing one baby after another like a brood mare. Well, she wanted none of it. Jenna Reid was going places, and children just didn't figure in her plans.

Max arrived home to find his wife loitering in the hallway, her emerald eyes twinkling in the lamp-light. He smiled at her as he took off his coat and hung it up. Clearly she was dying to see what he had bought her.

When she couldn't see any carrier bags Jenna rushed over to Max, throwing her arms around him. "Darling, where are they? Where are my presents? Are they still in the car? You've left them in the car, haven't you?" she playfully punched him now and threw her arms around his neck. "Come on, Max, tell me where they *are*!" she demanded.

"Nope, it's not in the car, Jenna. There's no point looking for any bags either because I didn't bring any home. You'll just have to wait until tomorrow, won't you?" he teased. She glared at him as she realised that he was perfectly serious. There were no gift bags from Harrods, or Tiffany or *anywhere*! "Oh, Max, you've forgotten!! How could you forget my twenty-first birthday? How could you?" with that Jenna ran upstairs and flung herself onto the king-size bed, sobbing tears of disappointment and frustration. She hated him. She fucking *hated him*.

CHAPTER FIFTEEN

It was Christmas Night and The Starlight Club was heaving with invited guests as they came together to celebrate Jenna Reid's twenty-first birthday. It had been a frosty Christmas indeed in the Reid household. Jenna had barely spoken to Max all day so disgusted was she that he hadn't even bothered to bring her a birthday gift. She would make him pay for this. By God, she would make him pay!

Last night he had tried to make love to her and she had pushed him away. "Not now, Max, I have a headache" she had lied. Inside she was seething with fury. How dare he forget her birthday?! She was his wife, for fuck's sake. How the hell does someone forget their wife's birthday, and her twenty-first birthday at that?

No, if Max Reid thought he was going to get away with this one, he had another think coming. Jenna knew exactly how to hurt her husband, and she was ready, willing and able. Christmas lunch had been strained with Max's parents struggling to keep the conversation going. Clearly there was a problem between their son and his wife, but they didn't feel it was their place to interfere. Max was a grown man after all.

*

Max was standing over in the far corner of the club chatting to a couple of business associates. He was thinking of purchasing another club in the summer and the men in question were the current owners. Max was confident he could get the place at a reasonable price, but at the moment the Richards brothers were holding out on him.

"Come on, Max, you know as well as I do it's a fair price, mate. You ain't gonna get a better deal anywhere. Just swallow your knob and shake hands on it eh, what d'you say?" Roy Richards winked at his younger brother, Paul, as the three men eyed each other warily.

Max had had dealings with these two fuckers before and he knew that they were bona-fide nutcases. One word out of place and he could wake up tomorrow to find The Starlight Club was no more than a huge pile of ashes. He had to get the brothers to come down a bit without seeming to take the proverbial piss.

"Tell you what, fellas, let's have another drink, shall we? I need to speak to my accountant, see how the land lies, if you know what I mean? Being married doesn't come cheap as I'm sure you know, Roy, and my Jenna's expecting something pretty special for her birthday. Its fair cleaned me out, if truth be told. I'm thinking I may have to pass on this one, if I'm honest".

Roy Richards took a large swig of his scotch and eyed Max Reid over the rim of his glass. He didn't believe one word of what this fucker was telling him. He knew Max Reid had more money stashed away than The Royal Mint, so if he was holding out on him it could only mean one thing – he figured he could get them to lower the price.

"No worries, Max, no worries at all, mate. I understand perfectly" Roy signalled to his brother now that it was high time they were going. "Sorry we can't stay to see Jenna unwrap her presents, Max, but I'm sure we'll catch up with her at some point in the future" The threat was subtle but Max picked up on it straight away.

Roy Richards was one nasty fucker and if he got it into his head that Max had reneged on a deal, even though no hands had been shaken at this point, he would think nothing of seeing to it that Jenna Reid never wanted to see her own reflection again.

"How's business, Roy? Struggling a bit over the past few months, I hear. Hope you got your Health & Safety certificates all up to date, mate - seems that Trading Standards are closing businesses down left, right and centre. Something about the Fire Safety not being up to scratch"

Max smiled now. If Roy Richards thought he was going to threaten him, and in his own fucking gaff at that, he needed his fucking head testing. Max drove his point home now. "Be a fuckin' shame if it all went up in smoke after all your hard work, eh lads?"

Roy and Paul Richards walked out of The Starlight Club under no illusions about Max Reid. They knew their card was marked, and one false move against him could bring retribution of epic proportions down on their heads. Max, for his part, felt that he'd made his point. He'd let them stew for a couple of weeks and then see how the land lay.

*

Jenna Reid was feeling decidedly down in the dumps! It was almost eleven thirty and still there had been no hint of a surprise gift for her birthday, let alone fucking Christmas. She was pissed off to say the least and was drowning her sorrows with a bottle of Cristal and a few lines of coke in the ladies restroom. Fuck her stupid, pathetic husband! She was going to go out there and tell him exactly what she thought of him, and fuck who heard her. She had been waiting all day for some hint that Max hadn't forgotten her. Well, she'd waited long enough!

Striding across the dancefloor toward her husband she took a swig from the almost empty bottle of champagne before rounding on him. "So, come on then, Maxie! Where's my fucking birthday present, then eh?" Max turned to see his young wife could barely stand. It was pretty obvious she was pissed but there was something else, something he couldn't quite put his finger on. She seemed too *full on* somehow, almost feral. Looking her in the eyes he suddenly saw it – she'd been snorting cocaine!

"For fuck's sake, Jenna, what the hell are you playing at, girl? Snorting that crap up your nose, as if you haven't drunk enough champagne for the pair of us – now you wanna go shoving that rubbish up your fucking beak. Where did you get it, eh? Tell me! Where the fuck did you get it?" Max's grip on her arm tightened as he struggled to hold his wife upright. People had heard the commotion and stood now, in small groups, watching and waiting to see what the outcome would be. Jenna Reid was known for her fiery temper and Max was pushing his luck bawling his wife out in public that way.

"Fuck off, Max, FUCK OFF!" Jenna screamed. "You couldn't even buy me a fucking birthday present, could you? I'm your fucking WIFE!" She threw the empty champagne bottle at Max's head, but luckily he saw it coming and managed to duck out of the way before it hit him. "Jenna! For fuck's sake, of *course* I got you a fucking birthday present. What the fuck d'you take me for, eh?" he pulled his wife over to where the deejay was busily trying to find a song which would drown out the sound of Max and Jenna rowing, and grabbed the mic off him.

"Ladies and gentlemen, friends…" He gestured with his arm now, sweeping it from right to left to encompass the room before him. "I would like you to join me in drinking a toast to my gorgeous wife, Jenna, on this – her twenty-first birthday - and to help her celebrate the start of her new business venture!"

With that he reached into his inside breast pocket and pulled out a long, white sheaf of papers. To the amazement of everyone, he went on: "My darling Jen, I wanted to give you something really special for your birthday. So - these are the deeds to your very own business. It's a chic little boutique in the High Street, and it comes with all the fixtures and fittings. There is a staff already in place, although of course that side of things will be up to you, darling. You can choose the stock you want to sell, but to be fair the stuff that's in there already is doing fantastically well. What d'you think, Jenna, you happy with it then, love?

Max Reid looked fit to burst as he handed the papers and a bunch of keys over to his wife, who stood open-mouthed as she tried to take in what he was saying. He'd bought her a shop? A *shop* for fuck's sake! Did he really expect her to go out to work for a living? Because that hadn't been what she had signed up for, it hadn't been part of the plan. She had married Max Reid fully expecting to be kept in the lap of luxury. She hadn't expected she would actually have to *work* for those luxuries!

She could feel the eyes of everyone in the room on her as she accepted the keys and the deeds to her new shop. She wanted to ram the deeds straight down his throat, along with the fucking keys too! This was too much; this really was beyond a joke. "I...I don't know what to say, I'm speechless". She stood with the keys in one hand and the deeds in the other as the crowd of invited guests, taking this as her delight, broke into rapturous applause.

One of the wives handed Jenna a glass of champagne to celebrate her good fortune. Jenna drank it down in one go, and promptly demanded another. There were murmurs of 'amazing' and 'fabulous present – so generous' amongst the guests as she struggled to fight back the tears. Max, seeing her eyes fill up, blindly assumed that they were tears of joy. "I'm so glad you like it, Jen" he shouted above the pounding music. Jenna raised her glass to her husband and spat "Like it, Max? Oh, I'm delirious!"

In the corner of the room Tommy McLaughlin stood watching the wife of Max Reid very intently. Tommy was a keen observer of people's body language and everything about Jenna Reid told him that she was unhappy, very unhappy indeed.

Tommy saw this as a challenge. He found himself wondering exactly what it might take to change that, to put a smile on her face. Then he smiled to himself. He knew exactly what would put a smile on the face of Mrs Max Reid and he had plenty of it. Never one to back down from a challenge – even a self-imposed one – Tommy decided there and then he would make the acquaintance of the young woman who stood wiping tears of apparent joy from her eyes.

Because Tommy McLaughlin recognised those tears for exactly what they were – total and utter misery.

CHAPTER SIXTEEN

Max Reid was puzzled. He had given his wife her own business, offered to pay for a total refurbishment to her liking and stock the place with the best clothing money could buy and yet, so far, she hadn't shown the slightest interest in opening the place. He had thought she would be overjoyed to have her independence but she simply refused to even go to the shop, let alone open it! Max was at the end of his tether.

"For fuck's sake, Jenna, what more do you want? I've paid out a hefty fucking wedge for that shop, the least you could do is take an interest" he stormed around the bedroom now, pulling shirt after shirt out of the wardrobe before flinging it on the bed and grabbing another. "Don't you want some independence, some money of your own?" He stood glaring at her now, angry and unsure of what to say to spark a bit of interest. Just lately his wife had been uninterested in everything, including him, and he feared for their marriage. "Look, if you don't want the place just say so. We can sell it if that's what you want to do. At least go down and take a look at it, see whether you like it. That way you can get a feel for what might look good, décor and that – we can employ a team to come in and do the place up exactly as you want it. What do you say? Will you at least pop down and have a look, love?"

"Yes, alright, I suppose it won't do any harm to look" Jenna smiled at him now. "I guess I just feel a little out of my depth in my own shop. I've not had any experience with business before, and I was *hoping* you might have wanted me at the club if I'm honest" Jenna eyed her husband sulkily now, determined to make her point. She had so wanted her name on the deeds of The Starlight Club - it was all she ever thought about. She figured she'd be a dab hand at running a nightclub, giving out the orders, but a clothes shop?!

"Oh, darling, you never said anything about wanting to work at the club. Besides, what on earth would you do there? There's no way I'd have my wife working the bar or the restaurant. I've already got a Manager in place and the book-keeper comes in twice a month so there'd be nothing for you to do" Max hugged his wife now and planted a kiss on her forehead. "Pop into the shop this afternoon, and we can discuss ideas for the refurb over dinner" Max picked up his jacket and keys and stopped to blow Jenna a kiss as he made his way out of the bedroom. "Bye, Jen"

Jenna gave her husband a half-hearted smile and rolled over in bed. Damn Max and that fucking shop! She was never going to convince him to let her run the club unless she learned how to run a small business first. Perhaps that was what he had in mind after all, she thought. Perhaps if she could prove herself in a small shop he would make her a partner in the club eventually. With that thought she jumped out of bed and went for a shower.

An hour later she parked in the side street adjacent to her new shop and strolled through the front door to find an assistant leaning over the counter, giggling and laughing with another young girl whilst chewing a mouthful of gum. Walking over to where the two girls were clearly sharing details of their latest boyfriends, Jenna stood waiting for them to notice her. They carried on chatting, oblivious to her presence. After a few minutes Jenna had had enough. She marched up to the counter and, pushing the friend aside, addressed the assistant. "I hate to interrupt your chat, love, but if you could possibly drag yourself away for a moment..." The girl looked up at Jenna with a sullen expression and smirked at her friend before saying "Yeah, what d'you want?" Jenna was livid. This was not the kind of assistant she wanted on the payroll of any business of hers! "What do I want? Well, let me see now" Jenna toyed with the girl as she stood staring at her, clearly unaware of who Jenna was. "What I *want* is for you to pop out into the back, or wherever it is you've hung your coat this morning, get your things and get the FUCK out of my shop – you're fired!" The girl's mouth dropped open as she realised that this young woman in front of her was in fact Mrs Jenna Reid, the new owner, and she was now looking for another job unless she bucked her ideas up.

"Look, Mrs Reid, I'm sorry like, it's just.... well....I wasn't expecting you, and I thought you was just a customer" the girl gabbled now, trying desperately to excuse her rude attitude. "Precisely!" Jenna spat "You thought I was a customer, and yet you treated me like vermin. I won't have that kind of attitude in my staff. Now get out, and take your friend with you" Jenna's determined expression brooked no argument and the girl stomped into the back, picked up her bag and coat and marched defiantly towards the front door of the shop, her friend following quickly behind. Opening the door, the girl turned to eye the woman who had just sacked her and her vitriol came spewing out as she pointed a finger at Jenna. "This place is shit anyhow, love. You'll be lucky to sell anything by the time I get through telling me mates about what you done to me. I reckon this fuckin' place will be closed within a month" and with that she turned on her heel and marched out of the shop, slamming the door so hard it made the windows rattle.

Jenna took a look around at the fixtures and fittings. The place could certainly do with a makeover. She envisaged sleek black chairs, crystal chandeliers and a gleaming new glass service counter. Moving into the back she eyed the two changing areas with disdain. The curtains were dated pink dralon and the lighting in the cubicles was poor. There were no hooks on the back of the door and nowhere to sit. Jenna found herself picturing the how it could look with new, brightly-lit cubicles and comfortable seating. The toilet in the back needed ripping out and replacing. As for the small kitchen area it, too, could do with replacing and perhaps the wall could be knocked down to make it a larger space for the staff to take their lunchbreaks. She imagined herself employing two part-time assistants, one covering the mornings and the other the afternoons. She herself would pop in every morning to oversee the new stock intake and keep an eye on things. Yes, she decided, this could work. This could actually work!

The first thing she needed to do was to decide on the new décor and advertise for the new assistants. She telephoned the agency and left the details of what she required – two sales assistants, over the age of 21, clean and presentable with impeccable manners. She gave details of pay and holiday benefits and a contact telephone number, saying that interviews would be held at the premises as early as next week if possible. The lady on the phone was very helpful and promised Jenna that she could have the two assistants in place for her within days if required. Jenna felt excited. She realised that Max had played a blinder buying her this shop. It was her own little domain, somewhere she would be in charge, and the profits would all be hers and hers alone. Locking up the shop, she made her way back to the car with a spring in her step.

Across the road, Tommy McLaughlin stood leaning against a lamppost and watched her intently. Sandra Jarvis had found him in the bookies, and mouthed off all over the place about the stuck-up bitch that had just fired her from the shop across the road. Tommy smiled inwardly. It seemed Mrs Jenna Reid had some backbone after all. Tommy liked feisty women, and it seemed this one was just his type. She was also married to Max Reid, and that only added to the appeal for Tommy. Never one to look a gift horse in the mouth, he promised himself that he would make the acquaintance of Jenna Reid first chance he got. He watched as she drove off down the road in her flash Mercedes convertible and decided there and then that, if he had his way, he would be taking the lovely Mrs Reid to bed one day in the not-too-distant future. He laughed out loud then. Tommy always got his way.

CHAPTER SEVENTEEN

The shop's opening day had been a grand affair. Half the town had turned out to celebrate with Jenna and the champagne had flowed freely. She had decided to name the shop after herself – Jenna's – and it seemed everybody loved the new fashionable lines she had brought in. There were some beautiful Italian leather jackets; designer dresses by Versace, Dior and Dolce & Gabbana. The range of footwear was stunning, if a little out of most people's price-range. Jenna had personally selected the Jimmy Choo and Manolo Blahnik shoes, taking great delight in the window display of top-of-the-range footwear and matching handbags. Jenna herself was dressed in a beautiful, classic Chanel dress and Laboutin shoes. The epitome of elegant chic, she chatted with her friends and prospective clients as they sipped Bollinger and smiled at her husband as he raised his glass in silent toast to her success. It really was a beautiful shop now that the refurbishment was complete and no one could have been more proud than Max.

Tommy McLaughlin wasn't invited to the opening of the shop but he had decided to pop along anyway. It wouldn't hurt to wish the new proprietor good luck and Tommy saw this as the perfect opportunity to make the acquaintance of Mrs Jenna Reid. He had been at her 21st birthday party, but only as the plus-one of an invited guest. He hadn't registered in her orbit yet, but today would put that little matter to rights. He had donned his best bib and tucker and slicked his hair back with Brylcreem before making his way to the High Street. If he hadn't already known just where to find the place, it wouldn't have taken him long. The crowd outside the shop was large and rowdy, champagne flowing freely and balloons floating around in the May sunshine.

Tommy pushed through the crowd of people outside and spotted Jenna Reid chatting to a group of women in the far corner of the shop. Strolling across the room, he picked up a flute of champagne and, downing it in one, made his way over to where the women stood. Coughing slightly, he apologised to the women for interrupting them, before turning to look at Jenna.

"Hello, Mrs Reid, you don't know me but I was at your birthday party on Christmas night, and I just wanted to congratulate you on the opening of the shop and wish you every success for the future" Tommy flashed a winning smile now, displaying perfect, white teeth. His deep blue eyes were twinkling in the light from the expensive Chrystal chandeliers and Jenna felt herself blushing as he took her hand. He was absolutely gorgeous!

"Thank you....um...." she realised that he hadn't told her his name. She paused, smiling into his handsome face.

"Tommy, Tommy McLaughlin, and it's a pleasure to meet you Jenna. May I call you Jenna?" he gushed now, aware that Jenna Reid was taken with his good looks and charm. Tommy could turn on the charm at will, and it had served him well over the years. He had woken up in many a woman's bed of a morning, unsure of her name or how he had gotten there in the first place. Drink was never a problem for Tommy when it came to getting it up. He just couldn't remember who the hell he had just fucked most of the time.

"It's nice to meet you, Tommy, and yes – you can call me Jenna" she smiled widely at him now, a pink flush creeping up over her neck – clearly she fancied him and Tommy could see it a mile off.

"Well, I just popped by to say hello, I won't take up any more of your time. It was lovely to meet you" Tommy held her hand in his and covered it with his other, looking deep into her emerald green eyes. He had her hooked. Now for the parting shot. "I really have to dash, I have a date with a beautiful young lady, but I hope to run into you again soon" he smirked knowingly. Jenna's eyes flickered slightly as she took in what he was saying. He was meeting someone. Damn! She would have liked to chat with him a while longer, get to know more about him, but it was not to be. Pulling his hand away he turned and strode confidently out of the shop. Jenna watched him go and wished he could have stayed a while longer.

Max had been chatting to a couple of his business associates and hadn't seen Tommy McLaughlin enter or leave the shop. Had he done so it might have given him cause for concern – Max was no fool when it came to other men – he would have seen the flirtatious way in which the bloke had taken hold of his wife's hand, caressing it lightly with his fingers as he gazed into her eyes. More importantly, he'd have seen the flush of attraction that had crept over his wife's face, and the way in which she had eyed the handsome young man in front of her, clearly taken with him.

Max was blissfully unaware of the encounter and, indeed, the importance of it. For that encounter would be the first of many between young Tommy McLaughlin and Max's pretty little wife. It was an encounter which would lead to untold pain and heartache for Max Reid in the future.

CHAPTER EIGHTEEN

The following Saturday Jenna arrived at the shop bright and early. She anticipated a good day's takings now that news of the opening day had filtered through to anyone who wasn't there. Word spread like wildfire in London and Jenna felt confident that her shop would do well over the coming months.

She had been in the shop for about ten minutes when the door opened and a young woman walked in carrying the biggest bouquet Jenna had ever seen. She smiled as she took the flowers from the delivery driver. Trust Max to think of sending her flowers on her first proper day. It was sweet of him.

Jenna suddenly felt irritated. That was Max all over – sweet. Oh, she couldn't fault him for the way he showered her with love and affection. It was just that it *irritated* her. She didn't really know why it did, but every time Max showed her his love just lately she felt strangely turned off by it.

Going into the small kitchen she took a cut-glass vase from under the sink and filled it with water. She would have time to trim the flowers before she opened up. Taking the small, white envelope from the bouquet she opened it and pulled out the card. No doubt it would be Max's words, but they would have been written by the florist. He never wrote the card out himself, another thing which irritated Jenna. Why the hell couldn't he make the effort?

Jenna gasped aloud as she saw who had sent the bouquet. The sender was not her husband, it was Tommy McLaughlin. The card inside was written in a masculine scrawl and simply read:

JENNA, GOOD LUCK WITH THE SHOP. TOMMY X

Jenna Reid suddenly knew *exactly* why she had felt so irritated when she had thought the flowers were from Max. It was because she had *wanted* them to be from Tommy. She was attracted to him, and she had been more than a little disappointed when he had walked out of the shop last week. Now he was sending her flowers, and not just any bouquet. This one must have cost him a small fortune. Jenna's pulse quickened as she re-read the card. Perhaps he, too, was attracted. Maybe this was his way of keeping her interested. She suddenly found herself fantasising about him as she cut the stems of the beautiful Grand Prix and Black Bacarra roses, the freesias and lilies. These flowers were more than simply a good-luck gesture. They had to be!

Jenna finished arranging them and took them through to the front of the shop and placed them centre-stage on the polished glass counter. She stood back to admire them. Clearly, Tommy had gone to a lot of trouble to get those flowers delivered so early in the day – it was barely nine o'clock. Jenna smiled wryly to herself. Well, if Mr Tommy McLaughlin wanted to make her acquaintance he was free to do so. He knew exactly where to find her after all.

CHAPTER NINETEEN

Disappointingly, Tommy did not put in an appearance on that Saturday morning. Nor did he show up over the next couple of weeks. Jenna had gone to the shop every day on the pretext of having stock-take to see to. The two young assistants found themselves wishing she would just take a day off. They couldn't sit chatting in the back whenever Mrs Reid was around, she preferred them at the counter all day, standing up and ready to serve with a smile.

Business was good, the tills were constantly full and Jenna could barely keep up with the demand for the latest designer gear. She sent the assistants to the manufacturers on more than one occasion instead of going herself which they found odd. After all, she was the owner – surely she wanted to see the goods before buying? Jenna had come up the excuse that she hadn't been feeling very well and had told the two sales assistants to take their time, go for lunch, anything they fancied doing, she just wanted some peace and quiet in the shop.

The truth was, Jenna was waiting for Tommy to show his face and she didn't want those two around if and when he decided to put in an appearance. She had decided that, if he did show up, she was going to feign feeling hungry and lock up the shop just after he arrived, thereby providing the opportunity for them to spend some time together. She would invite him to have lunch with her, spend an hour or two getting to know him. After all, he couldn't refuse a slap-up lunch at her expense, now could he?

By the start of the fourth week Jenna had given up any hope of seeing Tommy McLaughlin again. She figured he must have found another way to pass his time, probably the 'beautiful young lady' he had been in such a fucking hurry to meet two weeks ago. Jenna felt inwardly rejected. She had been certain that he had been as attracted to her as she had been to him. Now she wasn't so sure. Or maybe it was Max that was putting Tommy off. After all, Max Reid was well-known in these parts - Tommy can't have failed to have heard of him. Perhaps the thought of Max's anger should he discover that Tommy had been hanging around his wife was enough to put him off. Either way, Jenna Reid was gutted to think she was never going to see Tommy again. She was in the back room, pouring herself a large glass of Chardonnay with which to drown her sorrows when Tommy McLaughlin walked into the shop.

Seeing nobody at the counter he figured that Jenna was in the back. He had been standing watching the shop for almost an hour now, taking in who was coming and going before deciding to walk across the road. So far he had seen Jenna Reid go in, but no sales girls. Perhaps Jenna had given them the day off. Tommy smiled to himself. This was going to be easier than he had first thought. If the lovely Jenna was alone in the shop he would surprise her.

Turning over the 'OPEN' sign he clicked the lock closed on the door to the shop. It wouldn't do for anyone to walk into the place, not with what he had planned at any rate.

Walking quietly behind the counter he stepped into the small, brightly-lit kitchen area at the back of the shop where Jenna stood with her back to him sipping on a cup of coffee.

"Hello, Jenna" he spoke softly now as he stood close to her. Jenna recognised his voice immediately and her stomach fluttered as she felt him behind her. *He had come back!*

Placing the half-empty coffee cup onto the sink top she turned to face him. As she did so Tommy kissed her hard, his mouth covering hers with such a sense of urgency it almost took her breath away. Jenna responded with equal passion – she had longed for this, imagined it day after day. Tommy's hands were all over her now, squeezing her breasts, her buttocks, caressing her back. She could barely keep her hands off him, so badly did she want this man. When he lifted her up she let it happen knowing that this was the point of no return. He turned and carried her the three or four feet to the kitchen table where Jenna and the assistants took their coffee-breaks.

Lying her down on her back he first took off her shoes before sliding her dress up over her thighs, exposing her black lace panties. Tommy slid his hands under Jenna's dress and pulled them down, throwing them onto the kitchen floor. Jenna was writhing on the table now, clearly aroused and up for it. Tommy knelt down and lifted Jenna's legs over his shoulders before burying his head between her legs. She gasped out loud as his tongue found her clitoris and he teased her with little flicks before inserting a finger into her throbbing, wet vagina. It was all Jenna could do not to scream as Tommy fingered her slowly and rhythmically, building up speed as she started to cliMax. She shoved a fist into her mouth as he brought her to orgasm. This was incredible! Jenna had never experienced such an intense feeling of pleasure before. Oh, she had had orgasms with Max, but not like this. This was something else.

Tommy unzipped his flies and pulled out his throbbing cock. He had been very blessed by Mother Nature and his mates often joked that his cock was so big it was a wonder he didn't pass out every time he got a hard on.

Shoving it into Jenna Reid he pounded her hard for several minutes until he could feel the familiar rush starting in his balls. Suddenly he was at the point of no return and came inside her, grabbing her arse as he did so for good measure, making sure she felt every thrust.

A few moments later Tommy McLaughlin was zipping up his flies and smiling down into the face of Max Reid's wife. He couldn't help but imagine the look on Max's face if he could see his wife now - lying on the kitchen table in the shop he had bought her, her knickers on the floor and her face flushed with orgasm. He leaned over her now and whispered into her ear "You ever want more of the same, give me a call" before handing her a small, white card with the name 'Bryce Industries' printed in black letters and the name 'Tommy McLaughlin' below it with a mobile phone number. Jenna took it and smiled up at the handsome face of the man she had been obsessing over for the past four weeks. She couldn't take her eyes off him as he stood tucking his shirt into his trousers.

Tommy began to whistle quietly to himself now as he watched Jenna pulling on her panties. She really was a looker, and an extremely good lay.

What made her all the more appealing in Tommy's eyes though was the fact that she was the wife of the man he hated most in the whole world.

CHAPTER TWENTY

Tommy McLaughlin had moved to the smoke from Ireland some eight years ago, at the age of twenty-two. He arrived full of ambition and a burning desire to make a fast buck. Easy on the eye, and laid back in his approach to others, Tommy had found it easy to settle in and make new friends. The men seemed to like him and treated him as one of their own. The women found the young, brooding Irishman fascinating. With his black hair and deep, blue eyes Tommy McLaughlin could take his pick of any woman, and he certainly wasted no time getting acquainted.

What nobody could have known was that, deep inside, Tommy McLaughlin was nursing a grudge against a man from his past. That man was Max Reid, and Tommy had promised himself that first chance he got, he would take the man down. It didn't matter to him how it came about, just so long as he had his revenge.

It hadn't taken Tommy long to find work on one of the new housing developments as a labourer, but although the work was consistent the pay wasn't all that good and Tommy had found himself looking for ways to boost his earnings. Apart from the odd stint as a doorman at a few of the local clubs he hadn't had much luck until one night he had run into Les Bryce. Les was a small-time gangster of sorts, with a finger in every pie. He ran a couple of strip clubs in the East End and dabbled in a bit of drug-dealing. Nothing major, but enough to provide a very decent earn.

The night in question proved to be a fateful one for them both. Tommy had been working the door at the Blue Banana nightclub and the evening had gone without incident until, that is, Les Bryce pulled a hatchet on another punter.

The bloke had clearly said something to offend Les and an almighty row had broken out at the bar. The smaller of the two, Les appeared to be on the receiving end of some serious verbal as Tommy and a couple of the lads walked over to the bar. Fists hadn't yet started flying and the doormen intended to break it up before it got to the stage where they'd have serious ruck to deal with. Unfortunately, Les Bryce decided not to wait for them to break things up. He took matters into his own hands and pulled a meat cleaver from his inside coat pocket. The blade gleamed under the bright lights of the bar area and Tommy just had time to register the weapon before Les grabbed the other bloke by the wrist and, slamming it onto the bar top, separated him from his right hand. The blood was everywhere. People were screaming and running for the door. The place was in chaos. The severed hand, complete with gold sovereign rings, was unceremoniously thrown onto to floor where Les Bryce proceeded to boot it into a crowd of onlookers. Tommy and the other doormen, a big bruiser called Mikey O'Rourke and a wiry, hard fucker called Harry Dixon, grabbed hold of Les Bryce and dragged him out of the club, down the back stairs and through the exit door onto the street. Les seemed unbelievably calm, considering he had just amputated a bloke's hand, and hadn't given the three men any trouble. Tommy had never witnessed anything like it.

A couple of nights later Les Bryce had turned up at the front door of the club and asked for Tommy by name. The receptionist had phoned upstairs and told Tommy he had best come down right away. Clearly nervous, she had a sense of urgency in her voice and Tommy made his way down to the foyer where he could see Les Bryce waiting with a couple of the doormen. He was chatting amiable to them as Tommy approached the group.

A small, balding man Les Bryce was a power-pack of solid muscle. Tommy had felt his strength as he'd escorted him out of the club a few nights ago and he wanted no beef with the man. Tommy could see the bloke was deranged, a bona-fide nutcase.

"Alright, Mr Bryce, what can I do for you, then?" Tommy decided to play the nice-guy approach. He hoped that he wasn't going to have a fucking ruck with Les Bryce, because Tommy didn't much fancy his chances against him.

"Hello, son – Tommy isn't it? Let's step outside, I'd like a word with you in private if I may" Les began, taking a cigarette from a pack and lighting it. Drawing deeply on it, he blew out the smoke before continuing "I want to apologise, y'know, for the other night. The truth is the bastard has had it comin' for a long time. He owed me a lot of money and he tried fuckin' me over big time. The thing is..." he trailed off now, seeming to struggle for the right words. Tommy stood watching him, preferring to remain silent at this point, give the man some time to consider his next words. Because Tommy had his instructions already – it didn't matter what Les Bryce said tonight – he was out, barred for life. Tommy didn't relish the thought of having to tell him so either, but he also knew he couldn't show weakness now. If Les Bryce caught a whiff of fear he would try to use it to his advantage and Tommy was nobody's fool, least of all this fucking nut job.

"The thing is, son, I know me card's marked 'ere in the club. Truth be told, I only called in to see that cunt. I just popped by to see if you fancied a spot of work" Les Bryce eyed the young man standing in front of him and he knew that he was also being scrutinised. The two remained silent for a few moments until Tommy enquired "What kind of work, Mr Bryce? I'm always open to offers, if you know what I mean, but I warn you – I don't come cheap"

Les Bryce finished his cigarette before he spoke again. Clearly the bloke had balls, that much was obvious. Les had watched Tommy in action up in the club and had seen him take out many a hard case with apparent ease. Tommy was just the kind of asset he needed in his business dealings -a bit of muscle, a bit of a persuader when the need arose. Les smiled at Tommy now. He was a cheeky fucker and no mistake. "Alright son, how does a couple of grand a week sound? But, I warn you, you accept my offer and you work for me – exclusive, like – and no questions asked, okay?" Les lit another cigarette and puffed on it as he waited for Tommy to answer. He could see the cogs turn, see the lad totting up the cash in his mind. He knew what the answer would be already. He was right.

Tommy had worked for Les Bryce ever since and had racked up some serious wedge in the process. Always there as a back-up whenever one of Les' debtors didn't want to cough up their loan repayments, or the cash owed for drugs that had been supplied 'on lay' Tommy was a grafter and loyal to his boss. As a consequence he enjoyed fringe benefits that others on Les' payroll didn't. The main one being access to Les' drum whenever he was out of town for the weekend or abroad on business for a week or two.

Les Bryce had a twelve year old daughter, Ruby, with his ex-wife Carol, who lived with her mother in Brighton. Les drove to Brighton religiously every Friday evening, returning late Sunday night. Tommy had proved himself to Les on numerous occasions and, as a perk of the job, Les gave Tommy the run of the apartment whilst he was gone. It was an arrangement that suited them both.

Tommy's place was nice enough, but nothing compared to the luxury of the place Les Bryce called home. Equipped with the latest mod-cons and sixty inch high definition television, it was every bachelor's dream place, and Tommy was no exception. He had taken many women there for a night of passion, promising them the world and then kicking them out in the cold light of day.

Tommy was a womaniser. He hadn't one shred of conscience about the girls he used. As far as he was concerned they were old enough to know what they were getting into, and once he'd fucked them rigid for a few hours Tommy grew bored of their company. Jenna Reid, however, was different. Not only was she seriously fit, she also happened to be married to Max Reid, which made the prospect of shagging her all the sweeter in Tommy's eyes.

CHAPTER TWENTY ONE

Jenna Reid felt like the cat that had got the cream. Ever since the morning that Tommy McLaughlin had walked into her shop and fucked her on the back kitchen table, she hadn't been able to keep the smile off her face. Max had commented on it a couple of times and Jenna had put it down to being happy that the business was doing so well.

She had decided to take the day off today and go up to the West End for a spot of retail therapy, get her hair and nails done and have a bit of lunch. She had been working hard over the past week or so and felt she deserved a pampering session. Plus, she had plans to ring Tommy and see if he'd like to join her for a drink later in the day.

Towelling herself dry, she sauntered out of the master en-suite just as Max was putting on his jacket. She eyed her husband slyly. Did he know just how much she resented him? Could he possibly have a clue how she felt, left alone night after night whilst he played host at his club? Wasn't that the reason his first marriage had failed – because the great Max Reid couldn't take his eye off the ball for a fucking second? Well, Jenna thought, that's fine by me because I've got something else to keep me busy, someone else to keep me company. She blow-dried her hair and dressed in a flowery, silk Karen Millen dress and matching shoes. Jenna liked to look good and today was a special occasion. If things went according to plan she would be taking the dress off by tea-time! She shivered with delight as a memory from last week suddenly popped into her mind. God, he was big! She had gasped in disbelief as he had pushed inch after inch of hard cock inside her, and the thought of it now made her pulse quicken and her cheeks flush pink. Max noticed his wife was looking particularly gorgeous this morning and he bent over to kiss her.

"Mmm...You smell divine, you going somewhere special" his blue eyes twinkling as he smiled down at her.

"Just shopping, thought I'd go to the salon and maybe catch up with a friend for lunch. Nothing too exciting" she returned his smile now, eager for him to leave so that she could daydream about Tommy. She couldn't wait for their next session; her desire for him had built over the past week until it was all she could do not to scream. Max had noticed a definite improvement in their love-making, with his wife seemingly enjoying it more and more over the past week or so. Little did he know that every time he was inside her, she was dreaming it was Tommy McLaughlin!

"I know I've neglected you lately, babe. Let me make it up to you this evening eh? We can go to the club and have dinner, maybe dance the night away into the early hours if you're up for it?" He paused now, waiting for her reply.

"That sounds lovely, Max, but could we make it another evening? I'd planned on popping to see my Mum later, and you know what she's like. It'll be hours before I manage to get away; she always wants the bloody low-down on everything" Jenna hoped to God Max didn't call her at her Mother's later, because she had no intention of being there.

"Sure, yeah, course we can. Make it tomorrow if you like. I've got a business meeting at four but I should be back around six, so I'll pop in for a quick freshen-up and we can take it from there, okay?"

"Yes, fine" Jenna applied lipstick and sprayed Jo Malone behind her ears before making her way downstairs. Max had percolated some fresh ground coffee and she decided to have a cup before heading off. Waving her husband goodbye she settled herself in the conservatory with her coffee and a croissant before taking out her mobile.

As she dialled Tommy's number her hands shook slightly and her stomach filled with butterflies. On the third ring he answered in a lazy drawl.

"Yeah? Hello" She heard his voice and her stomach did a somersault. She was sure she was blushing as she coughed slightly before speaking. "Hi, Tommy, it's Jenna Reid here" she waited, holding her breath for a few seconds. The silence was deafening as she waited for some response. "Hello? Are you there?" she fumbled now, unsure of what to say. Tommy was smiling to himself on the other end of the line. He never liked to appear too available to a woman, not even for Jenna Reid. He wanted her to realise right from the start that it was him in control, not her. It wouldn't do to let her think she had him on a hook. No, he wasn't about to be caught and reeled in by any woman.

Jenna was just about to hang up when she heard Tommy speak. "Hi, Jenna, what can I do for you?" he was playing with her now. He knew precisely why the lovely Mrs Reid was calling, and he was happy to oblige if that's what she wanted. Only it had to be on *his* terms, not hers.

"I er....I'm popping up to the West End this morning, I wondered whether you might be free for lunch, say around noon?" She tried her best to sound casual, but inside her stomach was lurching at the thought of him.

"Sorry, no, love. I'm busy at lunchtime. You got a pen handy?" he waited now as Jenna fumbled in her handbag for a pen and a scrap of paper. Tommy seemed off-hand, and that made her want him all the more.

"Yes, sure, go ahead" Jenna waited, curious to know what it was he wanted her to write down – a bar perhaps; a café somewhere; an address?

"Write this down" Tommy ordered before reeling off an address in Kensington. "Three o'clock, sharp! See you there"

Jenna scribbled down the address and was about to ask whether she should park out front when she heard the line go dead. He'd hung up! *He'd actually hung up!*

Jenna had never had anyone hang up on her before. She knew that she should tell him to go to hell. She knew it, but she also knew that she wouldn't. The attraction was too great. She wanted Tommy McLaughlin and she had to have him. If that had to be on his terms then so be it. Jenna Reid smiled to herself. This afternoon she would be in bed with Tommy, and hopefully they would spend some time getting to know one another this time.

Tommy ended the call and sat back on the black leather sofa. He was grinning from ear to ear. So – Jenna Reid fancied getting shagged this afternoon, did she? Well, if that was the case he'd best get a move on! Tommy whistled to himself as he showered. Today was going to be just the start of things between him and Jenna. He had a really good feeling about it.

CHAPTER TWENTY TWO

Jenna arrived at Les Bryce's apartment bang on time. She hated being late as a rule anyway, but Tommy had demanded she be punctual and she didn't want the afternoon to get off to a bad start. She checked her make-up in a small compact, applied a slick of lipstick and sprayed on her favourite Jo Malone perfume. She wanted to look – and smell – attractive for Tommy.

Pressing the buzzer, she heard the intercom click and she pushed open the outer door. The address Tommy had given meant it must be on the top floor so she called the lift and, when it arrived, checked her appearance one final time. The nerves in her stomach were on over-time now, she could barely breathe such was her excitement. She had been practically licking her lips during the drive over - such was her desire to have Tommy McLaughlin once more.

Opening the door Tommy stood, barefoot, smiling seductively as Jenna stepped out of the lift. He was dressed in light blue jeans and a loose-fitting white shirt. His black hair was still damp from the shower and he smelt wonderful. Jenna noticed that he had already placed a bottle of Champagne in an ice-bucket, and that there were two flutes on the coffee table. Fantastic!

"You found it okay, then? Sorry, I was a bit short on the phone – business meeting – you know how it is" Tommy smiled his most seductive smile now, watching Jenna from deep, dark-blue eyes fringed with thick black lashes. Jenna returned his smile, all the while drinking him in. She could almost *taste* him, even at this distance.

Pouring them both a glass of Champagne, Tommy gestured for Jenna to follow him. She did so and found herself in a large, white-painted bedroom with the biggest bed she had ever seen. The drapes were half closed and it lent a subtle ambience to the room; the sunlight filtered through the venetian blinds just enough to let them see one another without being too glaring. Tommy gestured for her to sit down on the bed, which she did. Handing her a flute of Champagne he bent to kiss her neck as she took it from him. The contact of his cool lips on her warm skin was electric and Jenna shivered in anticipation. Sipping her drink, she watched him as he sat on a chair opposite and lit two cigarettes. Taking one from him, Jenna's fingers brushed Tommy's ever so slightly and she looked up to see him staring intently at her.

"What do you want from me, Mrs Reid?" he asked in a nonchalant tone. He drew deeply on his cigarette, taking the smoke into his lungs then blowing it out coolly. Jenna couldn't believe just how laid back he seemed when she herself felt like she was about to burst into flames right there in front of him, such was her desire.

"I would have thought it was obvious what I want" Jenna suddenly felt a little disoriented. After all, it had been Tommy who had told her to call him if she wanted a repeat performance. She felt foolish now, almost embarrassed.

"Tell me" He downed his drink in one and poured himself another, smiling like the proverbial cat that had gotten the cream. "Tell me what you want, Jenna" he teased.

"What do you mean – tell you? You know what I want. Don't play games with me, Tommy" Jenna had had enough now, her frustration was becoming evident. What the hell was the man playing at, for god's sake? Wasn't it obvious?

"I want you to tell me what you want, *exactly* what you want, Jenna. Nothing's going to happen until you do"

He stared at her hard now, and Jenna felt uncomfortable, like a school-girl who was completely out of her depth with an older man. What the hell should she say? She felt herself getting hotter as she tried, unsuccessfully, to meet his gaze. Damn the man! She wanted to tell him to forget it. She wanted to, but she knew she wouldn't.

Tommy enjoyed playing cat and mouse with the women he fucked. He liked to feel in control, liked to let the woman know who was boss. Why should Jenna Reid be any different? The silence between them was electric, and Tommy relished every agonising second as he watched Jenna Reid struggle with her pride. She would give him what he wanted, he was sure of it. There had never been a woman born who could resist his unique brand of charm.

"I'm waiting" Tommy stared at her now and she shifted position; she felt decidedly hot and bothered.

"For fuck's sake, what is this? Are you trying to embarrass me or what? Okay, you want to know what I want – I want to leave, that's what I want. Okay?"

Jenna stood up and Tommy leapt out of the chair and caught hold of her, spinning her around until they were standing face to face. His deep blue eyes smouldered as he continued to hold her gaze. Jenna glared at him now, willing him to kiss her, take her in his arms. He kissed the inside of her wrists – tiny, butterfly kisses that drove her wild with longing for him.

"No, you don't. Tell me what you want, Jenna. Say it, say it out loud" Tommy knew she was undone. He could feel it as he kissed her wrists. Her pulse was racing and she was breathing heavily now.

"I.....I want you to fuck me" She blushed now as she heard the words fall from her lips. She had never said those words to a man before. Tommy McLaughlin seemed to be having a strange effect on her. She felt the pull of him and began to smile. Clearly she was going nowhere, and she knew it.

*

Two and a half hours had passed since Jenna had first stepped out of the lift and walked into the apartment. Two and half hours, during which Tommy McLaughlin had fucked her in every position known to man. He had brought her to orgasm several times and, as a result, she felt totally satisfied. She had never felt pleasure like it! Tommy was certainly a skilled lover and had done things to her that Max had never so much as hinted at. She sighed heavily as he kissed her shoulders and back; planted light butterfly kisses on the back of her neck. He was turning her on again. She had thought she was done, but she felt the familiar throbbing between her legs and gasped aloud as she felt Tommy's hand push between her thighs. She really must go soon, otherwise there was the danger that Max might call her mother and then her alibi was blown, but how could she go when he was doing this to her?

Turning onto her back she took Tommy between her legs and wrapped them tightly around him as he entered her. She ran her fingers through his thick, black hair and nibbled on his earlobe as he thrust into her. When he came he held onto her so tightly that she wanted him never to let her go. Jenna couldn't understand what was happening to her. She felt so close to this man, in a way that she had never, ever felt with her husband. He knew exactly how to pleasure her, what to do to bring her to orgasm. With him it was effortless. Whatever it was that Tommy McLaughlin had she couldn't get enough of it that was for sure.

Jenna had never believed in love at first sight but it seemed that she had fallen hook, line and sinker for Tommy and there wasn't a damn thing she could do about it. What frightened her most was the thought that he sensed it, that he knew the hold he had over her, because if he knew that then he had power over her. And if there was one thing Jenna Reid had always said it was that no man would ever have power over her, never have control. She shivered slightly as she lay wrapped in Tommy's tanned, muscular arms. It occurred to her at that moment that she was playing with fire. She was the wife of Max Reid, and as such she should have known better than to jump into bed with Tommy McLaughlin, because if her husband were to find out he would kill Tommy, and quite possibly her too!

CHAPTER TWENTY THREE

Three months later

Jenna Reid was on her knees in the bathroom, throwing up for all her worth into the toilet and she knew without any doubt that she was pregnant. The enormity of the situation was not lost on her for a moment.

How the hell could she have been so stupid? She had been so caught up with Tommy that she had forgotten to take her pill on a couple of occasions, and now here she was – with a belly full of arms and legs.

The trouble was Jenna couldn't be sure who the father was. She wanted it to be Tommy's baby. She desperately wanted to be having his child, if she was to have one at all. However, she knew that there was just as much chance of Max being the father and the prospect of having his child filled her with dread.

The truth was she was in love with Tommy McLaughlin and she wanted out of her marriage. She wanted her and Tommy to make a go of things, with a place of their own and a child to love. Surprised by her own willingness to commit to motherhood, she stood and splashed her face with cold water. She was carrying Tommy's child. As far as she was concerned there was no other option. She would tell him the news later on today, when they met up for their afternoon session at Les' place. He would have no reason not to believe her, especially when she told him that her and Max had always been careful.

Showering under the hot, steamy water she allowed her mind to envisage life with Tommy, the kind of home they would have, the kind of life they'd have together. She had to admit she was nervous about telling him. She wasn't sure how he would react to the news that he was about to become a father. Tell him she would, though, because she wanted this more than she had ever wanted anything, and she wasn't about to let Tommy shirk his fatherly duty.

An hour later she made her way over to the apartment. Things had become more relaxed over the past couple of weeks. Tommy had even had a key cut for her, telling her that she was welcome to make herself at home any time from Friday afternoon until Sunday morning, and this she had taken on board. Tommy had explained how he looked after Les' place for him at the weekends, that it made sense for him to be in town. It gave him a good base from which to do business and Les, being the paranoid type, felt happier having someone there keeping an eye on the place.

She would cook for them tonight, something delicious, and after a good meal and a couple of bottles of wine she was certain that Tommy would receive her news in a favourable light.

She let herself into the apartment that afternoon feeling apprehensive but determined to convince Tommy that they had a future together. As she stood preparing the meal she sipped a cold glass of Chardonnay and told herself things would work out fine. After all, only last week when she had told Tommy that she loved him, he had said he felt the same. It had been after they had made love in the huge king-sized bed and Jenna had been so totally caught up in the moment that the words were out of her

135

mouth before she had fully engaged her brain. There had followed an awkward silence for a few, long moments until, taking her in his arms, Tommy McLaughlin had told the woman who was now gazing adoringly into his eyes that he, too, was in love. She had swallowed it hook, line and sinker too.

Tommy had lain back on the pillows and regretted the words almost as soon as he had uttered them. It was foolish to let Jenna get any big ideas about the two of them. He hadn't envisaged spending his life with one woman, not when there were so many more out there just begging for a turn in his bed. No, Tommy McLaughlin had never wanted marriage. He hadn't wanted commitment of any kind, but now that he had said those words they couldn't be unsaid.

*

Jenna hardly ate at dinner, her nerves had gotten the better of her and she gulped glass after glass of white wine. Tommy had noticed she seemed on edge but, until now, had decided not to mention it. He figured trouble found its own way to your front door – no need to draw it a fucking map. Now, though, Jenna was starting to slur her words and Tommy began to feel a tad concerned. After all, the silly mare had to drive home, didn't she? She was hardly going to make it in this state, and if the law pulled her over she would be in more shit than she could handle.

"Alright, babe, slow down a bit, eh? Anyone would think there was a fucking national shortage on the stuff, the way you've been knocking it back" Tommy took the glass from Jenna and downed the rest of it in one. Jenna felt suddenly angry and upset at the same time, not knowing which emotion to give room to first. "Give me another glass of wine, Tommy, NOW!" she flung her hand across the table and knocked one of Les' best crystal glasses onto the marble-tiled floor. It shattered into tiny, diamond-like pieces and Jenna promptly burst into tears. Tommy couldn't believe it. Les was particular about his possessions and he wouldn't take too kindly to finding one of his top-notch fucking crystal glasses finding its way into the garbage bin.

"Shit, Jenna, look what you've done, for fuck's sake! You know this place ain't mine, Les is gonna go fucking ballistic when he gets back" he raised both arms in the air as if to illustrate the sheer enormity of what she had done.

Jenna looked at him from across the dinner table and knew she couldn't keep it to herself a moment longer. It was now or never and, taking a deep breath, she prayed to a god she didn't really believe in and blurted out her secret.

*

"You're fucking WHAT!" Tommy was striding backwards and forwards now across the entire length of the lounge, shaking his head in disbelief. "Tell me you're fucking joking with me, Jenna, please. Tell me you're having me over" He glared at her now and she sat, dumbstruck, unsure of what to say to calm him down. She had never seen Tommy like this. Sure, she knew he had a temper – it was legendary in the clubs – but not with her, never with her. She could see he was on the verge of losing it big time and for the first time in two months of knowing Tommy McLaughlin she felt afraid. She actually felt afraid of the man she was in love with.

137

Because that was what she was – in love – and right now she was watching her whole world falling apart right in front of her eyes.

After what seemed like an eternity, Tommy finally slumped onto the sofa and lit a cigarette. Jenna sat stock still, numb with shock and disbelief, unsure of what to say to make things alright.

Tommy turned to face her now, his dark blue eyes flashing in the candlelight. "I take it's mine, then?" his expression brooked nothing less than a direct response, and Jenna knew that if she faltered now he would pick up on her uncertainty and that would be the end of her dream. "Yes, Tommy, it's yours" she stated firmly, knowing that she had to stay calm if she stood a chance of convincing Tommy that he was the father of her unborn child.

He seemed to accept the affirmation and sat quietly smoking his cigarette before stubbing it out and promptly lighting another. Jenna decided it might be a good time to try and talk to him, explain how easy things would be once she had told Max she wanted a divorce. She walked over to where Tommy sat, brooding, and sat down beside him. She wanted this man so badly. If it took a white lie to get him then so be it. After all, it might well be Tommy's baby. Her and Max hardly ever made love any more, he was always out until the early hours of the morning and she was usually asleep when he arrived home. If she wasn't, then she pretended to be. On the few occasions he had surprised her by arriving home early she had made excuses about having a headache, or an upset stomach. No, she and Max had only made love a couple of times over the past two months, whereas she and Tommy had been at it like rabbits. It was Tommy's baby. *It had to be!*

"Tommy, I'll leave him. I'll leave Max and we can be together, a real little family. Just picture us in our own drum, a nice place out in the country somewhere, just the three of us. It will be lovely, babe, I promise you. You'll see - I'll make you so happy, Tommy...."

Tommy could hardly believe his ears. "You're having a fucking giraffe, ain't you girl? You honestly think the great Max Reid is just gonna roll over and play dead on this one, do you? You must be fucking dreaming, Jenna"

Tommy shook his head at her now, clearly unconvinced. "Let me explain something to you, *Mrs Reid,* when your old man finds out about this little lot he will blow my fucking brains out, and yours too if he's got any sense. There is no fucking way he is just gonna let you up sticks and leave him, love. Even if he wanted to, he couldn't. Can you imagine how much business cred he will lose if people find out he just sat back and swallowed this; let his own wife walk out on him for the bloke she has been shagging behind his back for the past two fucking months. I mean, can you just picture Max being happy with that level of ridicule, can you, eh? This sinking in yet, is it, Jenna? There's not a cat in hell's chance you're leaving him any time soon, love. Make no mistake - Max will kill the pair of us before he allows you to do that"

Jenna Reid suddenly saw in stunning clarity the hopelessness of her situation. Tommy was right. There was no way Max would agree to a divorce. She had been foolish in the extreme to ever think he would. The tears rolled down her cheeks now, smudging her mascara and streaking her cheeks with little black rivulets of misery. She looked a mess, and she felt worse. The wine had given her the most dreadful headache and she began to feel sick. Whether it was from the alcohol or from sheer fright at the prospect of her husband finding out what she had done, she wasn't sure, but – as if things needed to get any worse – she promptly threw up all over Les Bryce's best Chinese carved rug.

CHAPTER TWENTY FOUR

Totally sobered up from the revelation of his impending fatherhood, Tommy had driven Jenna home in her car then caught a cab back to Les' place where he had spent nigh on two hours cleaning puke off of Les' rug. He wondered at his own stupidity in getting her pregnant. Why the fuck hadn't he worn a condom, for god's sake? It was basic common sense, but it seemed his had left him every time he had been nestled between Jenna Reid's thighs and now he was paying the price. In fact, once Max Reid found out what he'd done, he'd be paying a much bigger one!

Jenna had cleaned her face up at Les' before allowing Tommy to take her home. She felt utterly wretched and she knew that she had to cover her tracks with Max, not let him see the state she was in - otherwise he'd start asking some very awkward questions. The last thing she needed right now was for Max to find out she was pregnant. He would wrongly assume that he was the father and that he and Jenna were going to be parents together, which was the last thing on Jenna's mind.

Creeping barefoot up the ornate staircase, she listened for the sound of Max's breathing in the master bedroom. She couldn't hear a sound, so she tip-toed to the bedroom door and flicked on the light. Max was not in bed. Jenna breathed a sigh of relief. She had time to compose herself before he arrived home.

Jenna stripped off and pulled on a silk dressing-gown, feeling the small swell of her belly as she tied it around herself. She made her way downstairs and into the kitchen. She needed a drink, badly. Pouring herself a small glass of Chardonnay she sat at the breakfast bar for a few moments, sipping the ice cold liquid and trying to collect her thoughts. Tommy was furious. He had made no bones about it either. Jenna had hardly been able to believe her ears when he had told her not to ring him for the next few days.

"Tommy, I'm pregnant, for god's sake! I need your support right now. You can't just leave me to deal with all this on my own" she pleaded with him now.

"Don't start, Jenna!" he spat "You never told me there was a chance you could get fucking pregnant, did you? I thought you of all people would have been on the fucking pill, seeing as you're shagging away from home, love" He eyed her angrily now. "Don't call me, just go home and stay cool while I try and figure out a way out of this car-crash of a situation. For fuck's sake, do NOT show up at Les' place. The last thing I need now is him finding out I'm involved with Max Reid's missus. He'd have a fucking fit if he found out about this little lot, be assured of that. Les is many things but a philanderer he ain't. He don't approve of it, not since his own wife was caught with her knickers down in the arms of his business partner. Suffice to say, the bloke in question left his mortal coil shortly afterwards, on the end of Les' shotgun. Les sent a hefty wedge to his widow and promptly divorced his cheating wife. So, I'm warning you, don't make the mistake of phoning me or turning up on his doorstep. Because the first thing he will do is aim the pair of us straight over the fucking balcony, and the second thing he will do is phone Max and tell him he's a widower. We clear?" Jenna nodded, miserably, and got out of the car. Tommy didn't even bother to kiss her good-bye. He just turned on his heel and marched off into the night. Jenna had been distraught.

CHAPTER TWENTY FIVE

Eileen Kelly knew something was up. Jenna looked washed out and she was off her food. She had been waiting for the right moment to quiz her daughter, fearing there might be trouble in the marriage.

"What is it, love? You sickenin' for summat then or what?" she coaxed. Jenna eyed her mother sulkily over the rim of her mug of coffee. Her mother could be a nosey old cow at times. Jenna resented the way she wanted to know the ins and outs of a cat's arse most of the time. Just for once, couldn't she just leave well alone? The last thing she needed now was for her mother to learn of her pregnancy. She would, naturally, assume it was Max's child and the knitting needles would be out before Jenna could say first trimester.

"Nothing, Mum, I've told you, I just feel a bit off-colour that's all. For god's sake stop fussing, will you?"

"You've been lookin' a bit peaky for weeks now, Jen. It's not Max is it? He ain't playin' away is he? Oh, I fuckin' knew summat like this would 'appen. That's it, isn't it? He's shagging about isn't he? Gawd, no bloody wonder you look like death warmed up, girl. I'll bleedin' kill that bastard when I get me hands on 'im, I swear I will"

As usual, Eileen invented her own version of the truth before anyone had the chance to discount it. She asked the question and promptly answered it, all in the same breath. Jenna had long since given up arguing with her.

"After all I've done for the bloody bastard, welcomin' him into me 'ome, makin' him one of me roasts. Even let him 'ave the chair by the bloody fire, I did, and this is how he repays me! Well I'm tellin' you now, girl, he won't know what bleedin' day it is when...."

A sudden scraping of chair legs on the laminated floor jolted Eileen back to the present. She looked on in dismay as her daughter leapt from the chair and bolted for the door. Flinging it open, she ran into the hallway and took the stairs two at a time as Eileen stood, mouth open, at the foot of the stairs, her face a picture of worry and concern.

Then, as if struck by lightning, Eileen Kelly knew what was wrong with her daughter. She knew it as sure as she knew night followed day. Jenna was pregnant! It had been staring her in the face for weeks - she just hadn't bloody seen it until now. Eileen could barely contain her excitement. She was going to have a grandchild to love! Oh, God was good. Hadn't she always said so? Now here was the proof. Her daughter was carrying her first child. Eileen hurried to the kitchen and filled a glass with cold water from the tap. No doubt Jenna would be glad of it once she had finished being sick. There was nothing worse than morning sickness. Eileen herself had been lucky when she had been carrying her Jenna, only throwing up the one time – which had been a blessing in itself considering she had been hiding the pregnancy. Her own mother had simply put it down to an upset stomach and given her milk of magnesia. Some poor cows had it every morning, some in the evening too! Eileen hoped that Jenna wouldn't suffer the way she had heard some women did. According to the women down at the market, some of them were throwing up morning, noon and night. It was a wonder the baby managed to get any nourishment at all, so bad was the sickness.

"Oh, Jenna, why didn't you tell me, love? You know I'd do anythin' for you and that baby, don't you?" Eileen sat beside her daughter now, stroking the damp hair from her forehead as she sipped the cold water. How she loved this girl, despite how difficult she could be at times. Eileen had endured months of agony keeping her condition secret from her family, and lost everything when the time came to bring her into the world, but she wouldn't have had it any other way. Jenna was her baby, her only child, and she loved her unconditionally. What Jenna couldn't possibly have known was that, sitting right beside her, was the best ally she was ever likely to find. If only she could be honest with her mother, Eileen would stand by her daughter come what may. She wouldn't tell Max, she'd keep the secret such was her love for her daughter. Of course, Jenna didn't know that. She figured her mother would be the first to run and tell Max that she had been having an affair. She didn't trust her mother. In truth, Jenna Reid didn't really trust anyone, believing that trusting people led to bitter disappointment. She only had to look at her own mother to know that trusting people got you nowhere.

Eileen Kelly had kept the circumstances of her daughter's conception from her, preferring instead to create a more palatable version of the events that led up to her being born. She lied about Jenna's father too, telling the girl that he had been a sailor in the Merchant Navy. When Jenna had asked why they had never married, Eileen replied that they had talked of marriage during his last leave, and they had planned to marry when his ship docked in six months. Eileen had gently explained that

146

Jenna's father had been reported lost at sea, presumably swept overboard during a bad storm. His body was never recovered, which meant that Jenna couldn't ask to meet her father. Eileen had elaborated about the moment that she had told George Smedley (the name she had given her imaginary beau) that they were to be parents. She wanted Jenna to feel secure in the knowledge that she had been wanted, by *both* parents. She told her young daughter about the plans they had been making when he had been so cruelly taken from them both. She felt sure that her child had grown up feeling comforted by that knowledge.

Unfortunately, and unknown to Eileen, Jenna hadn't believed a word of it. For starters, how come her mother hadn't kept any of George Smedley's letters? How come she had no photographs to show her, claiming that they had all been lost over the ensuing years? Jenna wasn't stupid, she suspected that her mother had been sucked in by some married bloke, some philanderer who had sweet-talked the knickers off of her. Well, she had decided very early on in life that the same fate wasn't going to befall her! No, she was going places, and she would hold on to her virginity until the ring was on her bloody finger.

"Does Max know, Jen?" Eileen eyed her daughter now, puzzled at the hunted look on her face. Something was troubling her- that much was obvious. "I take it he isn't happy about it, then?" she pushed. Jenna spun round in her seat and, pointing a carefully manicured finger at her mother, she spat angrily "He is TOTALLY happy about it, you silly cow, why wouldn't he be, eh? I'm his *wife* aren't I? I'm not some cheap bloody whore who dropped her knickers to the first man that came along. Of course he is happy about it, and I don't want to hear another bloody word

147

from you about it okay? This is *our* business, mine and Max's. So keep your nose out of it, and keep your stupid comments to yourself in future, alright?!"

Eileen watched as her daughter picked up her coat and bag and flounced out of the front door, down the path and into her S Class Mercedes. She smiled to herself as she poured a cup of stewed tea from the pot.

"Definitely a boy" she said out loud. "It's definitely a boy".

CHAPTER TWENTY SIX

Tommy sat chewing his fingernail and tried his best to look interested as Les wittered on about his weekend with his daughter. She was a lovely little thing by all accounts, and Les clearly adored her. The only fly in the ointment being that the child was the spitting image of her mother, something which seemed to piss Les off no end.

"Typical isn't it, Tommy, eh? I have one child in my life and she don't look anything like me. The girl gets her looks from her mother, poor cow. I only hope she grows out of it" he laughed loudly now as he poured himself a large Scotch on the rocks in one of his favourite crystal glasses.

Tommy had long suspected that Les wasn't the girl's father, but to say so – to even so much as *hint* at it – would mean a parting of the ways between his shoulders and his head. Les was proud as punch of his daughter, Ruby, and if he had ever doubted paternity he had certainly never voiced those doubts.

Tommy wished Les would shut the fuck up. For the past three days he had been trying to think of a way out of his current dilemma and Les prattling on was seriously hindering his thought processes.

The way Tommy saw it he had three options: One, he left town and never came near London ever again. Two, he told Jenna that he wasn't interested and that she should return to her husband. Three, he swallowed his knob and accepted responsibility for the child he had helped create and stick by Jenna.

149

The trouble was every option left him either seriously broke, or seriously broken. If he left the smoke it meant starting all over again, making new contacts and building a new line of business. That could take months, and Tommy didn't have the kind of funds required for a long, drawn out wait. Plus he needed to be close to Max Reid.

If he dumped Jenna she could decide to bite the bullet, tell Max that she had been playing away and hope for his forgiveness, blaming Tommy for the whole thing. Jesus, she might even claim that Tommy had raped her! In which case, Max Reid would pull the trigger first and ask questions later.

So, the only option that seemed to make any sense was the last one. The trouble with option three was money, or rather the lack of it. If he and Jenna were to leave and make a life for themselves they'd need money, lots of it. Tommy had a few grand put by but nothing like the kind of money it would take to buy a decent place and raise a child, let alone cater for the needs of a high-maintenance woman like Jenna Reid. No, if he was going to go down the route of starting a new life with her then he needed to figure out a way of raising some serious wedge, because once they left London they were on the run for good. Max Reid wasn't the kind of man to forgive and forget.

Jumping up from the sofa he made his excuses and left. He needed to think, needed to work out a plan, but he couldn't do this on his own. He needed to know that if he was going to commit to a new life that he wasn't pissing in the wind. It was time to call Jenna.

CHAPTER TWENTY SEVEN

"It's not that simple, Jenna, we can't just up sticks and move away, for fuck's sake. This has got to be planned down to the last detail." Tommy was feeling exasperated with how naïve Jenna was being. She thought that, so long as they were together, the rest of it was sure to follow. In the real world, however, the only thing that was likely to follow was Max Reid and a van load of serious aggro. Tommy didn't relish the thought of being parted from his testicles whilst hanging upside down in a dis-used warehouse. Jenna clearly wasn't getting the picture.

"Look, love, we need to figure this out properly, okay? We need to have enough money behind us so that we can take off, out of the country, and never look back. Because – trust me – your old man ain't gonna like it too much when he finds his lovely wife has fucked off with another bloke, now is he?"

Jenna pondered this for a moment. She had been so relieved when Tommy had called this morning she had broken down, and it had been a full five minutes before Tommy had been able to get any sense out of her. She was happy just being with Tommy. She didn't care about anything else, so long as he was going to stand by her.

They were sitting on an old, leather sofa in Tommy's place. Jenna was sipping a cup of hot, steaming tea and Tommy a can of Budweiser. Jenna thought the place was nice, but it wasn't Les' apartment. The walls needed a lick of paint and the furniture was shabby and dated. Tommy explained that he spent his weekends at Les' so hadn't really wanted to splash out on this place. Truth be told, Tommy didn't really have the cash. Oh, he had a few grand stashed away, but once he started spending on new sofas and plasma televisions it would eat a huge hole in his savings, and Tommy liked to have readies; he didn't particularly care for all mod-cons. Not if he was footing the bill, at any rate. Most of his earn had been frittered away on booze, weed and women.

"Max is loaded, Tommy. If I could figure out a way of getting my hands on some of his cash then all our troubles would be over" she looked at Tommy now as though she had just solved the problem in one go. Tommy despaired of the silly mare at times. Jesus - women! He stretched his arms above his head now for maximum dramatic effect.

"Oh, I know, Jen. Why don't you ask him for the combination to his safe, love? Or better still, why don't you ask him to write you a big, fat cheque and buy us a fucking pram while he's at it, eh?" Tommy strode into the kitchen and pulled a can of beer from the fridge. He was fast losing his patience, and – truth be told – his temper into the bargain.

Slumping back down onto the sofa, Tommy opened the can of beer and downed half of it in one. He needed to get pissed. When he was pissed he thought more clearly. Right now his brains felt like mush. Tommy put it down to the fact that he had consumed a fair amount of cocaine over the past couple of nights and this was his brain's way of letting him know he had overdone it.

He'd spent the past couple of nights shagging and snorting anything he could get his hands on, unbeknown to Jenna of course. Jesus, if she found out what he'd been up to there'd be hell to pay, and Tommy was all for a quiet life.

Last night had been particularly enlightening. Tommy had taken two Malaysian sisters, who were not averse to a bit of three in a bed, and a large supply of coke back to Les' place and they had kept him up until the early hours, one way or another. Tommy lit a cigarette and passed it to Jenna who took it and drew deeply on it as she considered their position. He then rolled himself a decent sized joint. He needed to relax, and right now having Jenna wittering on in his lug-hole was driving him to distraction.

After a few moments silence, Jenna turned to look at Tommy with a wide grin spreading over her face. "So, let me get this straight, Tommy" she began. "What you're saying is – we need to find a way to screw a hefty amount of wedge out of Max, but at the same time we need to do it in such a way that there are no come-backs?" She paused now, watching Tommy intently as he smoked, and waited for his response.

After a few seconds Tommy put the joint down in the ashtray and turned to face her. "That's about the size of it, darlin', yeah. Why? You got any bright ideas then, have you?'" he drawled sarcastically.

"Well isn't it obvious, Tommy?" Jenna sat bolt upright now, her emerald green eyes flashing with excitement as she waited for him to cotton on to her plan. God, men could be so thick at times, she thought to herself. Much as she loved Tommy, he wasn't exactly the sharpest knife in the drawer when it came to getting what he wanted out of life, whereas she, on the other hand, was an expert at it.

Tommy didn't think it was at all obvious. In fact, he hadn't got a fucking clue what she was on about. If the truth be told he was tired and all he wanted to do was crawl into bed and sleep last night off. At that precise moment, he felt like telling her to fuck off but he figured he'd have to humour her now if he didn't want her to end up crying snotty tears all over his couch. All she seemed to do lately was cry. Tommy figured it must be the hormones.

"Go on then, Jenna, let's hear it, girl. I'm dying to know just how the hell you plan on duping old Maxie boy into parting with his hard-earned cash. I'm all ears, love. What do you reckon will have Max Reid parting with at least half a million in readies without batting so much as a fucking eyelid, eh?"

"Well" Jenna paused now for effect. "There is *one* thing that Max would give up everything he owns for, without as much as a second thought. Something he would pay through the nose for and be glad to do it into the bargain, *actually*." She emphasised the last word now, determined to get it through to Tommy that she was a smart cookie and that he needed to take her seriously.

Tommy decided to play along, anything if it shut her up! He lit the joint and took a deep drag on it, holding the smoke in his lungs for a full five seconds before blowing it out noisily.

"Oh, yeah, and what might that be, then, Jen?" he drawled sarcastically.

Jenna Reid had thought of the perfect plan to ensure that she, Tommy and the baby she was carrying would walk away from this with a small fortune and Max would be more than happy to hand it over.

"Well, it's simple really, Tommy. The thing Max values most, the thing he would pay any amount for, especially if he thinks I'm carrying *his* child, is me!"

CHAPTER TWENTY EIGHT

Max Reid was pissed off. He had been avoiding Roy Richards for months, with his staff under strict instructions not to put his calls through when he rang, and now the bloke had had the front to turn up at the club, uninvited, for a meet. To make matters worse, the new receptionist had blabbed that Max was in the building, so now Max had no choice but to agree to see him. Fuck! This was all he needed.

No doubt Roy was after a handshake on the sale of his club but, after taking advice from his accountant, and giving it much consideration, Max had decided once and for all that he would not be buying the place. Business had taken a nose-dive by all accounts and it seemed as though Roy Richards thought he could pull the wool over Max's eyes and palm him off with a non-starter. Well, he had another think coming!

Max poured himself a scotch and called down to his Manager, Rob, to bring Richards upstairs to the office. Rob Marsden had been Manager at the Starlight Club since it opened and Max considered him a friend as well as an employee. Anything Max asked of the bloke, he gave readily. Max knew he could rely on him to be discreet. He also knew that Rob was pretty handy with his fists if push came to shove, and whilst Max was no pushover when it came to business, he didn't fancy his chances alone in his office if Roy Richards decided to get nasty. Max had been dreading this meeting for months, and now the bloke was here. Like a bad smell, he just kept coming back.

A few minutes later, Rob Marsden knocked at the door to Max's office and ushered Roy Richards in. The look that passed between Max and Rob spoke volumes, and they both knew that once this fiasco was over they'd share a drink and have a good laugh about it. Right now, though, both men wore serious expressions as they sat down with Reynold. Both men knew that, if Richards heard something he didn't like, the atmosphere could change in a heartbeat, and they were feeling on edge as Max poured the three of them a drink.

"So, Roy, what brings you to this neck of the woods?" Max sat back in his leather office chair before lighting a cigarette and drawing deeply on it as he waited for Richards to start his spiel. Rob Marsden had quit the fags six months ago, but right now he was sorely tempted to light one up. The tension in the room was palpable.

"We had a deal, Max. You told me you were interested in buying my place. I took it that your word was enough, seeing as we are both gentlemen" Roy drove his point home now. "The thing is, mate, I need the cash. I'm investing in a couple of properties abroad and right now the extra wedge would come in handy, so I'm here to ask you to hold up your end of the bargain" Roy smiled now at Max, and Rob shuddered as the image of a rattlesnake came to mind.

"Whoa, let's slow down a bit, eh Roy? I seem to remember saying I *might* be interested in buying your gaff. At no point did we shake hands on a deal. In fact, if I recall correctly, I told you on Christmas Night that I may well have to pass, seeing as I'd just forked out for a shop for my wife" Max stared hard at Roy, daring the man to contradict him. Max was many things, but a liar he most certainly was not, and pissed or sober – he never forgot a thing he may have said when it came to business.

Max Reid was known for being a fair man, a man true to his word, so the fact that this cunt was now sitting in his office implying that he had somehow reneged on a deal left a bad taste in Max's mouth. He took a swig of scotch and waited for Roy to recall the conversation. At that point, Rob shifted uneasily in his seat and Max, sensing the bloke's discomfort, offered him another drink. Rob accepted, relieved to have something to do. Taking the glass from Max, he took his seat and tried to calm his nerves as the two men stared each other out.

Roy looked away first. Max saw on the man's face that he had now, indeed, remembered the conversation at the Christmas Night party. However Roy Richards wasn't going to let him off the hook as easy as that. He had come here to seal the deal, and he was damned if he was just going to leave without putting up a fight.

"Maxie...come on mate. I'm offering you a real bargain here, you can't lose. Come on let's shake on it, eh? What d'you say?"

Roy had changed tack now. He knew Max Reid had the dosh, all he needed was a quick sale and he could pay off his gambling debts and start over. Business hadn't been too good at his place lately, but he figured someone like Max would have no trouble getting it up and running again without too much trouble. He had borrowed heavily at the Casino and owed a hefty few grand to a loan shark who was now beginning to scare him, if the truth be told.

Roy's wife, Andrea, had answered the door to a caller last weekend only to find herself looking down the barrel of a handgun. Poor Andrea had wet herself with fright as she was unceremoniously shoved out of the way. The bloke with the gun had marched into their lounge, had a good look around and then gone upstairs to check if Roy was hiding in one of the bedrooms.

Satisfied that Roy wasn't on the premises he left him a chilling message with Andrea – pay up or else. Andrea had gone ballistic on the phone to Roy, screaming and ranting for a full ten minutes before Roy could make any sense of what had happened. When he realised just how close he had come to getting himself blown to kingdom come, Roy Richards had leaned back against the wall of the local betting shop and promptly slid down it onto the stained, threadbare carpet. He knew that if he didn't come up with the seven grand he owed the bloke, it wasn't just his neck on the line, it was also Andrea's.

Roy couldn't bear the thought of anyone hurting his wife. She might be a gobby cow at times, but after twenty two years of marriage Roy still got butterflies whenever she walked into a room. No, he wasn't about to let anything happen to Andrea, not if he could help it.

Max eyed Roy now from behind the desk. The bloke was hot under the collar - sweating like a dog on heat - and Max had a feeling the man was more than a little desperate for cash. Nonetheless, Max was no fool and he wasn't about to buy into a non-starter, particularly now when he needed to invest wisely for the future.

"Roy, the business has nose-dived, mate. You know it and I know it. Fact is, I've had a couple of my lads take a look at the place over the past couple of months and they've reported back to me that the club was half empty last Saturday night. Now, Thursday night I could live with it being a bit down on its luck, mate, but Saturday? Nah, it's a non-starter Roy. Bottom line is – I ain't interested. Sorry"

Max stood now. As far as he was concerned the meeting was at an end. Coming from behind the desk he held out his hand to Roy, hoping to end things on a good note. That was how Max Reid did business. Keep things civil, stay on good terms. He believed in good manners and he expected no less from anyone who came into his orbit. Roy, however, didn't share his natural bonhomie.

Standing up, Roy glared at the two men, his pale blue eyes rimmed red from too many late nights and too much hard drinking. The past few months had seen him lose almost two stone in weight such was the worry of his mounting debts. Andrea had urged him to see a doctor, but Roy was adamant he could sort things out. He needed her to trust him, believe in him again. Roy knew that if his wife got a hint of how much he really owed out she'd leave him, and that fact alone was the reason he drank himself into a stupor every night. He was terrified of losing Andrea. Nothing in the world could be as bad as his wife leaving him, of that Roy was sure.

"So, that's it then, is it? You're going back on everything you promised, Max? I held that club for you, d'you know that? I had offers coming in left, right and centre but I told them – 'sorry, fellas, the place is sold'. That is what you told me, Maxie boy. You said you wanted the fuckin' place" Roy raised his voice now as his despair gave way to anger.

Max knew full well that Roy hadn't had any offers for the place. He wasn't about to fall prey to emotional blackmail, despite the fact that he also knew Roy Richards was up to his eyes in unpaid gambling debts. Word on the streets was that Richards was a bad risk, and any self-respecting businessman avoiding him like the plague.

Rob Marsden stood up, hands held out in supplication, trying to appeal to Roy's better sense. The man was raving now, ranting at them both about how he could have sold the place ten times over, how he had lowered the asking price as a personal favour to Max, thinking that they were friends. In truth, they were nothing of the kind. Max Reid couldn't stomach the bloke, never could. He saw Roy the way most people did – a born loser.

Suddenly, without warning, Roy took a swing at Max. Max saw it coming and ducked out of the way, leaving Roy punching at thin air. Clearly up for a fight, he swung again. This time Max managed to ward off the blow by smashing his forearm against the inside of Roy's right arm and knocking him off balance. Roy was mad as hell, spittle flying out of his mouth he screamed at Max. "You fuckin' turncoat bastard, I'll fuckin' kill you"

Rob Marsden stepped in-between Max and Roy. Before Roy knew what had hit him, Rob had floored him with a right upper cut that took him clean off his feet and onto his arse. Roy sat down heavily, his back slamming against the side of the mahogany desk and his right foot catching the edge of the glass coffee table, causing the three glasses, still half full of scotch, to empty all over the thickly carpeted floor. Clearly humiliated, he closed his eyes for a few moments before pulling himself upright. Straightening his crumpled suit jacket, he glowered at Rob Marsden who held his gaze levelly. Rob wasn't scared of Roy Richards. He wasn't scared of anyone.

"Get out, Roy. Just get the fuck out of my office and out of my club. We're done here. In fact, we're done full stop. Don't ever darken my fucking doorstep again, I mean it. You come round here again and you'll be met with some serious aggro mate, make no bones about it" Max kept his cool as he opened the office door and gestured for Richards to leave. Roy made his way slowly towards the door and as he walked through it he muttered "Be seeing you, Max. Be seeing you" Max laughed then, as he retorted "Not if I see you first, Roy".

CHAPTER TWENTY NINE

Jenna Reid opened her eyes to see her husband walking into their bedroom carrying a breakfast tray, smiling like the proverbial cat that had gotten the cream. He had never felt happier in his whole life. In a few short months, he was going to be a father, and nothing – nothing – could spoil his mood right now. He felt like the luckiest man alive.

When Jenna had told him last night that she was expecting their first child he had thought he was dreaming; he had almost given up hope of ever being a father, and now here it was. Max was finally going to have it all – a beautiful wife, a thriving business and a child to complete the picture. What more could he possibly want?

Jenna smiled weakly as Max placed the breakfast tray in her lap and kissed her on the forehead. "Good morning, my darling, how are you feeling?" he enthused. Inside, he felt like a teenager again, such was his delight.

"I'm sorry, darling, I feel a bit queasy this morning. Breakfast is off the menu at the moment, I'm afraid" she took the cup of coffee and sipped the hot, strong liquid. Last night had been tiring. From the moment she had told Max she was pregnant things seemed to escalate into a flurry of excited phone calls and endless questions about how far gone she was, what she thought the sex of the baby might be and when did she find out. Jenna's head was swimming by the time she had fallen into bed and she had slept fitfully, her dreams being of Max and Tommy and babies without arms and legs.

Jenna had woken in the early hours drenched in sweat, terrified that in some way her guilt might be harming the baby. She had lain awake, next to her sleeping husband, listening to his peaceful breathing and telling herself that she must try to remain calm. Everything depended on her behaving like any other excited wife who had just found out that she and her husband were to welcome their first child together.

Max could not have any reason to doubt that she was as happy about the baby as he was; that her excitement about them both becoming parents together was equal to his own. She could play the part, she felt sure, so long as she knew Tommy was on board. It had taken all her powers of persuasion to convince him that her plan was the only way out of this mess. He had taken a hell of a lot of convincing, but now she felt certain he would play his part when the time came.

*

Five miles away, hungover and bleary eyed, Tommy McLaughlin was delighted to discover that the girl in his bed had a penchant for sucking cock. As she slid down beneath the duvet murmuring words of appreciation at the size of his erect member, Tommy thought briefly about Jenna Reid before closing his eyes and letting his desire take over.

When Jenna had first come out with the plan to fake her own kidnapping Tommy had looked at her as though she had just grown two heads. He hadn't been able to get his head around the fact that he was expected to phone Max Reid and make menacing ransom demands, all the while knowing full well that Jenna was perfectly safe and sitting next to him on the sofa! It had to be the craziest fucking thing he had ever heard.

He had thrown back his head and laughed until he cried when she explained how Max would pay what he asked just to keep her and the baby safe. It all seemed just a bit too good to be true as far as Tommy was concerned. Jenna, however, was adamant. This was going to be their passport to a new life, so it was important that he got it right. When this was all over, Jenna had insisted, it would just be the three of them – and half a million of Max Reid's money.

CHAPTER THIRTY

Tommy was on pins waiting for Jenna to call him. They had both agreed to put the 'kidnap' off for a couple of weeks to give them time to plan it properly. Plus, Jenna wanted Max to get used to the idea of impending fatherhood, that way he wouldn't hesitate to pay up once he thought there was a risk of him losing everything. Jenna had promised to call this morning to confirm that she had told Max about the baby and that things were going according to plan.

Suddenly, Tommy's mobile sprang into life and he snatched it up, expecting it to be Jenna. He was disappointed to see it was Les calling. Shit! The last thing he needed now was Les keeping him gabbing for half an hour. Tommy debated whether or not to simply ignore it, but he figured it was best not to. Les might have a bit of work for him and right now he needed as much cash as he could get his hands on.

"Alright, Les, what's up?" Tommy wasn't in the mood for Les right now. He hadn't slept properly last night, tossing and turning until the early hours, and now his head was banging.

"Tommy, I need a favour, son" Les always referred to Tommy as 'son'. It pissed Tommy off no end. It made him feel as though Les saw him as a kid, a no-mark, a subordinate. Tommy had his pride - he didn't like being talked down to by anyone, least of all his boss. He decided to overlook it now though. He had bigger things to worry about.

Les went on "I've arranged to take Ruby away to Disneyland Florida for a couple of weeks. Her mother has been on at me, non fuckin' stop, the past couple of months about takin' her on 'oliday, and I can't let the poor little mare go back to school without givin' her a proper 'oliday now can I, eh?" Les didn't pause for breath before he said "I want you to look after me gaff, son. Two weeks, startin' next Friday, which means I need you to be on the premises twenty-four-seven, if you get my drift?"

Tommy got his drift alright. Les wanted him to look after the place because, unknown to the Inland Revenue, Les Bryce had nigh on a million quid stashed in his safe. The way he figured, what the bastards didn't know wouldn't hurt them, and he didn't see why he should hand over hundreds of thousands of pounds in taxes when it could be spent furnishing his lavish lifestyle.

Tommy had to agree with him. Les was an entrepreneur of the highest calibre. Anything he touched seemed to turn to gold and, over the years, he had made some very sound business investments with his portfolio now worth something in the region of fifteen million pounds. Les was a shrewd character when it came to investing, often making a killing because he got in there first. 'The early bird catches the worm' was his favourite anecdote. Tommy envied him his lifestyle, but he knew deep down he wouldn't have the business acumen to do what Les did. No, he was happy to work for the man. He paid generously, far above the going rate, and allowed Tommy the use of his luxury penthouse apartment every weekend. Tommy saw their arrangement as a fair one, and both of them were happy for it to continue indefinitely.

"No problem, Les" Tommy knew that Les trusted him implicitly and that by telling him about the million quid in his safe he had proved it. Tommy understood the gravity of having Les' trust, because he also understood that if Les ever found out that his trust had been misplaced he would have no qualms about putting a hatchet into Tommy's skull.

"I'll be over Thursday night, that way you can get an early start on the Friday morning, if that suits?" It did suit, and Les ended the call, relieved to know that Tommy would be there keeping an eye on the place in his absence.

As soon as Tommy put the phone down it sprang into life again, and this time it was Jenna Reid. She sounded anxious and wanted to know why Tommy had been on the phone when he knew she would be calling.

"Calm down, Jenna, it was an important call. In fact, it might just be the perfect solution to our plan. When you coming over?"

Tommy wanted to tell Jenna that they had the run of Les' place for two whole weeks, which meant that they could use the place to stay in whilst they screwed Max Reid out of his money. It couldn't have come at a better time. Tommy didn't really care about the state of his own place – he figured it suited his needs and it was really just a place to sleep. He knew, however, that Jenna hated the shabby furniture and the tasteless wallpaper. Several times he had seen the look of disgust as she wrinkled up her nose at the smell coming off the threadbare carpet. She would complain constantly about the state of the place, demanding to know why Tommy didn't at least give it a fresh lick of paint and replace the flooring for some new, clean laminate. Tommy humoured her. She was a bossy, stuck up little cow at times, but the truth was she turned him on. He couldn't quite figure it out, the hold she had over him. He had screwed hundreds of women over the years, older ones, younger ones. They all wanted a piece of him in one way or another, and Jenna was no different on that score. Christ, she was having his kid, for fuck's sake! If that wasn't getting a piece of him, Tommy didn't know what was.

There was something about her, though, that had him hooked. At first he had been blasé about the whole thing, but now he had developed a real passion for her. Tommy knew it wasn't love. He saw it for what it was – pure lust and nothing more. Jenna did things to him that drove him insane. She wanted to please him yes, but she demanded things from him too. Maybe that was what he found so irresistible, the fact that she made demands of him. Every other woman he had been with just did whatever he told them to. Jenna Reid was no pushover. She was not the kind of woman you gave orders to. Tommy had to admit he held a grudging respect for her because of it despite the fact that, at times, he could cheerfully throttle her.

"When you comin' over, Jen?" Tommy was keen to make plans, and he didn't trust mobile networks. They could be traced, and that was the last thing they needed. He had gone out and bought two brand-new, untraceable mobile phones. He figured that it was best they didn't talk on their own phones from now on, in-case Max Reid decided to ignore instructions and involve the Old Bill. Tommy had watched too many films where the kidnapper had insisted on no police involvement and the first thing the aggrieved partner did was call them in. No, he decided it was best to err on the side of caution and stay off their mobiles until this thing was all over.

"I'll be there at twelve, Tommy. I need to shower and grab some breakfast first. Max is downstairs now making me scrambled eggs" She laughed now as she blew kisses into her handset and Tommy jokingly told her she was a silly cow for doing it with her husband downstairs. Jenna didn't care at that moment. She loved Tommy so much.

CHAPTER THIRTY ONE

"So we're going to stage the kidnap at Les' place then?" Jenna was beaming now at the prospect of not having to spend the few days she'd be 'missing' at Tommy's flat. She loved being with him, but she loved her home comforts just as much and Tommy didn't really go in for luxury and mod-cons. She intended to put that right once they were out of here and settled into a new place of their own. She wanted the best that money could buy and she didn't see why Tommy shouldn't learn how to be a bit more discerning when it came to décor and furniture. Yes, Jenna had it all figured out. Once they had a place of their own she and Tommy would fill it with the best furniture, the finest crystal and the most beautiful fabrics.

Jenna didn't do shabby. She had decided from an early age that only the best would ever be good enough for her. She was going places, and Tommy needed to buck his ideas up if he wanted to be with her. Tommy smiled at her now. He could read her like a book. "Yep, in the lap of luxury!" he laughed. He was nervous about the plan, but he knew that his hands were tied. He couldn't back out now, Jenna had set her heart on them being together and the alternative didn't bear thinking about.

He was in no doubt as to the consequences of him walking away from her. Several times he had questioned the decision he had made to stand by her. Several times he had reached the same, unavoidable conclusion. It really hadn't been his decision at all. He had no choice, did he? So how could he call it his decision? Tommy had lain awake night after night mulling over the events of the past couple of weeks. More than once he had mentally kicked himself for allowing himself to be trapped. Why the fuck hadn't he used protection? Why hadn't he made sure that there was no possible chance of a pregnancy? He always used protection, always insisted on it, so why hadn't he with Jenna Reid?

The answer- albeit not the one he had wanted to acknowledge - had come to him in the early hours one morning as he lay in bed smoking a cigarette. It was staring him in the face and as much as he tried to deny it, Tommy now had to admit to himself that he had *wanted* to make her pregnant! He had *wanted* this to happen!

As he drew deeply on the cigarette, he lay staring up at the ceiling thinking about the way things had turned out. Tommy's conscience was battling with his subconscious mind, trying to block out the real reason that he had fucked the wife of Max Reid without using a condom. He liked to believe he was a good man, a decent man, but right now he was having a hard time convincing even himself of it.

He had rolled over and fallen into a fitful sleep, in no doubt whatsoever that the truth – hard as it would be to stomach - would be there waiting for him come morning.

CHAPTER THIRTY TWO

Max was like a dog with two tails. He told everyone in his orbit the wonderful news of Jenna's pregnancy, his face a picture of happiness as he regaled them with updates and plans for the future. Nobody was in any doubt about how much Max wanted the child - they could see his joy for themselves.

Max had instructed the decorators to begin work on the nursery almost as soon as Jenna had announced the pregnancy, and they had spent hours poring over fabrics and carpet samples. He had insisted that Jenna take it easy from now on, only working part-time at the shop until they could find a buyer.

Jenna had explained to Max that she wanted to be a stay-at-home Mother, insisting that they sell the shop so that she could concentrate on her pregnancy and taking proper care of herself and their unborn child. Max had readily agreed, after all this was their first child and he wasn't taking any chances.

Jenna sat in the conservatory sipping Earl Grey tea and feeling very pleased with herself. Max had fallen for her plan hook, line and sinker. His face had lit up with pride as she waffled on about how important it was now for her to concentrate all her energies on keeping fit and healthy. He had readily agreed that she didn't need the added stress of running a business on top of carrying their first child. She had chosen her words carefully, playing on the need for caution as this was her first pregnancy and so much was at stake. Max had been so proud of her. She really seemed to be over the moon about the baby and her wish to take things easy just endeared her to him even more.

If only Max Reid could had known that the child his wife was expecting was probably not even his. If only he could have known that in a few, short days, his happiness would be shattered into a million pieces; that his wife and her lover were planning to con him in the cruellest possible way.

Had he known, he might not have driven into Bond Street that morning, grinning like a Cheshire cat, and bought his wife a stunning Tiffany eternity ring to celebrate the news of their first child together.

He wanted to give her something special to say 'Thank You' and also 'Sorry' for neglecting her lately. Deep down he knew she had been unhappy at the amount of time he was spending at the club. He vowed to make it up to her, with the promise that things would change from now on. God knows he adored Jenna. She was the best thing that had ever happened to him. Even their love-making was back on track since the announcement, and Max just put the past couple of months down to his wife being in the first few weeks of pregnancy. He had understood perfectly that she hadn't felt like having sex even though, secretly, he had longed to take her in his arms. He wanted her to know just how much she meant to him and tonight, over dinner, he was going to surprise her with the stunning diamond ring which now nestled in his inside pocket.

"Alright, boss, you want me to bring up some coffee?" Rob Marsden was pleased for Max. The bloke deserved some happiness, after the way his last marriage had ended. There had been many a night when Rob had carried Max upstairs to bed after he had drunk himself into a stupor over his ex-wife. Rob despaired at times, truly believing that his boss, and his friend, would never get over the divorce. Then Max had met Jenna Kelly and within a few days the change in him had been noted by everyone who knew him. Gone were the late nights in his office, often drinking Scotch until the early hours of the morning only to be discovered, slumped over his desk, by one of the cleaners.

Max had a spring in his step again and no-one was more pleased to see it than Rob. Now it seemed the union was to produce a baby son or daughter and Rob couldn't think of a better birthday present for Max, who would be turning forty next month.

"Cheers mate, I'm fucking parched" Max took the cup from Rob and took several mouthfuls of the hot, black coffee before leaning back in his leather office chair, arms behind his head and a wide grin spreading across his face.

"There's something I want to speak to you about, Rob" Max sat, stony faced now, as Rob waited, his attention focussed on the man that he respected more than any man alive.

Rob's own father had passed away when he had been just fifteen, and Rob had become the man of the house overnight. He had quit school and gone to work in a local betting shop to earn money for his mother and his seven year old sister.

After a couple of years of barely scraping by he had been ambling past a newsagents on his way home one evening when he noticed the shopkeeper was pinning and advertisement onto the noticeboard in the front window. Curious, Rob had waited until the shopkeeper had finished before walking up to take a look. It was dark now, and the street light opposite kept blinking on and off, much to Rob's annoyance, so he had been forced to press his nose right up against the glass in order to read the wording on the ad. The advertisement read:

WANTED – CELLAR MAN FOR LOCAL NIGHTSPOT - MUST BE HONEST AND HARD-WORKING.

There was a number scribbled underneath which Rob tried to memorise but, realising that by the time he arrived home he would likely have forgotten it, he asked the shopkeeper for a pen and paper to write it down. Wasting no time, Rob called the number from a phone-box and was invited for an interview by the owner, a Mister Max Reid.

That had been almost ten years ago, and Rob had worked his way up from cellar-man to Manager within a few short years. Now he had the trust of his boss, and counted the man as a friend. He knew Max viewed him in the same way. They had spent many hours exchanging memories and telling stories over a bottle of malt. Rob, being twenty-seven, looked up to Max not as a father-figure, but more as a big brother. They worked well together and Max had come to rely on Rob for his loyalty and his discretion which was why it gave him a lot of pleasure now to be able to have this particular conversation with the man he had come to regard as a close friend.

"Ok Max, whatever you need, mate" Rob sat patiently waiting now. It didn't matter what his boss had in mind, it was a given from the get-go that Rob would be only too happy to agree to it. Max never asked anything of Rob that he wouldn't be happy to do himself. He figured that a boss was only as good as the people he managed, and Rob was one of the best.

"The thing is we're going to have to make a few cut-backs, mate. Things have been a bit tough lately. I was wondering how soon you'd be able to find something else"

Rob looked as though he had punched in the face. "You're letting me go, boss? Fuck's sake, what the hell...I thought business was up if anything. I don't understand!"

Max could barely keep a straight face. He had been planning to wind Rob up all morning, but now it was proving difficult. Rob sat back in his seat, ashen faced, shaking his head in total disbelief.

"Chin up, Rob, it's not all bad news. In fact, come to think of it, I've heard of a position that I think would suit you down to the ground, if you fancy it of course" Max's sides were aching now as he struggled to contain his laughter.

"Oh, yeah, what's that then?" Rob Marsden looked like he'd lost a grand and found a fiver.

Max couldn't hold it in any longer. He burst out laughing as Rob looked on, bewildered. The tears ran down Max's face as he struggled to get his words out. "We.......we're looking for a ...oh my god...a godparent...for our baby, if you're interested" Max was laughing so hard now his shoulders were shaking. Rob stared at his boss like he'd lost the plot.

Suddenly the penny dropped and Rob was out of his chair, cuffing Max around the back of the head, the two men laughing like a couple of kids. "YOU FUCKIN' BASTARD!" Rob was shouting and laughing now, shoving his boss flying as the two men wrestled good-naturedly. "You had me goin' there, mate" he laughed.

"Seriously, mate, we'd love you to be our son or daughter's godfather, if you're up for it" Max was serious now. He hadn't hesitated when thinking of who should be the godparents to his first child. He wanted Rob, and Marcus Graham and his wife, Sally-Anne. Max and Marcus had known each other a long time, and he liked Marcus' wife very much. Strangely, when he had suggested the three to Jenna she had agreed without putting up a fight. Max had expected her to have someone in mind that she would like to ask herself, but she had seemed happy with his choice.

"It would be an honour, Max, really it would. Fuck me, mate, you had me going there for a minute" Rob grinned now as he shook Max by the hand and patted him on the back. "Thanks for asking me, Max, I'm over the moon. Who knows eh? It might be me asking you the same thing if things work out with Lucy"

Rob had been seeing Lucy Adams for the best part of a year now, and he was head over heels in love with her. Unbeknown to anyone, even Max, Rob was planning to propose to Lucy on Christmas morning this year. Lucy worked in Harrods as a beauty consultant and earned a hefty commission from sales. She was the most independent girl Rob had ever encountered, insisting on paying her way whenever they went out. She didn't like the feeling it gave her whenever a man footed the bill. She preferred to be seen as an equal, and therefore Rob should treat her as such. At first, Rob had found this hard to swallow. He had wanted to show his new girl a good time, splash his cash a bit, but Lucy was adamant. Either she paid half the bill or that would be their last date. Rob had reluctantly agreed.

Max had met Lucy a few times and she and Rob had recently been over to have dinner with Jenna and himself. The two women hadn't hit it off though and Max had asked Jenna what the problem was. Jenna shrugged, claiming not to know what was wrong, however she knew only too well the reason behind Lucy Adam's dislike of her.

Halfway through dinner, Jenna had excused herself from the table and headed upstairs to the bedroom claiming that she felt unwell. Lucy, feeling concerned, had offered to go upstairs and check on her whilst the men talked business. As she made her way across the landing towards the master bedroom, Lucy had overheard Jenna on the phone. She couldn't make out all of what was being said but, as she neared the door she heard Jenna Reid call someone 'Darling' and murmur words of love to the person at the other end. Who the hell was she speaking to? Did Jenna Reid have a secret lover?! Unsure of what to do, Lucy was about to turn and make her way back across the landing when the door to the master suite opened and Lucy found herself staring at Jenna Reid.

"Heard enough, have you?" Jenna didn't mince her words now. She knew that if Lucy Adams were to open her mouth it could ruin all her plans. "Didn't anyone ever tell you it's rude to eavesdrop on other people's conversation? She was challenging Lucy now and the younger girl began to visibly colour, much to her dismay.

"I..er..I just wanted to come up and check you're okay" she faltered. Lucy could hardly look at Jenna, so acute was her embarrassment. She attempted a half-hearted smile now, which was not returned.

Jenna's heart was hammering in her chest now as she tried to remain composed. Had the girl been outside the bedroom door the whole time? How much had she heard? She decided to brazen it out. She figured the girl couldn't have been outside the door for longer than a few seconds anyway.

"Thanks, I'm fine" Jenna snapped. "Just having a chat with my Mother, if you must know, alright? Let's go downstairs and have a drink, shall we?" Pushing past her, Jenna left Lucy at the top of the stairs as she skipped down them, seemingly unfazed by the encounter. Perhaps she *had* been talking to her Mother after all, Lucy pondered.

Lucy followed Jenna back into the sitting room and, still shaken from what she had overheard upstairs, she couldn't look Max in the eye as she took her seat. She whispered to Rob that she had a splitting headache and asked him to take her home. Rob was a bit put out that the evening had come to an abrupt end but, not wanting to upset his girlfriend, he made his apologies and left with Lucy, ushering her protectively into his BMW before setting off to Lucy's apartment in Maida Vale.

As he drove, Rob felt puzzled as to why the headache had seemingly come on so fast. One minute they were all sitting around the dining table, laughing and joking, and the next they were outside on the gravel driveway bidding their hosts goodnight. Rob felt distinctly uneasy about the sudden and abrupt way Lucy had called 'time' on dinner.

"What's wrong, babe? Did something happen between you and Jenna? It's just you seemed okay one minute and the next we was heading out the door" Rob eyed Lucy discreetly as he drove, he didn't want to put pressure on his girlfriend but clearly there was more to this than met the eye.

"No, honestly" Lucy lied "Everything's fine, Rob, I just drank a bit too much wine that's all. It's been mental busy at work and I've been a bit stressed lately with our new Manageress always on at me about sales targets and what have you. Honestly, darlin' it's nothing" Lucy tried to act nonchalant and hoped that she sounded convincing. The last thing she needed, or wanted, now was for Rob to push her into spilling her guts about what had really happened upstairs at the Reid's house. She didn't want him running and telling Max Reid that his little wife was playing away from home, because clearly that is what she was doing and Lucy fully intended to keep well out of it.

Whatever was going on in Max and Jenna Reid's marriage, she wanted no part of it. She vowed there and then never to repeat what she had overheard. Not to Max. Not to Rob. Not to anyone.

CHAPTER THIRTY THREE

One week later

Tommy and Jenna had decided that the 'kidnapping' would take place this coming weekend, which left just three days to finalise the details. They had met twice over the past few days to discuss exactly how and when they were going to stage it, and what Tommy would say to Max during the ransom call. Jenna had told him that he should use a thick cloth to cover the receiver of the payphone, thereby disguising his voice a little. She also suggested that he faked an accent, however Tommy had insisted that he wasn't willing to risk it as he would be nervous enough just making the call. In the end, it had been agreed that he would simply use his own, natural speaking voice.

Jenna had joked that she found him quite sexy when he had practiced the deeper sounding, menacing voice, and Tommy had told her to pack it in otherwise he wouldn't be able to do it without laughing.

The only thing left to do was to open up new bank accounts for them both, under false identities, which Tommy had said he would sort out, and book the flights to Mexico. Tommy told Jenna that had a contact in Puebla who could, for a price, provide them with fake passports, driving licences and a place to stay until they could find a house of their own.

Tommy had warned Jenna that it wouldn't come cheap, this new life of theirs, but assured her that there was a substantial amount of money which he himself could to add to the funds and that once they were out of the country they need never look back.

They had decided on Mexico because it was hot, and Jenna liked hot weather. Tommy would have preferred Spain but, as Jenna had pointed out, Max would have no trouble finding them there. Max knew Spain like the back of his hand, but Mexico was alien to him and Jenna felt they stood a better chance of starting a new life there without any kind of comeback.

They had agreed that they would meet up again on Thursday afternoon, just to finalise everything, and after that it would be the day itself - the day that they planned to screw Max Reid out of half a million pounds and head for a new life in Mexico City.

CHAPTER THIRTY FOUR

Thursday Afternoon

Tommy finished his joint and took a long swig from a can of Fosters. He felt wired, even though he had been on the weed since a little after six this morning. He figured it was nerves getting the better of him and tried to play it down to Jenna who was sitting curled up on the sofa at his place, a scowl on her face as she glared at him.

"For god's sake, Tommy, lay off that fucking stuff will you? It'll turn your brains to mush if you keep at it the way you're going! Jenna was beginning to worry now. The last thing either of them needed was for Tommy to suddenly get an attack of the giggles in the middle of speaking to Max, and the way Tommy was rolling one joint after another did nothing to inspire confidence in him. She knew that if Max were to believe the ransom demand was real, Tommy was going to have to sound mean and menacing, and at the moment he looked and sounded about as mean and menacing as a three week old kitten.

"Lay off me will ya, girl? I'm just relaxing before Saturday, that's all. You don't need to worry your pretty, little head darlin'. When it comes to makin' that phone call Max Reid is gonna know I mean business alright. He ain't gonna wanna mess with me, darlin', that much I can promise you!" Tommy grinned now, the epitome of confidence, and Jenna decided that she was worrying about nothing. It would all work out. It had to.

Once they had pulled this off there would be no going back, not for either of them. Her emerald green eyes flashed as she smiled at him.

Suddenly Jenna leaned across and wound her arms around Tommy's neck. "Make love to me, Tommy" she whispered, as her lips found his. She felt closer to Tommy at that moment than at any other time, and she figured it was down to the fact that they were planning to screw her husband out of his hard-earned cash. Jenna loved drama - it was an aphrodisiac to her.

"I want you Tommy, I really do" she urged, in her most seductive tone.

Tommy, despite the copious amounts of weed he had smoked that day, felt himself getting hard. He hadn't had a decent shag for three days, and that hadn't been much cop if he was honest with himself. The girl had been eager enough, but Tommy hadn't really been up for it.

At first he had blamed it on the booze he had consumed – laughed it off inside his own head. After the third attempt, he had told the girl to fuck off, said she wasn't doing it for him.

The girl, a young Lithuanian called Monica, had been seriously pissed at having to leave in the early hours of the morning and had helped herself to a few hundred quid from Tommy's kitchen drawer as he fell into a drunken stupor.

Tommy, for his part, didn't seem to give a shit. So he hadn't been able to get it up –no big deal. He figured that as soon as he sobered up his todger would stand to attention again, no worries at all.

Deep down, though, he suspected that his lack-lustre performance in the bedroom was down to something far more serious, and that was anathema to a man like Tommy McLaughlin. He had tried to tell himself that he had it all wrong, that he must be going off his trolley or something to even entertain the thought. Nonetheless, when he awoke the next day he knew, without a shadow of a doubt, the true reason why he hadn't been able to do the business the previous night.

For the first time in his life Tommy had developed a conscience, and a strong one at that. He felt guilty, and nobody could have been more surprised by the sudden change in his way of thinking than he was.

CHAPTER THIRTY FIVE

Eileen Kelly had her knitting needles out again, and this time she was going to take a chance and knit blue.

Jenna's morning sickness had subsided now, thank God, and she seemed to be feeling a lot better in herself. Of course, Max had been on the phone morning, noon and night wanting to talk babies and, although Jenna hadn't really communicated as much to her mother, Eileen felt sure that her daughter was every bit as thrilled about the new arrival as her husband clearly was.

"So, Max, tell me – have you thought of any names for the baby yet, then?" Eileen had a few suggestions which she threw in for good measure, but she knew that none of them would be chosen. Her Jenna would probably opt for something posh –sounding like 'Toby' or 'Jonathan' knowing her! Max, on the other hand, seemed to favour more traditional names with 'Harry' his current favourite. Eileen didn't care what they decided to call him, or her, just so long as the little one was healthy. That was really all anyone could wish for, really, she told Max.

Max had agreed wholeheartedly with his mother-in-law, and they had chatted on for almost an hour about this and that; about the colours they had chosen for the nursery; the kind of bedding Jenna had chosen for the crib. Eileen was in her element as she listened to Max describe how lavish the christening would be – a real East End knees up he called it, and Eileen was already thinking that she would splash out on a new two-piece outfit especially for the occasion.

"As soon as we decide on a name, Eileen, I promise you'll be the first to know" Max Reid liked his mother-in-law. She may be a bit rough and ready but she had done a sterling job of raising his Jenna on her own, and he fully appreciated the many sacrifices the woman undoubtedly would have had to make over the years.

Max had twice offered to buy Eileen a new house, something a little bit more 'up-market' as he put it, but Eileen had politely but firmly refused. "I was left this house by a very dear friend, Max, it was home to me and my Jenna when we 'ad no place else to go. So, it's very nice of you, son, but I'll be staying put" Eileen had been so grateful to Old Mary for the house all those years ago. It wouldn't seem right to just disregard it now, just because her daughter had married into money. No, Eileen was happy as a pig in clover in her little two-up, two-down terraced house.

"'Ere, you ain't goin' to be 'avin' one of them big, posh prams, are ya? I mean, I can barely make it up the stairs, Max, the way my hip's playin' up. Gawd knows I wouldn't manage one of them big Silver Cross things at my age. I mean, I wanna be able to take the little one out now and again for a walk, don't I?"

Eileen could hardly contain her excitement at the thought of wheeling her new grandchild around in a posh pram. She planned to take the child down to the market and show him off to all the stall-holders and regulars that she had come to know over the years.

Max assured Eileen that, when it came to purchasing a pram for her first grandchild, they would consult her first. Eileen was delighted at the prospect of being 'consulted' even though, deep down, she knew Max was just being polite. It meant a lot to her though, that her son-in-law thought to say it. It showed her that he cared, that he respected her, despite her humble stature in the world. Eileen had ended the call with Max feeling on top of the world. She felt important, valued, and soon she would have a little grandson to lavish all her love on. Because it *was* going to be a boy, Eileen was certain of it.

As she sat by the fire knitting jumpers and cardigans for her first grandchild Eileen's mind would sometimes wander back to the night that her Jenna had been conceived. She would never forget that night, or the awful thing that happened to her, but she had learned to deal with it over the years.

Every time Eileen re-lived that terrible, fateful night she would thank God that He had seen fit to spare her, knowing that she might well have ended up on a mortician's slab if Fate had dealt her another hand. She thanked the Almighty for her baby girl, her Jenna, and for Old Mary who had given her a roof and put food in their bellies when her own mother and father had turned their faces away from her in the street.

Eileen Kelly was a woman who knew how to be grateful for what she had. She didn't waste time feeling sorry for herself, nor did she feel envious of others and what they had. The way she saw it everybody had their own cross to bear, and just because someone else's life might seem perfect to those on the outside It wasn't always the real story.

No, all in all Eileen Kelly felt grateful for her lot in life. She hadn't had to struggle to buy the things her child had needed over the years, thanks to Old Mary's generosity. She hadn't known the hardship of trying to hold down three jobs just to pay the rent and put food on the table.

Eileen Kelly felt that she was a blessed woman, a very blessed woman indeed.

CHAPTER THIRTY SIX

Saturday Morning

"At least let me get Billy to drive you, darling'" Max Reid felt concerned about his wife this morning. She had told him she was meeting a prospective buyer for the shop this afternoon, but she seemed vague about the man's name or where he came from. Max felt uneasy about his pregnant wife meeting a total stranger at the shop, even if it was in broad daylight.

"Honestly, Max, you treat me like a child at times" Jenna snapped. Today was 'D' day, and she was impatient to get things started. Max wittering on was getting on her nerves. She didn't need him messing up her carefully laid plans by getting his chauffeur to drive her! "I'll be just fine on my own, promise" she smiled at him now.

Max couldn't put his finger on it but something didn't feel right. He had been watching his wife carefully over the past two days and every time the phone rang, or there was a knock at the door, she visibly jumped. He worried that the pregnancy was affecting her, but when he questioned her obvious nerves she just laughed it off and told him he was being silly. "I'm fine, Max, really" she had lied.

The truth was she was dreading Lucy Adams turning up, spilling her guts to Max about what she had overheard on the night of the dinner party. She suspected that Lucy may well have confided in her boyfriend and, knowing how close Max and Rob were, she figured it was only a matter of time before her secret was out.

So far she had managed to avoid any further contact with Lucy and Rob, playing on her pregnancy and claiming that she was too tired to entertain. She told Max that, once the baby was born, they could get back into the whole social thing. Max for his part had accepted his wife's reassurances, and put it out of his mind for the time being. However, this morning she seemed more jumpy than ever, and Max was seriously concerned about her safety if she intended to go and meet this prospective buyer alone.

"Well, look, make sure you take your mobile with you, ok? Any problems, anything at all, just give me a ring and I will send Billy over to pick you up" Max picked up his car keys from the dresser and kissed his wife's head as she sat brushing her long, auburn hair in the mirror.

'Send Billy over' Jesus, that was so typical of Max, she thought angrily. It was never 'I'll come and pick you up', always 'I'll send Billy'. Jenna scowled at her reflection now as she brushed furiously.

"Well, fuck you, Max, because after today you won't be sending Billy to pick me up ever again!" she said out loud.

*

Tommy McLaughlin's nerves were beginning to get the better of him. Where the hell was Jenna? She should have been here at one o'clock and it was now almost two fifteen.

Downing his scotch in one, he swiftly poured himself another. Why hadn't she shown up? Had she bottled out of it? Had Max found out the truth about the affair, about the child Jenna was carrying?

Tommy felt as though he might actually throw up at the thought of what Max Reid would do to him if he *had* found out. He knew the bloke would inflict on him the worst possible kind of protracted agony if he had discovered that he, Tommy McLaughlin, had been bedding his wife for the past three months, and had gotten her pregnant into the bargain!

Lighting a cigarette, Tommy paced the floor of Les Bryce's apartment like a caged animal, trying to decide what to do for the best. Should he get the hell out of here now, cut his losses? Or should he hang around a while longer, giving Max Reid plenty of time to find out his whereabouts? Tommy was like a cat on a hot tin roof, his every sinew stretched taut, his nerves frayed at the edges as he drew deeply on the cigarette. He was feeling decidedly paranoid.

Suppose Max was on his way over here right now? Tommy would have no time to get away if he left it much longer. For all he knew, Max and a couple of heavies were in the lift, on their way up! Tommy suddenly pictured Les' face if he came home to find blood and bone all over his Chinese rug; brain matter and bits of skull embedded into his fancy, silk wallpaper. The thought did nothing to settle Tommy's stomach, which was somersaulting in waves of fear, as he envisaged himself being tied to one of Les' fancy dining chairs and having his fingernails pulled out one by one with a pair of pliers.

The warning light above the lift doors lit up red. Tommy's heart nearly leapt out of his chest. Fuck! This was it, they had found him! Tommy knew without a doubt that it wasn't Jenna - she would have called him en-route to let him know she was on her way. She knew Tommy would be waiting for her at the apartment, and that he would be worrying because she hadn't turned up. She would have called to reassure him that it was still on. Having received no call from her, Tommy figured that the cat was well and truly out of the bag and that their plan to take Max Reid to the cleaners had gone awry.

Quickly making his way to the master bedroom, Tommy ran over to the bedside table on Les' side and opened the top drawer. Pulling out the Glock 23 Gen 9mm, he dived across the king-sized bed onto the floor and, keeping himself low, he checked to make sure the gun was loaded. Les always kept the gun beside him whenever he slept. He had had dealings with some very unsavoury bastards indeed over the years and, as he once told Tommy, it doesn't hurt to assume the worst of people.

Tommy breathed a silent sigh of relief as he saw that the gun was, indeed, loaded. He knew that Max Reid would have come carrying, as would his henchmen. What he didn't know at this precise moment was how many of them were going to come out of those lift doors.

Some years back, Les Bryce had called in a top notch security team to fit a warning light above his lift. Whenever anyone pressed the Penthouse Apartment button in the lift, the red light would flash a warning, letting Les know that he was about to have unwelcome visitors. Les always insisted on a courtesy call before any meeting, so he always knew that, if he wasn't expecting anyone, the visitor in the lift was bound to be hostile. It had served him well over the years, giving Les extra piece of mind whenever he was at home. Les didn't like uninvited visitors. He considered it very bad manners indeed to just turn up at someone's gaff, unannounced and it nearly always spelt trouble.

So when one lazy Friday morning, before setting off to visit his beloved daughter, the red light had pinged into life Les had armed himself with the Glock and positioned himself in an armchair which sat directly opposite the lift doors. Tommy had often remarked at how the chair seemed oddly placed, being neither part of the dining room or part of the lounge. He just couldn't see the sense of having an armchair in the middle of a room, facing a lift.

Les, however, knew exactly why the chair was positioned that way. He himself had put it there and, on that particular morning, that decision had undoubtedly saved Les' life.

The lift doors had opened and out of the lift had come a lone, masked gunman – obviously sent by one of Les' many enemies with a grudge to bear – and he was pointing a pistol straight at Les' head. Clearly taken by surprise, the masked intruder stopped for a split second when he saw Les sitting staring right at him from the leather armchair opposite the lift doors.

That split second hesitation was all that Les Bryce had needed. He fired the Glock once, hitting the gunman right between the eyes, and then fired a second time, putting a bullet in the man's chest. A 'double tap' – the executioner's preferred method of despatch. Les had simply put down the gun, called his cleaning company and told them they would need to send someone over right away as the lift was in a bit of a mess.

No-one bothered Les about the killing. It had been self-defence, the bloke had come into his home pointing a gun, and he had every right to defend himself. The police asked a few routine questions at the time but, despite the fact that they would have loved to be able to charge Les with murder, they had no choice but to chalk this one down to experience.

Les Bryce was many things, but a fool he was not, and although the police kept a watchful eye on him hoping that one day he would slip up and they could throw the book at him, he kept himself well out of reach of the boys in blue.

*

Tommy lay on his belly, his head at the foot of the bed, thanking his lucky stars that Les had installed that warning light. The way he figured, if he could disable the first shooter with a well-placed head shot, then he might have a fighting chance of staying alive. His heart was thudding in his chest as he lay, hardly daring to breath, waiting for the first man to put in an appearance.

He heard the lift ping as it came to a halt and he knew he only had a matter of ten or fifteen seconds before Max Reid and his heavies found him. Tommy swallowed hard, the adrenaline taking over now as he heard the lift doors opening. The bedroom window was slightly ajar and the traffic, although some distance away, was loud enough to prevent Tommy from hearing the footfall of anyone who might be coming toward the bedroom door.

Straining his ears, he detected movement in the apartment lounge and knew that the men, however many there were, would be signalling silently to one another before making their move. The last vestige of hope that it was Jenna stepping out of the lift was gone. She would have called out his name. He knew now with certainty that she wasn't coming. His head was pounding now, the blood coursing around his veins as he prepared for the fight of his life.

Suddenly, to his horror, he heard footsteps approaching the bedroom. They were getting closer now. Tommy could just make out each tentative step as the first of the men made his way towards the master bedroom. He figured they must have done a quick, visual sweep of the lounge area and, seeing no sign of him, realised that he must be hiding in one of the two bedrooms.

Tommy swallowed hard again, his mouth as dry as a bone. If only he had left earlier when he had first thought about it, he wouldn't be in this mess now. He could be heading to the airport, booked on a flight to Spain and looking forward to starting a new life instead of lying here hiding beside Les Bryce's king-sized.

Tommy held his breath as the door was pushed open. He pulled back the safety on the Glock; he knew that he would have only a split-second to pump a bullet into whoever came through that door first before he found himself coming face to face with the second man. With a finger on the trigger, he held his position and waited.

Inch by inch, the door opened slowly and Tommy knew that he was possibly only moments away from death. Jesus, what he wouldn't give now to be sitting on a beach somewhere drinking cocktails with a young, Latino lovely. Why the hell had he *ever* allowed himself to be talked into this madness? Had he really thought he could screw Max Reid over and get away with it? Clearly he had, and now he was about to pay the price.

He figured that Jenna had bottled it at the last minute and confessed all to her husband. Why else would she not bother showing up? Tommy found himself rueing the day he had ever set eyes on the lovely Jenna Reid. He cursed himself inwardly for ever taking the route he had, knowing that there had been other options open to him. He hadn't needed to bed Max Reid's wife, he could have found another way to do this. Now, though, it was too late.

How did that old saying go? *'He who pays the piper calls the tune'* Well, he was certainly wasn't calling the fucking tune now, wasn't he? He was about to be taken out in a blaze of fucking glory, and at the hands of a man he hated. Tommy didn't know which bothered him the most – the fact that there was a very good chance that he was about to die, or the fact that it would be Max fucking Reid who got to do the honours. Either way, he knew that he was well and truly fucked!

Tommy could barely breathe as the first of the intruders stepped into the room. He gripped the Glock with his right hand, using his left hand to steady his arm and, pushing himself forward with his toes, he rounded the corner of the bed and took aim. This was it, there was no going back.

Aiming high, Tommy squeezed the trigger.

CHAPTER THIRTY SEVEN

Jenna Reid was out of breath. She should have been at the flat over an hour and a half ago, and she had only just managed to get away. Tommy would be worried sick, thinking she wasn't coming.

She had been about to call him when she had heard a knock at the front door. Rushing to open it, she figured she would get rid of whoever it was by telling them she was late for a hospital appointment.

Eileen Kelly stood on the doorstep, carrying an armful of packages and smiling expectantly at her daughter. Jenna's heart sank. Jesus, why on earth couldn't her Mother ever call before popping round? This was most inconvenient!

"Sorry, Mum, I was about to go out" Jenna began. Eileen didn't appear to have heard her and hurried past Jenna into the kitchen. Jenna tutted loudly, irritated at her unexpected visitor. She *had* to get to Les' apartment!

Eileen had brought some little hand-knitted jackets over for the baby and had wanted to stay for a coffee and a chat. Jenna explained that she had an appointment with a prospective buyer for the shop and that she was already late, but Eileen didn't seem in any hurry to leave.

"Half an hour won't hurt, will it Jen?" Eileen was desperate to see her daughter. It had been weeks since she had found out that her first grandchild was on the way, and she hadn't had so much as a phone call from Jenna.

"Fifteen minutes, okay? I'll call the buyer and let him know I'm running late, but as soon as you've finished your coffee I must dash" Jenna poured her Mother a cup of coffee from the percolator and sat down at the breakfast bar, unable to conceal the fact that she didn't want her Mother there.

"Gawd, Jenna, you might look pleased to see me, love! Look, look at all this stuff I've brought for the little one...I've got some lovely bargains here. There's a pair of little bootees, and a winter coat too!" Eileen felt thrilled with her purchases. She had loved every minute of her shopping trip this morning, telling anyone who would listen that she was about to become a Grandmother for the very first time. The shopkeepers had seemed genuinely pleased for her.

Jenna, seeing her Mother's obvious delight, softened a little. "Thanks, Mum, they're lovely. Really nice" she patted her Mother's hand now in appreciation and Eileen smiled at her daughter, feeling that the bond between them would surely improve once the little one arrived. Eileen missed the early days, when Jenna was still a babe in arms. She had had her whole life in front of her then. Now she felt the best times were behind her, so the arrival of a new baby to shower all her affection on was like a miracle sent from Heaven to Eileen Kelly.

Jenna decided that she would text Tommy to let him know that she was setting off shortly. Fishing in her bag, she pulled out her mobile only to discover that the battery was dead. Shit!

201

Plugging her mobile in to charge, Jenna poured herself a fresh orange juice from the fridge and sat back down. She figured she might as well make an effort with her Mother, after all – she wouldn't have the chance to chat with her once she left the country. Tommy had been insistent on them having no contact with anyone back home. He told Jenna that, if they were to make a go of things, it needed to be a clean break with the past, and all that they knew now. Jenna had agreed that it made sense.

Finally, at almost two-thirty, Jenna had stuck her foot down and told her mother that she had to go.

"For god's sake, Mum, the buyer will have left by the time I get there, I'll have lost the sale thanks to you wittering on" Jenna glared at her mother now, willing her up off the kitchen stool and out of the front door.

"Alright, alright, I'm goin'..I know when I'm not wanted" Eileen sniffed. She didn't know what had gotten into her Jenna this afternoon - the girl was a bag of nerves. "'Ere, you alright, love? You seem a bit on edge, like" Eileen eyed her only daughter as she pulled on her coat. "You ain't sickenin' for somethin' are ya" she persisted.

"NO! I'm not sickening for anything, Mum, I'm just fucking LATE!!" Jenna bellowed at the top of her lungs.

Eileen was taken aback at her daughter's attitude. It seemed that she didn't want to talk about the baby, or any of the plans she and Max were making. Something was wrong. Something was definitely wrong. Eileen knew her daughter better that anyone and she was not behaving like a happy woman, about to give birth to her first child.

Sensing her Mother's hurt feelings, Jenna promised that they would have a catch up soon, to finalise the plans for the nursery. She figured that would serve to stem her mother's nosiness just long enough for her to get her out of the door. It seemed to work, and Eileen climbed into her car and drove off down the road, happy in the knowledge that she and Jenna were going to have the chance to sit down together and discuss the baby some more.

Eileen loved her little red Mini. It had been a Christmas present from Jenna and Max last year, although Eileen suspected that Jenna had had little to do with it. Somehow, she couldn't see Jenna thinking that one up all by herself. No, it would have been Max's idea, and Jenna would have simply gone along with it to keep the peace.

When they had invited her over for Christmas Day lunch and, afterwards, taken her outside to the big double garage, Eileen had wondered what on earth was going on. She couldn't imagine why they should want her to traipse out to the garage in the snow, when they could all be sat by the fire drinking sherry.

When Max had opened the garage and Eileen had seen the Mini, all wrapped up in a huge, golden bow, she had naturally assumed that the car was a gift from Max to his wife. Although Eileen had secretly wondered to herself what Max was thinking buying her Jenna a Mini, when she drove a top of the range Mercedes!

It wasn't until Eileen realised that Max and Jenna were standing staring at her, waiting for a reaction, that the penny finally dropped. Eileen almost fell over with the shock. The car was for *her!*

"Oh Jen, Max – I..I dunno what to say, I really don't. You do know I can't drive, don't you love?" she laughed now as Jenna handed her a pair of scissors to cut the giant bow away.

"Well, that's what we thought, so we sorted out some lessons for you too" Max handed her a white envelope which Eileen opened to discover that Max and Jenna had paid for a week's crash-course followed by her test.

"Oh, my giddy aunt - I don't believe this is happening!" Eileen had shrieked before jumping behind the wheel; she couldn't believe that in a few short weeks she would be driving her very own car. Eileen had never seen herself driving, but now it was being offered she could barely contain her excitement. All in all, it had been one of the best Christmases she had ever had.

Waving as her mother pulled away, Jenna felt a pang of guilt. There would be no meeting up to discuss the baby. No chats about the nursery, or the names for the baby. There would be no more of anything after today, because Jenna would be in Mexico with Tommy, looking forward to the start of a new life together.

Little did Eileen know, as she drove home in that afternoon, that it would be the very last time she would ever see her only daughter.

CHAPTER THIRTY EIGHT

Tommy watched, horrified, as Jenna Reid slumped to the ground, blood pouring from a hole in her chest. The next few moments seemed to happen in slow motion as Tommy's brain struggled to register what had just happened. He had shot her. *He had fucking shot her!* This couldn't be happing! He continued to stare, as though he were in a trance, as she lay on the ground, her expression a mixture of bewilderment and hurt.

"T...Tommy...Tommy,..help me..." Jenna's voice was barely audible now as she lay clutching her chest - her eyes wide open in shock. What the hell was Tommy thinking, why had he shot her? Jenna couldn't quite believe that she was lying on the bedroom floor in Les Bryce's apartment, covered in blood with a gaping hole in her body.

"Jenna! Oh, my God, Jenna, I'm sorry, I'm so sorry...I thought it was.....I didn't know....Jenna, I thought..." Tommy's words were garbled now. He was having trouble stringing a sentence together. He crouched beside her and cradled her in his arms. She groaned loudly as he lifted her, the pain in her chest unbearable.

The bullet had hit Jenna just below her throat and shattered her sternum, making it almost impossible to breathe properly. She was clutching at the hole in her chest, trying desperately to stem the flow of deep, dark red blood that was gushing out of her body and soaking into the cream, wool carpet beneath her.

Tommy told Jenna to lie very still, to try and stay calm, and he would go and ring for an ambulance. Jenna looked up into his eyes as he stroked her damp forehead; a single tear escaped from her right eye and trickled down over her cheek and into her hair. She thought that she must be dreaming because it seemed that Tommy had just fired a gun at her, and yet she knew that Tommy would never do such a dreadful thing to her. In a few moments she would wake up from this terrible nightmare she was having and everything would be alright.

"Tommy....the baby...help me...my baby..." her words came in short, breathless gasps now as she felt the panic start to rise. Why wasn't he calling a doctor? He said he would ring for an ambulance. Why was he just sitting there when she was obviously bleeding to death and her unborn child was dying inside her?

In that moment, as Tommy looked into Jenna's eyes, he saw with stunning clarity the hopelessness of his situation. If he called an ambulance, the truth would come out and he would be a dead man walking. He knew, without a doubt, that he could not get caught with Jenna Reid; that if anyone were to find out about this then he would pay with his life. He sat with his back to the wall, stroking Jenna's hair, as she lay in his arms.

In that moment, Jenna Reid's fate was sealed. She would die here, in Les' apartment, and Tommy knew that he would have to get out of the country as fast as he could. He couldn't call an ambulance, couldn't call anyone. He had to let her die. The way he saw it, there was no other option open to him.

Jenna's breaths were coming in short gasps now and she reached up and dug her fingernails into the back of Tommy's hand, the fear apparent in her emerald eyes, desperate for him to do something.

"Tom...Tommy?" she whispered, unable to believe what was happening. He wasn't moving, wasn't calling for help!

He didn't want her to die. He didn't want the child she was carrying to die, but as he sat cradling her head in his hands, feeling the sting of her nails in his flesh as she desperately clung to life, he made his decision.

Closing his eyes, Tommy tried to ignore the pain in his hand as Jenna's nails drew blood. Inside his mind, a voice was screaming for it to be over. There was no way back from this now.

It was done.

CHAPTER THIRTY NINE

Jenna Reid died in Tommy McLaughlin's arms on that Saturday afternoon, frightened and bewildered. She hadn't been able to comprehend that the man she loved was doing nothing to help her, nothing at all.

She had thought of her unborn child as she lay, taking her last breaths, in the arms of the man she had believed loved her every bit as much as she loved him. Even in those final moments, she could not quite believe it was happening. He loved her! He had told her that he loved her, so why wasn't he getting help? Why had he been hiding in the bedroom with a loaded gun in the first place?! None of it had made any sense.

*

She had driven through heavy traffic to the apartment, an overnight bag with a couple of changes of clothes in the boot of her car. After setting off she had decided to call and let Tommy know that she was on her way. Reaching into her bag she could not feel her mobile phone. Pulling over, she searched the bag thoroughly. Damn! She had left her mobile, still charging, on the kitchen worktop.

No matter, she thought, she would be there in five or ten minutes and then they would be able to proceed as planned. She could barely contain her excitement as she weaved her way through the afternoon chaos, tapping her fingers on the steering wheel as Radio One played the latest chart hits. She felt happy and in love.

Jenna had told Max that she would be home in time for dinner, so she figured that when she hadn't shown by around six o'clock, Max would start to feel worried and try to call her. Of course, she had planned to switch off her mobile at Les' place, but with the phone still at the house that wouldn't now be necessary. Max would be angry that she hadn't taken her mobile with her, but ultimately it didn't matter because she wouldn't need it now, anyway.

Arriving at the apartment block, Jenna had been careful to park her car well out of sight and had made her way in the lift up to the Penthouse. She had been so excited, knowing that this time would be forever, that she and Tommy would be on a plane to Mexico in a few short days.

Smiling to herself, she had checked her appearance in the lift's mirror and applied a fresh slick of lipstick. She wanted to look her best for Tommy. She planned on drinking champagne and taking her lover to bed until it was time to make the ransom call to her husband. She and Tommy had agreed that they would make the call around midnight at which point her husband would be out of his mind with worry.

Stepping out of the lift, she couldn't see Tommy in the apartment and figured he must be in the shower, or maybe he was having a nap to prepare for the long night ahead. Yes, that would be it - he'd be in bed asleep.

Wanting to surprise him, Jenna had not called out to Tommy. Instead, she had crept quietly towards the bedroom door, a mischievous grin spreading across her face as she pictured slipping into bed beside the man she loved and waking him with her mouth around his cock. She knew that

209

Tommy loved her to wake him up that way, and she had to stifle the urge to giggle as she neared the bedroom door.

Tommy was a heavy sleeper, particularly if he had consumed alcohol, and on the way into the apartment Jenna had seen a bottle of scotch and an empty glass on the coffee table, so she knew that he had been drinking before her arrival, probably to steady his nerves. No matter – it would all be over soon.

Slowly pushing open the bedroom door, so as not to disturb Tommy, she inched forward and peered into the room. The bed hadn't been slept in. She couldn't see Tommy, so she figured he must be in the en-suite bathroom. Well, she would just surprise him in the shower! She loved it whenever they took a shower together, often making love under the hot, steamy water. Yes, that's where he would be!

Pushing the door open, Jenna stepped forward into the room and suddenly found herself catapulted backwards against the wall. Puzzled, she felt an acute pain in her chest and instinctively clutched her hand to where it was coming from. She noticed that there was a strange smell filling the room and wrinkled her nose as it grew stronger.

Looking down at her chest, Jenna saw that there was thick, red blood gushing from a wound there. She stared at it in horror, astonished at just how much blood there was on her hands. Her clothes were also drenched in blood, which was dripping now down onto the bedroom carpet. Suddenly feeling very light-headed, she struggled to remain standing upright, and a few moments later collapsed onto the bedroom floor.

Jenna didn't quite understand what had just happened. She didn't understand it at all. Because a moment ago, she had been walking into the bedroom, excited and happy, looking forward to spending the rest of her life with the man she loved. Now here she was, lying on the floor, covered in her own blood.

*

Jenna saw Tommy leap up from behind the bed, holding a gun in his hand. What the hell had he been doing down there, hiding behind the bed? Why was he holding a gun? Jenna felt very confused now as she watched Tommy rushing over to where she lay. He kept mumbling something about being sorry. What was he sorry for? Had he shot her? Yes, that was it, it must be. Tommy had shot her. Her mind, however, refused to accept this as fact. It was ridiculous to think that Tommy could have done such a thing. He loved her. Why on earth would he shoot her?

The pain in her chest was excruciating now and she was struggling to breathe. Tommy had his arms around her and was saying something about an ambulance. Yes, that was it - he was going to call an ambulance. Help would be here soon, very soon, and she would be alright. Her baby would be alright. Tommy would bring help.

Tommy was just sitting on the floor, stroking her forehead, and muttering words that she could not understand. She thought she heard him apologise again, but couldn't fathom why he hadn't called for an ambulance yet. She was feeling weak and confused, her breathing was laboured and she feared she was going to die if help didn't get there soon.

She couldn't die! She was having Tommy's baby. They were going to be a family!

As if to shock Tommy into action, Jenna gripped his hand with all the strength she could muster and dug her fingernails into his flesh, willing him to snap out of his stupor and ring for the medical help that she so desperately needed. Surely he could see that she was bleeding to death. Couldn't he? She willed him to get up and make the call.

The last image Jenna Reid ever saw was the face of Tommy McLaughlin – the man she adored - his eyes tightly closed, with silent tears rolling down his cheeks. She had wondered for a moment why he was crying. Was it because he knew that there was no hope for her and the baby? Did he know she was dying? Was it guilt because he had been the one to shoot her? Had he wanted out of their arrangement? Why was he just sitting there, doing nothing to help her?

All of these questions whirled around Jenna's mind as she slipped away, questions to which she would never know the answers.

Jenna Reid's last thoughts were of her unborn child. The child that she would never get to meet, never get to hold or love. The child she never, ever thought she would want until the day she had met Tommy McLaughlin.

CHAPTER FORTY

Max Reid stared down at the mobile phone on the kitchen worktop. She hadn't taken it! For fuck's sake, how the hell could she have gone to that meeting without her mobile? How could she have been so stupid?

He thought back to this morning and how jumpy his wife had been. Who had she been meeting and, more importantly, where was Jenna now? It was almost seven-thirty in the evening and he hadn't heard from her all day.

Making his way into the lounge, he stopped to pour himself a brandy and settled into an armchair. He would scold Jenna for forgetting her phone, good-naturedly of course. She never left her mobile at home. Clearly she had been in a hurry this afternoon. He reached for the house phone and dialled the number to the shop. It rang out ten, twenty times, but nobody was picking up. Had Jenna left already? Yes, that would be it Max decided, she would be on her way home.

Turning on the television, Max settled into the armchair by the fire to wait for his wife.

*

Max opened his eyes and realised that he had been asleep. Checking his watch, he saw that it was gone eleven and he wondered where Jenna was. Stretching, he got up and made his way to the kitchen. There was no sign of her. Perhaps she had gone straight up to bed. He took the stairs two at a time and strode into the master bedroom, only to find the bed was still made and Jenna was nowhere to be seen.

An icy cold finger of fear crept up Max's spine now. Where the hell was she? Why wasn't she home at this time of night? Had something happened to her?

Max took a deep breath and decided that he would begin ringing around, to check whether or not anyone had seen Jenna today. His first call was to Eileen Kelly.

"Hello, Max. Jenna? No, I've not seen her since lunch-time, love. She was goin' to meet someone, she said" Eileen sounded concerned now as Max explained that she had not returned home, and that she hadn't taken her mobile phone with her. He instructed Eileen to call him the moment she saw Jenna - if she saw her at all - and ended the call.

Eileen sat by the fire, clutching her hands tightly to her chest, worried for her daughter's safety now. Where on earth could she have gotten to? It wasn't like her to just take off like this - she was always at home for dinner of an evening. Eileen Kelly couldn't possibly have known that her daughter was never coming home again.

Max rang around Jenna's friends, the staff from the shop and a few others he thought might have seen Jenna that day, but nobody could tell him anything. The girls at the shop said that she hadn't been in today, which Max questioned. Were they positive that they hadn't seen her? Wasn't she meeting a man there this afternoon about a possible sale of the premises? The two young sales assistants claimed to know nothing of

Jenna's meeting and insisted that Mrs Reid hadn't been into the shop all day. In fact, one of them told Max, they hadn't seen their boss all week, not even for the stock-take which Max knew was something Jenna always liked to supervise personally.

Max was starting to feel seriously concerned about his wife's safety now. She was missing, at this un-godly hour and almost four months pregnant. Could something have happened to the baby? His heart was racing now as he dialled the number for the local hospital. Could Jenna have miscarried their child and been rushed into hospital this afternoon? Surely, they would have called him, though, if that were the case. Unless...Max couldn't bring himself to think the worst now. She was alive, she had to be! If anything had happened someone would know to call him. Jenna must have her bank cards and driving licence in her handbag. She was easily identifiable as the wife of Max Reid.

Comforted by that thought, he spoke to the operator on the hospital switchboard, explaining that his wife hadn't come home and that she was pregnant. The operator transferred him through to A&E where the staff nurse he spoke to assured him that no-one matching his wife's description had been admitted. She then patched him through to the Maternity Ward and, again, Max was given the same answer. Nobody of Jenna's description had been admitted onto the ward today. Max replaced the receiver with a feeling of dread. Something had happened to his wife, he felt certain of it now.

Fearing the worst, Max called Rob Marsden.

CHAPTER FORTY ONE

Tommy McLaughlin was sitting in the lounge of his boss' apartment with a glass of scotch in his hand and a dead body in the bedroom.

He didn't know how long he had been sitting there, but he had consumed most of the bottle of whiskey and felt numb with shock. Not only had he mistaken Jenna for some lunatic with a gun, hell-bent on blowing his brains out, he had shot and killed her and her unborn child. As if that wasn't bad enough, he had allowed her to die. He hadn't tried to help her as she lay, bleeding to death from her injuries, in his arms. Instead he had thought only of himself and his own sorry arse.

Tommy couldn't think clearly about anything right then. His mind seemed to have switched off as he sat there, drinking and crying in equal measure. What the hell was he going to do now? He knew he could stay in the apartment for a while at least. Les wasn't due back from Florida for another week.

Les! Jesus, Les would kill him when he found out what he'd done. Pouring himself another glass of whiskey, Tommy lit a cigarette and drew deeply on it, trying to steady his nerves. He had to think, had to plan his next move.

The bedroom floor was covered in blood, Jenna's body still lying where she had died. Tommy hadn't even bothered to cover her up. He had waited until he was certain she was dead and then he had simply laid her head back onto the cream carpet and got up off the floor. What could he do? She was dead, and he was responsible for it.

Tommy finished his cigarette and lit another. Smoking seemed to relax him a little. He would have given his right arm now for a spliff, such was his state of mind. Tommy knew it was unlikely anyone would have heard the sound of the gunshot, the apartment was sound-proofed throughout (something Les had insisted on, to keep out the noise from the neighbours below)and as far as he knew the people downstairs had moved out recently anyway. No, he figured that he was safe enough here in the apartment for now, just as long as he kept his head down.

He hadn't wanted things to go this way, hadn't planned on this at all. Waves of guilt washed over him now as he faced up to being the coward that he truly was. Despite everything he had said, every promise he had made her, he hadn't planned on being with Jenna Reid for much longer. He hadn't purchased two plane tickets to Mexico, as he had told Jenna. Instead, he had planned on booking himself on a one-way ticket to Spain, and he had been planning on making the trip alone. No, Jenna Reid hadn't been part of his plans, but he sure as hell hadn't wanted to kill her!

He had intended to tell her the truth, the whole truth, once the ransom money had been paid into the Banco Santander account that he had opened online last Monday. Using a false identity, Tommy had set up the account in his new name and all that he would need to do was produce his passport at the bank once he got to Spain. The new, fake passport had cost him a few thousand but he figured it was well worth it. The five hundred grand would be in his new account, and he would be untraceable. He would be home and dry.

After that, he hadn't much cared about what happened to Jenna Reid if the truth be told. The way he saw it, she had brought this all on herself. He would take pleasure in telling her exactly what he thought of her which, if he was going to be brutally honest, wasn't much at all.

Tommy hadn't originally planned any of this. The idea of taking Max Reid's money hadn't occurred to him at all. He had been happy in the knowledge that he was shagging Max's wife. Occasionally he would try to imagine the look on Max's face if he ever found out about the two of them. Of course, he couldn't ever find out. Tommy knew that Max would kill him if the affair ever came to light, but it had been enough for now just knowing that it was he, Tommy McLaughlin, who was pleasuring Jenna Reid on a regular basis and that her husband was none the wiser.

The rest of it would come later, once Tommy had worked out a plan. He would see that bastard rot in hell if it was the last thing he ever did! It was that thought, and that thought alone, that had kept Tommy McLaughlin going.

No, it had been Jenna herself who had come up with the idea to screw her own husband out of half a million pounds so that she and Tommy could play at being happy families. At first, Tommy had laughed in her face, not believing for one second that they could pull it off. However, over the past couple of weeks, Jenna had managed to convince him that her plan would work. In fact, she had assured him, it was a dead certainty.

"Tommy, he loves me" she had told him. "Max adores me. Once I tell him about the baby he will be over the moon. There is nothing, *nothing,* he wouldn't do to ensure my safety, especially when he believes I'm carrying our first child. Oh, don't you see, Tommy, it's so perfect!" Jenna had thrown back her head and laughed out loud at the whole thing. Clearly she had thought she was clever, cooking up a plan like that. She had talked of nothing else once the idea had come to her. Tommy had been reluctant at first but, after a while, he began to see that this could be a very profitable way out for him. He figured that if he just played along for a while he could be looking at a small fortune within a matter of a few weeks, and Jenna Reid would be left, quite literally, holding the baby.

The truth was Tommy had seen Jenna Reid in a whole new light as they had sat on his old, battered leather sofa drinking beers that Thursday afternoon. He had always thought women were devious bitches, out for what they could get, but this whore was taking it to a whole new level!

She was perfectly prepared to dupe her husband into thinking that she was having his child (which was bad enough in Tommy's eyes) and then scheme to arrange her own 'kidnapping' in order to fleece him out of five hundred grand! Tommy McLaughlin had heard some things in his time, but this one took the proverbial biscuit. Clearly, Jenna Reid only thought about herself, her own wants and needs. Well, Tommy had decided, two could play at that game!

He had appeared to go along with her plan, dutifully playing the part of the devoted lover and father-to-be. He would gaze adoringly into Jenna

Reid's emerald eyes as she talked of their future together, making plans for the two of them, all the while thinking to himself that she was nothing but a sly, manipulative little cow. He had played his part to perfection, and Jenna Reid had died still believing that Tommy McLaughlin was in love with her.

After a particularly torrid bout of love-making one evening, Tommy had lain awake as Jenna slept and wondered whether or not he really was the father of the child she was carrying. 'After all' Tommy had thought to himself 'if Jenna can lie to her husband, trick him so cruelly into believing that the child she is carrying is his child, just to further her own ambitions, then it stands to reason that she might also be playing the same trick on me'

Tommy had closed his eyes, certain in his own mind that Jenna Reid would never be anything more to him than the means to an end, his passport to a better life. With that, he had fallen into a deep sleep, more settled in his mind than he had been at any time since meeting her.

The irony of the whole situation was not lost on Tommy, however. It was Max Reid's own wife who was out to con her husband out of half a million quid. Tommy couldn't have planned it better if he had tried.

*

Now though, all of Tommy's carefully laid plans had back-fired on him. Now he had no way out of the mess he found himself in, plus he now had a dead body to contend with. Not for the first time, Tommy berated himself for ever becoming involved with Jenna. He should have found another way, a better way, to deal with Max Reid.

As he sat feeling sorry for himself, an unsolicited thought began to work its way into his addled brain. At first he struggled to make sense of it and then, once he had made sense of it he immediately dismissed it as utterly ridiculous. He'd have to be fucking crazy to try it. It would never work - never in a million years! Tommy laughed out loud at the ridiculousness of the whole idea. Jesus, he must be really fucking pissed to have thought *this* one up!

However, the longer he sat there mulling things over, the more the idea began to take shape in his mind. The more it took shape, the more he became convinced that maybe it wasn't quite as crazy an idea as he had first thought.

He could do this, he could pull it off. All it would take was for him to keep his head, and he'd be home and dry.

Feeling suddenly optimistic, Tommy walked over to the kitchen sink and, turning on the cold tap, he splashed his face. The freezing water brought him back to life with a jolt and suddenly he was able to see things far more clearly than he had been able to over the past couple of hours.

'Yes' Tommy thought to himself, 'Why not?! After all, what have I got to lose? As the old saying goes – *nothing ventured, nothing gained'* Whistling softly to himself, Tommy found a half-smoked spliff in one of the kitchen drawers and promptly lit it, taking the smoke down into his lungs and holding it there a while. He decided that perhaps tonight wasn't going to end up a total disaster after all. In fact – it might just turn out to be the best night he'd had in a long time. Sitting down at the dining table Tommy picked up Les' house phone.

All he had to do was convince Max Reid that his wife and child were still alive and he'd be quids- in. He would demand the ransom just as he would have done had she been sitting beside him, and Max would be none the wiser.

Mentally congratulating himself on the brilliance of his plan he began to dial the number. It was almost one thirty on Sunday morning, way too late for most people to be receiving phone calls. However, something told Tommy that this particular call would be welcomed. He felt certain this was one call that the recipient would be positively dying to receive.

CHAPTER FORTY TWO

Rob Marsden had been in bed asleep when the phone on his bedside table sprang into life. Upon hearing the anguish and worry in his boss' voice he had jumped up, got dressed and headed straight over to Max's place. He figured the least he could do was to keep his friend company as he waited for news of his wife. Lucy was away for a weekend spa break with friends however Rob sent her a text letting her know that Jenna was missing.

When he arrived Rob found Max already on the driveway, clearly at his wits end. Rob threw his arm around his boss and reassured him that everything was going to be alright, Jenna would be home before he knew it. Deep down, though, Rob was deeply worried. For Jenna to have disappeared without a word to anyone was out of character. Yes, she could be head-strong, but she wasn't a fool. She would be only too aware of how worried Max would be, so it made no sense at all that she would stay out for this long without at least calling to tell him she was safe.

"I'm having a brandy, Rob, d'you fancy one?" Rob rarely touched the stuff these days. He and Lucy had decided to get fit for their holiday in Cyprus and Rob was under strict instructions to lay off the booze. Now, though, seeing the forlorn expression on his best mate's face he decided to join him. The man was clearly worried sick, and Rob tried his best to reassure him. Max, for his part, was grateful to have his friend there with him. God knows he'd have gone stark, raving mad if he'd had to sit here on his own throughout the night.

Max had decided not to telephone his parents at this late hour. He was acutely aware of his father's failing health - James Reid had suffered a second heart attack twelve months ago. The last thing Max wanted to do was put his father under any unnecessary stress. Jenna could well turn up unharmed (although Max didn't hold out much hope of it) so the way he saw it there was little point in worrying his parents until he knew for sure that there was something to tell them.

"I take it you've phoned around everyone you can think of, Max?" Rob watched his boss over the rim of his glass now, seeing the pain and worry etched on the man's face. He didn't know what to say to give him any comfort.

"Yeah, even people that Jenna hasn't seen In years, Rob. Nobody's seen or heard from her since yesterday lunchtime. It doesn't make sense. I mean, she wouldn't just go off like this, mate, there's no reason to"

Rob knew his boss was speaking the truth. If there had been anything wrong between Max and his wife he knew the man would be open with him about it. The one thing Rob Marsden could bet his life on was Max's honesty.

"I'm thinking of calling in the law, Rob. The way it's looking, she ain't coming home. The longer I leave it the worse it'll be. If they need to start looking for her then the sooner I give them the nod, the sooner they can start" Max Reid looked forlorn now as he sat cradling his brandy between both hands.

Standing up, Rob walked over to the fireplace and put a couple of logs into the wood burning stove. The way he saw it they could be in for a very long night and he didn't see any point in freezing to death while they waited.

Seeing his friend stoking up the fire, Max smiled thinly at him and downed his brandy before pouring himself another. He decided he might as well get pissed, because he had a feeling that come the morning he might be glad of it.

"I'll give it until two, Rob and then I'm calling in the boys in blue. I can't see any other option. If something has happened to Jenna I need to know for sure" he looked across at his friend now, his face a picture of abject misery.

"She's four months pregnant, for God's sake. Why would anyone want to harm a pregnant woman, Rob?" Max, at the very thought of someone actually hurting his wife and unborn child, broke down. His shoulders heaved with great, wracking sobs as he allowed the emotion of the past few hours to leave his body. Rob sat, helpless, watching his boss fall apart. Never in his life had he seen a man cry like this. Sensing that Max would want a moment to pull himself together in private, Rob muttered something about needing to use the bathroom and left him alone, head in hands, as he struggled with the thought that his wife and child may be lying somewhere, butchered to death.

Ten minutes later, Rob returned to find that Max had switched off the lamps in the lounge and was sitting staring into the fire. The flickering flames bathed the room in a cosy glow and Rob thought briefly of Lucy and wished that she were here now. She would know what to say to Max better than him. Lucy always knew just what to say, it was part of what he loved most about her. She had a natural way with people and seemed to make friends very easily, which was why Rob had been so confused by the apparent awkwardness between her and Jenna.

Rob had wanted to meet up with Max and Jenna over the past week or so, but each time he suggested it Lucy would make some excuse about having to work late, or meeting friends for a catch-up. Rob couldn't understand it. He thought that the four of them had gotten along famously, but all of a sudden it seemed the Reid's were off-limits.

Taking the armchair opposite Max, Rob took a sip of brandy and decided to put the whole Jenna/Lucy thing to the back of his mind. Now was not the time to broach the subject and, if he knew Max, chances are his boss wouldn't have even noticed the rift. Perhaps it really was nothing. Perhaps Rob was just imagining it.

Suddenly the phone in the study sprang into life, the shrill ring-tone snapping the two men back to reality. Max leapt out of his armchair and rushed to answer it. Snatching up the receiver, his heart felt as though it would leap out of his chest as he said, breathlessly, "Jenna?"

Silence on the other end of the line. "Jenna, Darling, is that you? For God's sake, say something!" Max gasped.

Hearing the anguish in Max's voice, Rob was out of his seat and strode into the study to find his boss holding the receiver to his ear with a look of sheer terror on his face.

"Max! Max, what is it? What's wrong?" Rob shook Max now. "What's happened?" he asked, his voice strained in the quiet of the study.

Max Reid replaced the receiver slowly before turning to face his Manager and friend.

"It's Jenna" he said, his voice almost a whisper, his face white with shock. "She's been kidnapped!"

CHAPTER FORTY THREE

Tommy McLaughlin had lifted the phone and replaced it three times before finally finding the guts to make the call.

He had debated how he should word things. Should he simply say 'I have your wife' and then demand a ransom? Should he wait until Max Reid asked him what it was he wanted? These, and many other, questions needed to be answered in Tommy's mind before he made the call. He needed to have everything worked out to the last detail, so that there was no room for error. He needed to take control, make sure that Max Reid knew who was calling the shots.

He had sat mulling things over for a little while, trying to recall movies he'd watched in which somebody had been kidnapped. He had no idea what to say, the right words to use. He wanted to sound menacing, believable, and he knew he would only have one chance to get it right. If he could make Max Reid believe that his wife was in danger, that their unborn child was in danger, then he stood to make a lot of money. He had to convince the man to do exactly as he was told without question. The only way to do that was to instil fear into him.

Once he had settled on the wording of the call Tommy took a deep breath and, remembering to dial 141 before the number so that the call couldn't be traced, he dialled Max Reid's home phone. He heard the call connect. His heart was hammering in his chest; sweat began forming on his brow and the adrenaline pumped through his body as he heard the ring-tone. One, two, three rings - then someone answered the call. Max sounded breathless – clearly he had run to answer the phone – and Tommy heard the desperation in his voice as he spoke.

"Jenna?"......Tommy waited now, his heart beating wildly in his chest. "Jenna, Darling is that you? For God's sake say something!" he urged. Tommy smiled to himself. He had Max Reid's full attention now.

"Max Reid? We have your wife" he said matter-of-factly. "If you want to see her and your kid again, you'll do exactly as you're told. No police! You go to the police and we'll kill her. We'll be in touch at eight o'clock sharp! Make sure you stay by the phone, *Maxie boy*" Tommy sneered as he said the last two words. How he hated Max Reid! How he would love to be holding a gun to the bastard's head, and then blow it clean off.

For now, though, he would settle for half a million quid. Revenge could wait a while.

*

Rob could hardly believe his ears. "She's WHAT?!" he sounded incredulous now as he paced the floor of Max's study. "You've gotta go to the police, Max. You can't handle this on your own, mate". Rob was visibly shaking as his imagination went into overdrive. He had heard storied of how people were murdered, despite the ransom money being handed over. He didn't fancy Jenna Reid's chances at all.

Max glared at Rob now. "Are you havin' a laugh, Rob? I go to the law and they'll be sending Jenna home in a fucking body bag. She's *pregnant* for fuck's sake! D'you honestly think for one second that I'd take any chances with Jenna's *life* when the bastards could just cut her fucking throat? Well... DO YOU?" Max was irate now. The veins in his neck were standing out and a rapid pulse was beating in his temple.

Rob realised he'd said the worst thing he could have said. "Max, I'm sorry mate, I wasn't thinkin'...me and my big mouth..." his voice was low now as his words trailed off, he didn't know what to say for the best so he figured he would keep quiet.

Max, realising that he had just yelled at one of his closest friends, stood up and went over to where Rob was leaning against the wall. Patting him on the shoulder, he smiled wanly and said "Sorry, mate, sorry...it's just.....you know" Rob nodded his understanding. He thought of Lucy and what he would do if it were him in Max's shoes right now. He had to admit to himself that if, God forbid, he should ever have to take a call like the one Max just had then he wouldn't go to the police either.

"Who would do this, Rob? Who the *fuck* would want to hurt Jenna?" he sat down heavily now and reached for a pack of cigarettes in his desk drawer. Lighting one, he drew deeply on it as he mentally dissected a long list of names; business associates, clients, friends – Max went through them all one by one. He didn't have any enemies that he knew of. He'd always played by the rules, been fair-minded, open and honest with anyone who came into his orbit. Why on earth would anyone want to do this to him and his family? Who could possibly be so upset with him that they'd sink to this level, set out to destroy him and those he cared most about in the world?

Suddenly, Max leapt up out of his chair and, stubbing out his cigarette in the ashtray, he turned to face Rob - his face a mask of fury.

Rob, sensing that Max was on to something, raised his eyebrows. "You figured something out, Max?" Rob Marsden didn't like the look in his boss' eyes now. The man looked fit to commit murder.

Nodding furiously, Max Reid grabbed his car keys from the hall table and beckoned for Rob to follow. As the two men climbed into Max's BMW he turned to Rob and said "I know exactly who's behind this, mate. There's only one cunt that would be capable of anything like this; only one piece of devious, low-life scum that would get any kind of enjoyment out of seeing me suffer. We're going to pay the bastard an unexpected visit, and when I get my fucking hands on him he'll wish he'd never been born!

CHAPTER FORTY FOUR

Andrea Richards was dreaming. She was dreaming about her brother-in-law, Paul. It was a recurring dream that happened every few nights, particularly after a few gin and tonics. She would dream that she and Paul were having a torrid affair and that he was desperate for her to leave Roy and run away with him.

Andrea had fancied Paul Richards from the first moment she had clapped eyes on him, which just so happened to be on her wedding day. Everyone had been there at the church – everyone, that is, except the best man. Roy had been frantic, phoning everybody he could think of to ask if they'd seen his errant younger brother, but no-one had anything to tell him. Andrea's parents were livid, especially when the usher told the driver to go around the block a few times because the best man hadn't yet put in an appearance!

Paul Richards had been living in Spain until a week before the wedding, running a beach bar and restaurant in Cala Ferrera. When he heard that his only brother was about to get hitched he had left the manager in charge and boarded the next flight out of Palma. Paul loved a good piss-up, and this was going to be the piss-up of the century!

Finally, almost forty minutes after the service had been due to start, with Andrea threatening to call the whole thing off if she had to go around the block one more time, Paul arrived at the church with a cheeky wink at the bridesmaids and an even cheekier grin to his brother, who by this point was ready to throttle him with his bare hands.

At last, the bride was informed that the best man had arrived and that she could now make her grand entrance. Feeling a little worse for wear, thanks to several large glasses of champagne at the hotel, Andrea Taylor almost tripped over the hem of her white, duchesse satin wedding dress as she swept into the vestibule. Clutching her father's arm for support she teetered down the aisle towards her husband-to-be, grateful that things were finally under way.

Andrea, having only seen old photographs of the best man up until that point, almost fell over backwards when she reached the altar and clapped eyes for the first time on her intended's younger brother. She thought he must be quite the most handsome man she had ever set eyes on. His deep blue eyes twinkled mischievously as he turned and smiled at her. For a split-second, Andrea felt like telling Roy that she had made a huge mistake, that she couldn't marry him after all. Not when she might have this god that was standing in front of her now, looking like something that had just stepped out of a magazine. He was an Adonis in Andrea's eyes, and at that moment she regretted telling Roy Richards that she would become his wife. Poor Roy, completely oblivious to his fiancée's dilemma, beamed approval at his bride's choice of wedding dress and thanked his lucky stars for Andrea Rose Taylor.

"You look beautiful, Andrea, truly beautiful" Roy had whispered as they stood together in front of the minister. Andrea pouted at him, realising that she had settled for what she could get with Roy, when what she *wanted* was standing right beside him holding the wedding rings.

"Shut up, Roy, for god's sake! You'll only start blubbing if you carry on like that" she had hissed.

The minister, who had no trouble with his hearing, frowned as he surveyed the couple standing in front of him. He had heard the exchange of words between the two and wondered, not for the first time in his long career as the parish priest, how on earth these two had made it this far. He couldn't help thinking that Roy Richards looked like the proverbial lamb to the slaughter, and inwardly chuckled to himself as he acknowledged that in this marriage it would most definitely be the wife who wore the pants.

He had begun with the customary 'dearly beloved' and ended by telling Roy Richards that he could now 'kiss the bride', although if he were being honest he'd have told the poor bastard to run now, whilst he had the chance.

*

Moaning softly in her sleep as she dreamt of Paul Richards, Andrea was suddenly jolted awake by the sound of breaking glass. Opening her eyes, she blinked a few times until her eyes became accustomed to the dark. Everything seemed to be exactly as it had been when she had switched off her bedside lamp some three hours ago. She turned to check on her husband, who was snoring softly, and was irritated to see that he was wearing those awful striped pyjamas that his mother had given him last

Christmas. Tutting to herself, she rolled over and pulled the duvet up over her shoulder, her eyes heavy as she began to fall back to sleep. She decided that it must have been a cat, somewhere, knocking over the empty milk bottles on a doorstep. Or perhaps it had been a car, back-firing. She began to drift back into a peaceful slumber, her body grateful for the comfort of the brand new bed that she had insisted they buy last month. Beneath the plump feather and down duvet she sank into blissful warmth, completely oblivious to the two men who were currently letting themselves in through her kitchen door.

*

Rob Marsden found that disabling the alarm system wasn't as difficult as he had imagined it would be. One snip of the phone line with his Swiss army knife and they were home and dry. It seemed that Roy Reynold's budget didn't stretch to one of the new-fangled, wireless alarm systems. He still had the kind of system that was powered by a telephone line and a battery in the outside box. Unfortunately for the sleeping occupants, the battery was dead. Andrea had been nagging Roy for weeks to buy a replacement and the fact that he hadn't bothered would prove to be a costly mistake if Max Reid had anything to do with it.

Wrapping his jacket around his arm, Max elbowed the glass in the kitchen door a couple of times before he heard a satisfying 'crack' – one gentle push and he was able to knock out the bottom corner and reach through the hole. Taking care not to cut himself on the jagged glass still protruding from the door frame, Max felt for the key in the lock.

"Oh, look" he whispered to Rob "They've left the key in the fucking door – must have been expecting us"

Taking a deep breath, Max gripped the key between thumb and forefinger before giving it a half turn. As the door clicked gently open, Max turned to Rob and smiled. "Right, let's give old Roy the surprise of his miserable fucking life, shall we?"

Rob could barely disguise a grin as he stepped over the threshold. It never ceased to amaze him how many idiots left their key in the lock. It was like a welcome invitation to a house burglar. They might as well roll out the red carpet and put up a big fuck off sign saying 'Come on in and help yourself'. Max Reid silently beckoned Rob Marsden to follow him upstairs. He was going to give Roy Richards the shock of his life, and no mistake. He would kill the bastard in his bed, right there and then, if he didn't get the answers he wanted. If this fucker thought he could pull a stunt like this and get away with it well, he had another think coming!

Max had always regarded Roy as a no-mark, a man he would just as soon cross the road to avoid whenever possible. The man had no scruples, which was anathema to a decent, hard-working bloke like Max Reid. This, however, was an all-time low even for Richards. After the incident in his office Max had had it in the back of his mind that he might need to watch his back in the future, but *this*? This was breaking new ground for Roy Richards.

It was bad enough that the bastard had taken a swing for Max, but to do this – to snatch his pregnant wife and then think he could get away with it? Well, it was nothing short of suicide as far as Max was concerned.

Tip-toeing softly up each carpeted stair in total darkness they reached the landing and looked around, their eyes slowly beginning to adjust to the limited light available. At the top of the landing, there was a small, rectangular stained-glass window through which a pale moon offered some respite from the pitch black surroundings. Trying to figure out which door led to the master bedroom. Rob gently pushed open the two doors directly opposite the stairwell, which turned out to be the toilet and family bathroom. He left the doors wide open and the light from the streetlamps, which were dotted along the avenue at the rear of the property, came flooding in through the small, opaque windows.

They crept quietly across the landing and, as they reached the first of three bedroom doors, Rob put his ear against the first but he couldn't make out any sound coming from inside the room. He shook his head at Max, who stepped silently towards the second door. This one, he noticed, was slightly ajar. If this was the bedroom where Roy Richards slept then they both needed to be prepared. For all they knew Richards might have a gun in the bedside drawer and, if he were already aware of their presence, they could find themselves unexpectedly coming face to face with it.

Signalling to Rob, Max reached into his waistband and pulled out his pistol, a Sig Sauer P226 9mm, capable of doing some serious damage at close range. Rob Marsden carried his own gun, a Glock 19, in a shoulder holster beneath his leather bomber jacket. He reached inside the jacket now and pulled the weapon out, clicking the safety off as he did so. Rob nodded to indicate that he was ready to roll and Max acknowledged him in return. Raising the weapon he held it close to his chest, one finger curled around the trigger, and gently pushed open the door with one foot.

The door swung open without a sound and Max inched around the frame, trying to get a look inside the room whilst keeping well out of the firing line. As he stepped gingerly inside the doorway he heard a loud coughing sound which stopped him dead in his tracks. Only the sound wasn't coming from this bedroom - it was coming from the one next door.

CHAPTER FORTY FIVE

Roy Richards was having difficulty catching his breath. He coughed and coughed, cursing the twenty cigarettes he smoked daily and thinking, not for the first time that year, it was about time he thought seriously about quitting.

Sitting up in bed, he wiped his hand across his mouth and with it the spittle that had collected on his chin. Reaching across to the bedside table he was about to switch on the lamp when the door to the bedroom crashed open and two figures, unidentifiable in the darkened room, came flying into the room shouting obscenities and ordering him to get up or they'd blow his head off.

Roy Richards was not a brave man. He would sooner talk his way out of an argument than start a fight. He knew, deep down, that he was all mouth and no trousers as the saying went. Oh, he could talk the talk – sure he could, especially after a few beers – but when it came to walking the walk Roy would just as soon walk in the opposite direction. On the few occasions that he had attempted to get the better of anyone with his fists, usually after a couple of scotches, he had always ended up on his arse before things had really got out of hand. So the sight of two unknown intruders flying through his bedroom door turned Roy Reynold's innards to jelly.

Suddenly, feeling two strong hands gripping him by the arms and dragging him up out of his bed, Roy began to protest loudly. He was petrified out of his wits but he was damned if he was going to go quietly without a fuss.

"What the fucking hell is going on? He was shouting now, more out of panic and fear than anger.

"More to the point, what the FUCK are you doing in MY house? If it's money you're after then you're out of luck!"

"Shut the fuck up, you low-life piece of shit" Max spat, smashing his pistol into the side of Roy's head. Blood sprang from the wound and Roy instinctively put his hand up to protect himself from a further assault. Recognising the voice as that of Max Reid, Roy was astonished as to why the man should be here in his bedroom at this time of night, and more importantly he was dumbfounded as to why Max was attacking him in this way. Sure, he'd pissed the bloke off that day in his office but surely to god it didn't merit this kind of retribution?

At this point, Andrea Richards woke, switched on the bedroom lamp, and wished she hadn't. The sight that met her eyes terrified her to the point of rendering her speechless (a rarity indeed for Andrea Richards!) and she stared, open-mouthed as her husband was dragged unceremoniously out of bed and thrown into a quivering heap onto the floor.

"R...Roy? Wha...what's going on? Turning to face her husband's assailants she hissed "What the hell do you think you're doing coming into my home in the middle of the night and...Oh my God – Max? What are *you* doing here? Would someone mind telling me just what is going on?"

"What's going on, Andrea? I'll tell you what's going on! This piece of shit that you're married to has signed his fucking death warrant tonight, that's what!" Max was shouting now, his face contorted with rage. "Where is she, Roy? Where the fuck are you holding her? Did you really think I wouldn't figure it out, you conniving cunt? Thought you could screw me out of a few hundred grand to pay off your fucking gambling debts, did you? Well I've got news for you, you slimy piece of shit. You'll be lucky to see the light of fucking day after this, my old son. Now – for the last time, before I make your wife over there a fucking widow – WHERE THE FUCK IS SHE? "

Rob, hearing no response, promptly kicked Roy in the ribs. "Answer the man, dickhead, or I'll blow your fucking nuts off and shove them down your throat" With that he grabbed a handful of Roy's hair and yanked him into an upright position. "Well, you fucking ponce, where is she, eh? Who are you working with?"

Roy stared up at Max Reid in total bewilderment. He had absolutely no idea what was happening. Where was *who?* What the hell were they on about? Roy's sleep-starved brain was having great difficulty understanding what on earth was going on. He decided to try and reason with Max, try to talk some sense into him. Whatever it was, whatever had happened, Max clearly had gotten hold of the wrong end of the stick. Oh, they'd had words the last time they'd met, sure, but Roy truly believed that in time Max Reid would be calling him up again - keen to do business with him – never in his worst nightmare could he have imagined Max taking umbrage with him like this!

Roy didn't fully comprehend the dislike that Max felt for him and his kind. In his world there were no standards, no principles or moral values, just the next opportunity. It didn't matter to Roy that he broke every promise he ever made in business; it didn't register that people judge a man on his honour and integrity. As far as Roy Richards was concerned, it was all about making a fast buck and if he had to let a few people down, or tread on a few to get where he wanted to be, then so be it. After all, business was business.

"Look...Max I don't know what you're talking about...honest. Come on fellas...we're all friends here, aren't we? Whatever this is about I'm sure it can all be sorted out. It was just a misunderstanding when all's said and done. You know what I'm like when I've had a few, Max. There's no need for any of this surely? Why don't we all go downstairs and have a drink, eh? What d'you say?" Roy's eyes were pleading now, desperate to put an end to the terrible situation he now found himself in. He figured Max Reid must have lost the plot, coming around here pointing a gun in his face. Either that or he must be on drugs. This certainly wasn't the same Max Reid that Roy had known for over ten years. That Max Reid was a reasonable, straightforward kind of bloke, whereas the lunatic currently standing over him in his own bedroom was anything but.

Max couldn't believe his ears. "Have a fucking drink, Roy? You're offering me a fucking *drink* when you've got my *wife* locked up somewhere! You bastard, I'll kill you Richards. I swear to God if you don't tell me right now where the hell she is I will blow your fucking brains out here and now!"

242

Andrea Richards covered her mouth with her hands. What the hell had Roy done this time? Surely to God he hadn't done anything to Max Reid's wife, had he? She didn't have long to ponder the question. Max Reid was pointing a gun at her husband's temple and she heard the click of the safety catch as it was released.

At which point Roy Richards, terrified out of his wits, felt his bowels loosen and promptly passed out. He slumped into a heap at the foot of his own king-sized bed, an ominous wet appearing at his crotch – much to his wife's disgust.

CHAPTER FORTY SIX

Andrea Richards poured Max Reid a large brandy and told him to sit down. The man was clearly a wreck, and right now he needed their support, despite his unwarranted entry into their home in the middle of the night.

After Roy had passed out, Andrea had spoken to Max quietly but firmly and asked him to explain his reasons for breaking into their home in the early hours like this. She had appealed to Max's better nature, told him to calm down and tell her what was wrong, and it seemed to do the trick. Max had told her of his suspicions surrounding the disappearance of his wife; how he had received a telephone call over an hour ago telling him that Jenna had been kidnapped. He explained that, in his considered opinion, her husband was the only one who had any kind of grudge against him following the incident in his office. Rob told Andrea how Roy had taken a swing at Max when his boss had refused to buy the club from him, and how the whole thing had left a nasty taste in all their mouths.

Andrea, putting two and two together, realised that there was more to Roy's ill health than she had realised. She now knew that her husband was in more trouble than he was letting on, and despite his reassurances to the contrary, things were most definitely not rosy in their garden.

She assured Max and Rob that she and Roy had been together for the entire weekend and, despite what Max might think of her husband, she was one hundred percent certain that even he could not stoop so low as to harm a pregnant woman – no matter what the provocation. So vehement was her defence of her husband that Max had accepted it without question.

Which left him right back at square one!

Roy and Andrea Richards had not been blessed with any children, however Andrea saw in her husband a deep desire to become a father and her failure to get pregnant had caused them both a great deal of heartache over the years. Finally, after almost ten years of marriage, the Richards had seen a consultant and he had agreed to run some tests. When the results came back Roy was left in no doubt that it was in fact he, not Andrea, who was to blame for their childlessness. Roy, it seemed, had a very low sperm count and at that moment he had been convinced that his wife would walk out on him.

To his surprise, and relief, Andrea Richards didn't walk out on her husband. However, she did make it perfectly clear that after all the insinuations she had suffered about it being her fault, she would fully expect him to 'make it up to her'. Roy had nodded his agreements. "Of course I'll make it up to you, girl, goes without saying".

 "After all, Roy" she said with a sniff as they drove home that afternoon "it's the very *least* you can do!"

The irony of his wife's comment had not been lost on Roy.

*

Max lit a cigarette and pondered this sudden turn of events. He had been so certain that Richards was behind his wife's disappearance. It hadn't

245

occurred to him for a second that he might have been totally barking up the wrong tree.

Roy looked decidedly sheepish as Andrea applied witch hazel to the cut on his head.

"Keep still, won't you! You keep fidgeting like that and we'll be here all bloody night, Roy" Andrea dabbed at the cuts a little too hard now and Roy winced in pain. "For gawd's sake, love, take it easy eh? My head feels like I've been kicked from here to Hampstead Heath and back again!" Roy wasn't exaggerating either – his head throbbed so much he could barely focus on the two men sitting opposite at their breakfast bar.

"So, Max, what's the plan then? Are you going to be bringing the law in on this or what?"

Max looked at Roy as though he were something that had just come in from the garden on the bottom of his shoe.

"Look, Roy, I'm sorry about what has taken place here tonight, god knows I am, but that doesn't suddenly make us bosom buddies. The truth is, I don't like the way you do business, and I don't much care for you either. So you can save the chit-chat for someone who's fucking interested, understood?"

Roy did understand. He understood perfectly. Max Reid was out of his league and always would be. He had thought he could play with the big boys and enjoy the kudos that such a lifestyle could bring, but in truth he was a non-starter and everyone knew it. He had failed at every opportunity in business, running up hundreds of thousands of pounds in debt and making more enemies than any one man needed along the way. Christ, he couldn't even get his own wife pregnant! No, Roy Richards was a born loser if ever there was one and, deep down, he knew it.

Unfortunately, after tonight's little fiasco, Andrea knew it too.

Standing up, he made his excuses and went back upstairs to bed. Andrea could see the two men out. She seemed to have everything under control, as always. Not for the first time, Roy resented his wife for her confidence; that ability she had to talk to anyone. He just blundered his way through life, upsetting people as he went.

Hearing the three of them talking in hushed tones downstairs, a conversation that he was clearly not going to be invited to take part in, Roy lay on his pillow before closing his eyes and finally letting out all the emotions that he had been keeping bottled up inside for years.

The shame of having pissed himself with fright in front of Max, Rob and Andrea was almost more than Roy could bear. In addition, Max had just put him in his place, told him what a no-mark he was, and Andrea had heard every word. She hadn't uttered one word in his defence either.

At that moment, Roy Richards wished with all his heart that he could simply fall asleep and never wake up.

CHAPTER FORTY SEVEN

Back at his apartment, Max made some fresh coffee and poured Rob and himself a large mugful each. It was going to be a long night. They would need to keep their minds alert, keep their wits about them, if this was going to end well.

Max and Rob both agreed that the eight o'clock call, when it came, would involve a ransom demand. They sat now, sipping the hot, black liquid, going over the ramifications of paying the ransom.

"Suppose you pay what they want and they don't let her go? Suppose....." Rob didn't need to spell it out.

Suppose you pay the ransom and they kill Jenna anyway.

Max lit a cigarette and drew deeply on it. He had no idea how much money the bastards would want, but he wasn't stupid. He knew it would be a hefty wedge, given his reputation. People knew that Max Reid had money and plenty of it. Up until now, though, nobody had thought to try and take some of it for themselves.

"The way I see it" Max began "someone's going to have to drop the money off, which will give us a golden opportunity to find out who is behind this. The caller used the word 'we' – that could mean two, or it could mean ten. Until we know what it is they want from me, we're just going to have to sit here like a couple of fucking lemons and do nothing. If I involve the law, Jenna's dead for sure. If I agree to their demands, we have a fighting chance of getting her home alive. Either way, Rob, I won't rest until I've put a fucking bullet in whoever's behind this, mate"

Rob could see that the strain of the past couple of hours was beginning to show on his boss' face now. Max had taken on the look of someone older than his years. His blue eyes were lined with worry, his complexion pale and washed-out. Rob's heart went out to him as he sat staring into the fire, clearly struggling to hold it together.

"Don't worry, Max, we'll bring her home safe. That's a promise, mate" Rob smiled at his best friend and patted him on the back. Max didn't answer him - he was too busy trying to work out just who could be behind this. Who did he know that bore him a grudge? Who would want to see him suffer like this? His mind raced back and forth, first one way then another, going over and over it in his head. He had missed something. He must have done!

*

Almost five miles away, Tommy McLaughlin was sleeping. He had consumed almost a full bottle of scotch on an empty stomach and, no matter how much he had fought against it, his eyes had closed and he had drifted off on the black leather sofa in Les Bryce's lounge. As he slept he dreamt of Jenna and the child she had been carrying, both happy and smiling and very much alive. The child in his dream was a boy of around two or three years with black, curly hair and deep blue eyes like his own. Tommy was playing football with him in the park and Jenna was lying on the grass, eating an ice-cream and laughing at her son as he tried to kick the ball to his father. The whole scene was idyllic and Tommy's eyes flickered in his sleep as he drank in the scene, happy and content.

Then, suddenly, the dream began to change. Above their heads the sky, which had been a brilliant summer blue, now turned dark and foreboding. Thunderclouds gathered as the rain began to pelt down onto their bare arms; stinging them, drenching them to the skin. Tommy called out to Jenna who, strangely, appeared to be further away from them now than she had been a few moments ago. He called her name but she didn't seem to hear him. As he watched her she gradually grew smaller and smaller in the distance, and then disappeared from view altogether. Tommy continued to stare as though in a trance. Where had she gone? Why had she left him and their child? Surely she wanted to be here with them, didn't she? He stood, mulling over the questions in his mind as the rain continued to pour down. Something felt very wrong.

After a couple of minutes Tommy turned to see that the child had wandered off towards the edge of the river and was skipping along the edge of the bank, totally unaware of the danger that he was in.

Running over to the water's edge Tommy just managed to catch hold of the child as he teetered on the edge, one foot flailing in mid-air. Swinging him up into his arms, Tommy berated the boy for wandering off like that and kissed him on his pink, wet cheeks. He felt an overwhelming sense of relief that his son was safe, that he had managed to get to him in time. 'Thank God' he whispered 'Thank God you're alright'.

As they started to walk back towards the park gates, where they had been playing football a few minutes earlier, Tommy heard an almighty cracking sound and looked up at the sky ahead to see forks of lightning shooting out from behind the heavy, black clouds.

Covering his son's head with his jacket, Tommy ran for cover underneath a huge sycamore tree and stood sheltering from the rain. Feeling the cold, he hugged the toddler tightly to him and buried his face in the child's wet hair. It smelt of apples and Tommy kissed his son on his head as the two of them waited for the rain to subside.   Suddenly, without warning, a bolt of forked lightning shot out of the sky, coming right at them. It hit the boy in the chest and Tommy felt the jolt as it threw his son backwards in his arms. He looked down at the boy, his eyes wide with fear, hardly able to take in what was happening.

"NO, NO!" he screamed "NO, DON'T DIE, YOU CAN'T DIE...." but it was no use, the child was lifeless in his arms. His head was hanging to one side, the innocent blue eyes staring ahead but seeing nothing. Tommy opened his mouth to scream but no sound came from his lips. Instead, as he tried to call for help, a thin trickle of blood began to fall from his mouth. He wiped it away but more appeared. He wiped it away again, but still more appeared. The trickle had now turned much thicker and faster until finally he began to choke on his own blood. Gasping for air as the metallic liquid filled his mouth, his throat, and finally his lungs, Tommy dropped to his knees with his son in his arms.

*

Tommy's eyes flew open in horror and for a few moments he felt completely disoriented. Where the hell was he? What the fuck had he just been dreaming about? As he started to come round the details of what he had been dreaming about became clearer and Tommy sat with his head in his hands, wondering if there really was a God in Heaven. More to the point, if there was – how long would it be before He had His revenge?

CHAPTER FORTY EIGHT

Eileen Kelly was in a state. It was five-thirty in the morning and still she had received no word from Jenna. She wondered whether perhaps her daughter had arrived back home and Max had simply forgotten to call her to let her know. She had sat up all night waiting for word, but she couldn't bear it any longer. If she woke them so be it.

Picking up the phone she called Jenna's mobile but it went straight to voicemail. Eileen ended the call then re-dialled, this time to Max and Jenna's house phone. It rang a couple of times and then Max answered.

"Hello...?" Eileen thought he sounded tired. Clearly he hadn't heard from his wife.

"Hello, Max, I take it you haven't heard from Jenna". Max debated for a moment whether to tell his mother-in-law the awful truth. He would have preferred to keep it from her but, given that he now knew that Jenna was in danger, he figured she had a right to know. He sat down at the dining table and took a deep breath.

"Eileen, I'm sorry love – you'd best sit down – I'm afraid I've got some bad news.

Eileen, fearing the worst, had to stifle a scream. She imagined that Max was going to tell her that her beloved daughter was dead. The truth, when it came, was only fractionally better. She sat down heavily in the chair, her stomach doing somersaults. Her Jenna – kidnapped? It was too much to take in.

"Oh my good Lord, who the hell would want do such a thing? Have you phoned the police?" Eileen's voice told Max that she was close to becoming hysterical and he urged her to calm herself.

"No, they said no police, Eileen. If I involve the law it could put Jenna's life in danger. We've just got to sit it out and wait for them to call at eight. It might be best if you were to come round here, sit with Rob and me. Can you drive or shall I send a cab for you?" Max felt concerned now that Eileen would ring the police herself if she were left sitting there alone, brooding. He needed her there with him, where he could keep an eye on things. Eileen agreed and ended the call, telling Max that she was okay to drive.

Ten minutes later, Eileen was on her way over to Max's apartment. As she drove she saw flashing images of her only child as a toddler, smiling and laughing, her auburn curls bobbing up and down as she skipped along in the park; images of Jenna on Christmas Day, opening her presents, her beautiful, emerald eyes shining with happiness.

'Oh, God, please – please don't let them hurt her' she prayed now, fighting back tears as she jumped a red light, barely noticing the other drivers on the road. An angry driver honked his horn as Eileen cut him up but she heard nothing, except the sound of her Jenna calling out to her. Eileen knew that Jenna would be terrified out of her wits, that under the cold, hard exterior she was just a frightened little girl. The tears that she had been fighting back now rolled down her cheeks. She couldn't bear the thought of anyone harming her baby girl. She had to do something! She pulled into the underground car-park and switched off the engine. Perhaps she could talk to whoever was holding her daughter. Perhaps if she appealed to them as a Mother they would let Jenna go, unharmed.

With that thought, Eileen pressed the button for the Penthouse Apartment. As the doors opened she saw Max, his face etched with worry, standing by the lounge window. Walking over to him she hugged him tightly, then took off her coat and offered to make them all some fresh coffee. Rob joined her in the kitchen.

"I'm so sorry, Eileen, you and Max must be worried sick. We've been racking our brains trying to come up with answers – who would want to do this, y'know, but so far nothing" Rob looked defeated now as he sat at the breakfast bar, head in hands.

"I know, son, I know" Eileen began "It's probably not personal, love. It's more likely to be some low-life scumbags who know that Max is worth a pretty penny and think there goin' to take advantage of the fact. There's no way this can be personal, Rob. Max doesn't have any enemies. You, of all people, should know that".

"You're right, Eileen, he doesn't. Everyone thinks very highly of Max, there's no way this is anyone who knows him personally, although we did think it might have been Roy Richards at one point"

"Richards! Why on earth would Roy want to do a thing like this? I mean, I know he ain't the sharpest bloody knife in the drawer but I wouldn't have thought him capable of doin' somethin' like this, love"

Rob laughed now, a hollow-sounding laugh that didn't ring true. "We paid him a visit after we got the first call, Eileen. Let's just say that Max is totally satisfied that Roy isn't behind this" Rob decided not to elaborate on the details of the visit earlier that morning to Roy Reynold's home. Eileen would freak out if she thought her son-in-law had broken into someone's home, brandishing a loaded weapon, only to discover that he'd got the wrong man. No, Rob decided that the least said about this morning's goings-on, the better.

"Why don't I make us all something to eat, eh? I could rustle you up some sandwiches if you like, Rob. You look like you haven't eaten all night, love" Eileen's concern was apparent now and Rob smiled gratefully.

"Thanks, Eileen, that'd be great. I don't suppose Max feels like eating but maybe you can have a word, try and persuade him to get something inside him" With that Rob carried the coffees back into the lounge and handed one to Max who was sitting at the dining table scribbling on a piece of paper.

"Here you go, mate" Rob sat down in the chair opposite and saw that Max was jotting down figures.

"The way I see it Rob, I could get my hands on a few hundred grand no trouble. The rest of my money is tied up in property. I mean, there's this place, the shop, the club and the house I bought for my parents in Hampshire, but other than that I reckon I'd be pushing it to find more than four hundred k if I'm honest. I'm stuck between a rock and a hard place if they demand any more than that, mate"

Rob could tell that Max was worn out. He had spent the past ten minutes doing sums, trying to figure out how much disposable income he could lay his hands on and, clearly, the man was worried sick. He would do all he could to help his best friend, no question. He knew that Max would do the same if the roles were reversed.

"Listen, Max, I've got about three hundred and fifty grand in the bank. I've been saving up for a nice place for me and Lucy, y'know, when I pluck up the guts to ask her to marry me that is" Rob grinned now and Max couldn't help smiling as he pictured his friend going down on one knee. "You thinking of popping the question then, Rob?" Max was pleased for his friend, glad that he had finally found the right one. Lucy Adams seemed like a nice girl, if a bit high-maintenance, and Max hoped that when Rob did get round to proposing that the girl accepted him.

"Listen, mate, I know what you're going to say and it's fucking decent of you, but there's no way I'm taking your money alright? You need it for when you become an old, married man. Thanks, Rob, but this is something I've got to handle on my own, mate. "Chances are they will demand a couple of hundred grand, but if the worst happens and it's more I can go to my Dad" Max smiled at Rob now, grateful to have his support at a time like this. "You're a good mate, Rob, the best. I couldn't ask for a better one, believe me".

Just then, Eileen came in from the kitchen with a plate piled high with sandwiches. There was ham and tomato, cheese and pickle and chicken. She placed the plate in the centre of the table and, turning to Max, she said "Come on, Max, get something down you. It's a couple more hours 'til the bastards call again. You want to be wide awake when they do, and by the look of you you're ready for the knacker's yard" Eileen patted Max affectionately on the shoulder. Max took no offence, he knew that Eileen cared about him and that she was trying to put on a brave face; he acknowledged that she must be terrified out of her mind at the thought of losing her only child, the same way he was.

CHAPTER FORTY NINE

Les Bryce stroked his daughter's forehead and smoothed a couple of stray hairs off her face. Ruby Bryce looked pale and thin, having not eaten for almost 72 hours. The hospital had put her on a drip to keep up her fluids and try to flush out the bug from her system.

Les and his daughter had enjoyed a fresh prawn salad for lunch three days earlier, after visiting the Dolphin show, and both had fallen ill with a bad bout of food-poisoning as a result. Les, being of sturdy constitution, had managed to overcome it with a regular supply of bottled water and some pills from the local chemist. Ruby, however, had been admitted to hospital after Les told the doctor that she had been sick constantly since ten o'clock the previous night.

Once Ruby was settled and stabilised, Les had phoned her mother to let her know that he would be cutting short the holiday and bringing their daughter home as soon as she was deemed fit to travel.

Carol Bryce had gone off like a firecracker when Les told her that Ruby had contracted salmonella from freshwater prawns. She blamed him entirely, telling him that he was both stupid and a bad father. It was nothing Les hadn't heard before, but this time he wasn't in the mood. Slamming down the phone, he made his way back to his daughter's bedside and vowed to give Carol a piece of his mind once he knew that Ruby was safe.

Les loathed his ex with a passion. She had been a difficult woman to please throughout their six-year marriage, always complaining and contributing absolutely nothing other than giving birth to Ruby, who Les adored with as much enthusiasm as he hated the child's mother. Once divorced, Carol had continued to make financial demands on Les, ringing him at all hours of the day and night asking for more money. Often drunk, she would launch into a scathing attack if Les refused, telling him what a crap father he was and how she was planned to sell the house and emigrate to Australia, taking their daughter with her.

"You're gonna do what?" Les had bawled at her one Sunday morning. "Over my fuckin' dead body Carol! I'm warning you, girl, you try that one and I will hunt you down and put a fucking bullet into that thick fuckin' skull of yours!" He had bellowed so loudly that Carol had been forced to hold the phone away from her ear. She hated Les Bryce almost as much as he hated her. The only good thing that had come from that particular union was her child. Not that Carol Bryce was the doting, maternal type. She did as little as possible for the girl, but she made sure that Les paid her maintenance on time every month. Having Ruby had been the best decision she'd ever made.

Carol knew a good thing when she saw it, and giving Les a child had been her ticket to a comfortable life of sitting on her arse in a house worth just over a million quid and drinking Chardonnay all afternoon, whilst telling anyone who would listen what a hard life she had and how that bastard of an ex had left her almost destitute.

Most of Carol's friends humoured her. They, too, knew when they were onto a good thing and Carol came in very handy with a free line or two of cocaine here and there, or a few hundred quid when they were short. All they need do was wait until Carol was pissed and she'd hand over the cash sweet as a nut. Carol couldn't see that she was being used. She really believed that she was surrounded by a loyal bunch of friends. If she ever heard the way they talked about her behind her back, Carol Bryce would probably be finished.

Les decided he'd ring Tommy once he was back in the U.K. No point in disturbing him yet, he didn't know when Ruby would be discharged or which flight he'd be able to get them booked on. In the meantime, Les stayed at his daughter's bedside, often falling asleep sitting upright in the wing-backed hospital chair. This morning he had woken at six with a stiff neck and a grumbling belly. Les hated hospitals. In his opinion they all stank of disinfectant and old age.

*

As Les wandered around the hospital, looking for a café that might be open at this un-godly hour, Tommy was taking a hot shower in Les' apartment. He had covered Jenna's body with the duvet from Les' bed and had stepped over it to get to the bathroom. He didn't feel as bad today as he had yesterday. What was the point? It wouldn't bring her back would it? Besides, it was an accident. He hadn't meant to kill her. She was just in the right place at the wrong time. It was hardly his fault if the stupid cow chose to turn up over an hour and a half late with no phone call to tell him she was coming, was it? Tommy conveniently ignored the fact that he had let her die in his arms; that he could have rung an ambulance but hadn't. Right now, that kind of thinking wasn't going to get him anywhere. He needed to concentrate on the matter in hand - to take Max Reid for half a million quid.

Towelling himself dry, he put on Les' silk dressing gown which had been hanging on the back of the bathroom door and walked into the lounge. It was almost eight o'clock on Sunday morning – time to make the ransom call.

At the precise moment that Tommy McLaughlin picked up his house phone and dialled Max Reid's home number on it, Les Bryce was tucking into an all American breakfast of bacon, waffles and maple syrup.

Had he known that in his master bedroom Jenna Reid lay stone dead, covered up with his own feather and down duvet in a pool of her own blood, Les Bryce might have thought twice about ordering extra bacon on his breakfast that morning!

As it was he tucked in, blissfully ignorant about the mess that would be waiting for him when he got home and the inordinate amount of trouble it would cause for all concerned.

CHAPTER FIFTY

Max visibly jumped when the phone rang even though he had been waiting for the call, keeping a watchful eye on the clock. When it sprang into life, Max leapt out of the armchair and grabbed the receiver.

"Hello? Max Reid here" he could hear the sound of someone breathing steadily on the other end. "What do you want from me, why are you doing this? If you've hurt a hair on my wife's head I'll....."

"You'll do what, Max? Tell me. Tell me what it is you think you'll do" Tommy felt the bile rise in his throat now as he locked horns with the man he had hated for most of his life. "Listen to me, Mister Max *fucking* Reid, and listen good. You will *do* exactly as you're told, if you ever want to see that pretty little wife of yours again" he sneered.

"Just tell me how much you want, for fuck's sake, and let's put an end to this madness. My wife has done nothing to deserve this; she's four months pregnant! How much is it going to take to get her home?" Max was desperate to know how much money he would need to raise to ensure Jenna's safety. So far he hadn't informed his parents of the situation, but if these bastards wanted more than he had then he would have to turn to his father for the shortfall. Max balked at the idea of taking money from his parents. God alone knew how good his mother and father had been to him over the years, and now he hated the idea that he might just have to ask for their help all over again.

Tommy could hear the anguish in the other man's voice. He sensed that Max Reid would pay whatever was demanded just to get his wife and his unborn child back home in one piece. Tommy smiled to himself now. *His* unborn child – well, that was a laugh in itself. Because the truth was, Max Reid might not have been the father of Jenna's unborn child at all. It might well be *his* baby that was lying dead in Jenna Reid's womb. Neither of them would ever know for sure, unless Max ordered a post-mortem, and by that time Tommy would be long gone.

"Five hundred grand, paid into an account in 24 hours, the details of which I will give you in a moment" Tommy spoke now, an air of authority in his voice. He went on – "Pay it and your wife will be released, unharmed. Refuse and we'll put a bullet in her brain, but not before we've had our fun - if you know what I mean" he waited for the full impact of his words to sink in. Max knew exactly what he meant.

Tommy had realised that by using the term 'we' he had added to the perceived threat in Max's mind. Max now thought that he was dealing with a gang of ruthless kidnappers as opposed to just one man. Therefore, he would see the threat to his wife's safety to be much greater than if there had been just one man involved. One man he might have been able to negotiate with, but a group of men? No, a group posed a much bigger problem.

Tommy had mentally congratulated himself on that particular stroke of genius. He wanted Max to suffer, to imagine his pretty little wife being held by a group of mean, testosterone - fuelled lunatics. The implied threat that she would be raped and then killed would ensure that he paid up. Tommy was banking on it.

"Okay, but before we talk money – just one thing" Max knew now that he was taking a massive risk, but it was one he felt compelled to take. He needed to be sure that these bastards were going to let Jenna go once the money had been paid, and he needed proof that she was alright. His heart hammered violently in his chest. Max Reid wasn't a man given to fear, but now he felt truly terrified, more terrified than he had felt in his whole life. Suppose he pushed these men too far and they hurt his wife? He'd never be able to forgive himself. Nonetheless, he had to stand firm. If they wanted half a million of his hard-earned money, he needed proof of life.

CHAPTER FIFTY ONE

Eileen and Rob watched Max's expression change now as he demanded to speak to his wife. Rob had to admire the man for having the balls to make such a demand, given that these bastards held all the cards. Eileen wanted to grab the phone and plead for her daughter's safe return but she knew that it would be useless. She also knew that, if she interrupted the call, she could put Jenna's life in danger, so she bit her tongue and remained silent.

"Let me speak to my wife, that's all I ask" Max repeated. "Once I know she's okay you'll have your money" he said. Tommy was now faced with a problem. He could hardly agree to put Jenna Reid on the phone. She was dead in the other room. On the other hand, he wasn't about to give up that easily. He decided to brazen it out.

"That's not possible at the moment, I'm afraid. Y'see, your wife is a bit *'tied up'* at the moment, Max, know what I mean?" Tommy laughed now as he heard the other man's sharp intake of breath. "But don't worry I'm sure we can keep her entertained until you pay up. Unless of course you want me to go and tell her that her old man doesn't think she's worth paying the ransom for?" Tommy was baiting Max now, playing on his emotions and hoping that it did the trick. Somehow he had to convince Max that his wife was still alive otherwise it was game over.

Max didn't like the feeling that he was getting about this whole set-up. Something felt decidedly off kilter and he again asked to speak to his wife.

"I'm going to want proof of life before I part with any money. Surely you can understand that. I just want to be sure that she's alright, that's all" he said, trying to reason with the man on the end of the line. If he could just hear his wife's voice he would gladly pay up every penny they were asking for.

"DON'T FUCK WITH ME, MAX!" Tommy yelled into the receiver now. He was getting more and more pissed off with Max fucking Reid. Who the fuck did this bloke think he was, making demands on *him* – Tommy McLaughlin?

"Take down this number and pay the fucking money into it by midday, or I'll shoot the bitch where she lies" Tommy's head had begun to throb now, such was his frustration. He hadn't anticipated that Max would ask to speak to Jenna. How could he have been so fucking stupid?!

He realised now that if only he hadn't accidentally shot and killed Jenna Reid he could, in fact, have brought her to the phone and then killed her anyway as soon as he'd collected on the ransom. He wondered for a second whether he was capable of it. Could he actually put a bullet into someone, commit cold-blooded murder? As much as Tommy tried to tell himself otherwise he knew, deep down, that he was more than capable of it.

He reeled off the account number and sort code for his Banco Santander account, certain that Max would be writing it down as he spoke. Tommy, however, was in for a disappointment.

Max, certain that something didn't feel right about this whole set-up, made a decision that was going to cause him untold heartbreak in the not too distant future.

He told the man on the other end of the phone to go to hell.

*

Eileen Kelly, on hearing Max slam down the receiver, leapt out of the chair and grabbed hold of him by the shirt front. Shaking him violently, she screamed at the top of her lungs. "What the hell have you just done, Max? How could you be so fuckin' stupid?! My Jenna, my only child, is being held by those monsters and you hang up on them!" The tears were streaming down her cheeks now as she balled her hands into two fists and began beating them on Max's chest. Her anguish was palpable.

Max stood rooted to the spot. He didn't know what he could possible say to the woman to make her feel any better, when he himself felt like dying inside. Had he just made the biggest mistake of his life? Would they call back, putting his wife on the phone, or would they kill her as they had threatened to do? He didn't have the answers, he just knew that if the people who had taken his wife wanted money from him then they had better start listening, better give him what he asked for – the chance to speak to his wife.

CHAPTER FIFTY TWO

Tommy McLaughlin was incandescent with rage. Fuck Max Reid. *Fuck him!* How dare he hang up the phone like that, like he was dealing with some fucking low life scum? Well, he would show him. Yes, he would show him alright!

Lighting a cigarette he debated what his next move should be. If he called back demanding the ransom money the chances were Max Reid would again insist on speaking to his wife. If he did nothing then the bastard wouldn't suffer, and Tommy wanted Max to suffer. He wanted it so much he could taste it.

Drawing deeply on the cigarette, he paced the room thinking about what to do. He was damned if that was going to be the end of the matter. There was no way he was going to simply walk away from this with nothing. If he couldn't get Max Reid to pay one way then he was going to make damn sure he paid another way.

Suddenly, Tommy knew exactly what he was going to do. Running to the bedroom, he picked up Les Bryce's gun and headed back to the phone. He was going to give the fucker one last chance to pay up, or face the consequences. Tommy knew that, if he played this right, Max Reid would either end up five hundred grand lighter in the next few minutes, or out of his mind with grief, remorse and guilt. Yes, the idea of Max being riddled with guilt felt good to Tommy right now. It was no more than the fucker deserved. Tommy was in control. He would be the one to have the final say and he relished the thought as he dialled Max's home number.

Rob was trying to calm Eileen down. He poured her a large brandy and told her to drink it down in one for her nerves. He explained the situation carefully to her, all the while reassuring her that Max knew what he was doing.

"Eileen, love, Max needs to be sure that Jenna is okay before he pays any money. He needs to hear her voice, otherwise how will he know that...." his words trailed off now and Eileen looked at him, her eyes rimmed red from crying. He didn't need to say any more. Eileen knew exactly what he meant.

How will he know that she's still alive?

The phone rang and Max snatched it up. "Jen? Jenna?" he began.

"Sorry, Max, like I said – Jenna's a bit tied up right now. I'm giving you one last chance to pay the money into the account - one chance Max, before I blow her fucking head off" Tommy sounded deranged now as he waved the gun around in front of him. If this was what it was going to take to destroy Max Reid then so be it. If he couldn't get the money from him, he'd have his revenge another way.

Max thought for a moment. If he transferred the money, there was no saying that his wife wouldn't be killed anyway. If he didn't, there was a chance, however slim, that they would agree to bring her to the phone. Once he could be certain she was alright, he could try to negotiate. What he needed was time - time to get the money together, and time to execute a plan of his own.

If he could somehow convince the kidnappers that he had the money lying around the apartment in cash, then he might also be able to persuade them to let him drop off the money at an agreed location instead of just transferring it into an unknown bank account which could be anywhere in the world.

He was hoping against hope that he could pull it off, because it was his only chance of getting Jenna back alive. If he simply transferred half a million pounds she was as good as dead and he knew it. If they allowed him to drop off the cash at a pre-determined destination, he would have Rob keeping lookout as he drove to the spot. With luck he'd be able to get eyes on the guy doing the pick-up and follow him back to where the rest of them were holding his wife. It was a long-shot, but Max figured that, right now, it was all he had.

"Look" Max began "I can get the money to you in a couple of hours. You just say where and when and it will be dropped off. No funny business, no police, just five hundred grand – *cash*" Closing his eyes, Max prayed that his carefully chosen words would have the desired effect. He needed this fucker on the other end of the phone to believe that he was getting his money otherwise there was no knowing what he might do to Jenna.

"First, though, I need to know that Jenna is alive and well. I need to speak to her, make sure she's okay. You can understand that, surely?" Max appealed to the man's common sense now. If Jenna was still alive then he shouldn't have a problem bringing her to the phone. Not if he wanted his money at any rate.

Tommy now realised that Max was no fool. It was as plain as day that the bloke had no intention of parting with any money until he could be sure that his wife was still breathing which, unfortunately, she most definitely wasn't. Tommy would have to resort to plan B.

"Alright, Max, you wanna play it like that, suit yourself. Don't say I didn't warn you, though. Remember – I gave you every chance to avoid this" Tommy pulled back the safety on the gun and aimed it at the ceiling. He knew that, due to the noise of the rush hour traffic, there was little chance of anyone hearing the gun going off.

Les would have a fit when he came home to find bullet holes in his ornate plasterwork, to say nothing of the body lying on his bedroom floor, but right at that moment Tommy didn't give a fuck about Les Bryce or anyone else; just the cunt on the other end of the phone.

"Say goodbye to your wife and child, Max, and remember – you could have prevented this. You could have done as you were told and just paid up but you decided to gamble with their lives. I just hope you can live with your fucking conscience, Max, I really do"

As he said the words, Tommy was reminded of the reason he was doing all this; the reason behind all the hatred he felt for Max Reid and he began to cry silently, memories of that terrible day flooding his conscious mind.

As he pulled back the safety, a red mist descended over Tommy McLaughlin. In his mind's eye, Max Reid was on his knees in front of him begging not just for the lives of his wife and child, but also for his own life to be spared. Tommy fantasised that he was the man in control, in charge of the situation. He got to decide whether the bastard lived or died. Well, today was the day that he was going to make Max Reid wish that he *was* dead.

Tommy took the phone from his ear and held it up in mid-air. Then he fired the gun twice in rapid succession. The sound of gunfire reverberated around the room - an ear-splitting sound that echoed off the high ceiling - causing Tommy to drop the phone. It landed on the coffee table, bounced off it and ended up on the floor. Tommy put down the gun, placing both hands over his ears. The noise in this enclosed environment had almost deafened him.

Max heard the gunshot, rapidly followed by a second shot - a 'double tap' execution. Letting the receiver fall from his hand he collapsed onto the floor, his mouth falling open in a silent scream. Suddenly every thought, every emotion he had been battling to keep in check, came to the fore – concentrating his mind on the terrible, gut-wrenching truth. It was more than he could bear. The bastard had killed them – killed them both.

With a devastating sense of finality Max Reid knew that it was all over. Jenna was dead; their unborn child was dead, both of them murdered in cold blood and he had done nothing to save them. He had gambled with their lives and he had lost.

Max felt that he might actually stop breathing right then and there, such was his pain. He had lost his reason for living, the reason he got up every morning. Jenna had been his life's blood. He had worshipped her. Their child hadn't even taken his first breath and now he was gone from him forever.

He would never get to meet his first child. Never know the joy of fatherhood. Never hold his wife in his arms again.

At that moment, Max Reid did not want to go on living, and Tommy McLaughlin had his revenge.

CHAPTER FIFTY THREE

Sunday Evening

Eileen Kelly was sleeping in the spare room at Max's apartment. Following the phone call with Tommy, and realising that her daughter was dead, Eileen had become hysterical, screaming blue murder at Max and blaming him for the shooting. In her eyes, Max Reid was entirely responsible for her daughter's death. He had tested the patience of the kidnappers, refusing to pay them the ransom, and left them with little alternative.

"I fuckin' hate you, you bastard!" she screamed in Max's face now. "You...YOU did this. YOU KILLED HER!" she spat. "If she'd never fuckin' married you my baby would be alive today. I told her not to do it...I fuckin' warned her it would come to no good. Why the hell didn't you pick on someone else, eh Max? Why, in God's name did you have to marry my Jenna? She's dead because of you and your fuckin' money, because that's what this is about Max – money. She should never have gotten mixed up with you. Well, as far as I'm concerned you are as much to blame for her death as the bastard that shot her. You can rot in hell for all I care!"

All of Eileen's grief came pouring out at Max now as he sat with his back to the wall, holding his head in his hands. She wasn't thinking clearly, as is often the case when someone is in shock, and she needed someone to blame. It seemed to her that her son-in-law had caused Jenna's death by antagonising the man on the other end of the phone. She couldn't see that Max himself was utterly destroyed, that he too had suffered a catastrophic loss. All she saw was her baby, her only child, lying dead somewhere because Max had insisted on hearing her voice. At that moment she hated Max Reid with every fibre of her being. She wished it was him lying dead somewhere instead of her daughter; wished it had been him who had taken the bullet instead.

Max did not respond or try to defend himself against Eileen's accusations. How could he? Every word she had said was the truth. He may as well have pulled the trigger himself. Why the fuck had he tried to get one over on those bastards? Why hadn't he just paid the fucking ransom instead of trying to be a smart-arse? Now, because of him, his beautiful wife and unborn child were lying somewhere in a pool of blood, and he would probably never know where to find them. Max knew how people like them operated. They had probably been holding Jenna in a dis-used warehouse somewhere, a killing ground for maniacs like them; somewhere they could carry out their business with no questions asked, and then dispose of the evidence by torching the place to the ground.

Max's stomach lurched as he pictured them setting fire to the place with Jenna's body still inside. He wouldn't even be able to give them a decent burial. His heart broke as he thought of Jenna, picturing them both on their wedding day. She had been so happy that day, they both had. He had been the proudest man alive when he had turned to see his bride walking down the aisle on Marcus Graham's arm. Now all he had left were memories, and the guilt he felt about how she had died. He would go on blaming himself for the rest of his life.

*

276

Rob had called Max's family doctor and asked him to come out right away. Doctor Allinson was a little put out at being asked to attend a patient on a Sunday, but when Rob explained that Eileen had received some very bad news he had dropped everything and driven over to Max's apartment.   Eileen was sitting in the armchair by the fire, rocking to and fro, muttering to herself when the Doctor arrived. When asked what had happened, Rob told the Doctor that Eileen's mother had just passed away. He was under strict instructions from Max not to divulge the real reason for Eileen's current state. At that point, Max didn't want anyone else involved. He needed time to get his head around what had happened before he informed anyone else about the terrible events of that morning.

Doctor Allinson was a short, balding man in his early sixties with a sympathetic nature and the ability to know when to keep his nose out and his mouth closed. Upon arriving at the apartment he asked whether he might examine the patient. Rob assured him that it was better to leave Eileen be for now, that he could pop by in a day or so, once Eileen had come to terms with things. "She won't talk to anyone, Doc. She's in shock" Rob explained.

"Well, it's all very irregular, Rob. Strictly speaking, Eileen Kelly isn't my patient so...." Rob's expression brooked no argument. "Well, I don't suppose it will hurt, just this once. She will need to see her own G.P. though, I can only prescribe enough to get her through today" he warned. Rob nodded his agreement. "No worries, Doc, she's just a bit fragile today, you know". Handing Rob a couple of Diazepam, which he said should be taken right away, he wrote out a prescription for another six tablets and left it on the dining table. Rob thanked him and told him that he would pop out to the all-night chemist as soon as he had settled Eileen.

"So, Max and Jenna are not here, then?" Doctor Allinson asked congenially. Rob shook his head and tried his best to appear nonchalant. "No, they've had to go out. Someone needed to inform the rest of the family, y'know" he offered. The Doctor seemed to accept Rob's explanation and asked how Jenna was feeling during her pregnancy. Rob lied and told him that everything was fine, no problems as far as he knew. He hated lying to the Doctor, but he has his instructions. Max had made it perfectly clear he didn't want the Doctor to know anything.

Max had stayed in the bedroom whilst the Doctor was at the apartment. He was in no fit state to see anyone, least of all his own family Doctor, who would probably have taken one look at him and admitted him to hospital. The last thing he needed right now was to be asked any awkward questions. If the Doctor were to discover what had happened he would be forced to inform the authorities, and that would mean having the police crawling all over the place. Max couldn't deal with them asking him about what had happened. He felt his head would explode at any given moment. If he had to tell some nosey fucking copper that he had practically signed his own wife's death warrant he would lose it altogether, and probably end up being locked up.

No, he needed time to think, time to sort out what he was going to do next. He didn't need any additional aggro coming his way. Right now, Max Reid was hanging onto his sanity by a thread.

CHAPTER FIFTY FOUR

Les Bryce settled his daughter into the seat by the window and put the hand luggage in the overhead locker. It was Monday afternoon, ten o'clock local time, and they were on a flight out of Orlando International headed for London.

Ruby had fully recovered from her bout of food-poisoning and was as bright as a button. She was disappointed to be going home early but, as her father had explained, it was best to be on the safe side. The truth was he didn't really have any choice but to return Ruby to her mother. Carol had called him two days ago and told him in no uncertain manner that if he didn't book them on the first flight home once Ruby was discharged, she would ring the police and tell them that he had taken Ruby abroad without her permission. In theory, Les could find himself in serious trouble if the police chose to believe Carol's lies, as his ex was the custodial parent.

Les had wanted to apply for joint custody when he and Carol had been going through a bitter divorce. However Carol had threatened him more than once that if he crossed her she would make sure he never saw his daughter again. Not wanting to upset her any further, Les had agreed to Carol having sole custody, so long as he could have regular access at the weekends.

This arrangement had worked out well. Les would drive over to Brighton on a Friday evening and spend the weekend with his daughter whilst Carol went out with friends. It was an arrangement which suited them both and Les looked forward to a Friday evening when he got to spend time with his only child.

Carol, for her part, liked to party hard. She loved nothing more than getting dolled up and going out on the town with her cronies. Often ending the evening in a club, she wouldn't get home until the early hours which annoyed Les no end as she wasn't the quietest person in the world when she was letting herself in through the front door. Many times he had needed to put Ruby back to bed after her drunken, loud-mouthed mother had woken her up. In the end, it had been agreed that Carol would spend the weekend at one of her friend's houses, which meant that Les and Ruby could have the house to themselves.

Les adored his daughter. Nothing was too good for her in his eyes, and he loved nothing more than splashing out on her whenever they went out shopping together. She would drag him around toy shops, clothes shops and shoe shops, pointing out this and that before finally deciding on what to buy and Les would dutifully carry the armfuls of bags back to his car as his little daughter skipped merrily along.

Ruby was a lovely child, if a little spoilt. She knew how to wrap Les around her little finger, but she did it in such a cute way that he, although fully aware that he was being played for a fool, was only too happy to oblige. After all, as he often told anyone who would listen – "You can't bloody take it with you!"

*

Four thousand miles away, Tommy McLaughlin was blissfully unaware of the fact that his boss was sitting on a plane, about to take off, and would be in the U.K. later that same evening. As far as Tommy was concerned, Les wasn't due back until Friday, which left him with plenty of time to decide what his next move should be.

He had noticed that the corpse in the bedroom had begun to smell slightly. Finding another duvet in the spare room, he took it and threw it over the body before closing the bedroom door. Tommy hated death, and the fact that there was a dead body in the next room did nothing for his sleep. He had found it almost impossible to get any rest in the guest bedroom so had taken to sleeping on the sofa in the lounge. Large and extremely comfortable, it had provided Tommy with a place to rest his head and he had woken this morning feeling quite refreshed.

He sat now, drinking a mug of steaming, black coffee and smoking a cigarette. He had opened the curtains upon rising and found that the sunlight hurt his eyes so he had quickly closed them and turned on a table lamp. Sitting there, on Les' sofa, drinking Les' coffee Tommy knew that he needed to get away, and to do that he needed money and lots of it. Damn Max Reid! Why hadn't he just paid up, for fuck's sake? He could have been halfway to Spain now if things had gone according to plan. Tommy cursed Max under his breath, and lit another cigarette.

Tommy knew that Les Bryce had money in his safe - over nine hundred and fifty grand, to be precise. Getting his hands on it, though, was proving difficult. Tommy had tried every combination he could think of to unlock the safe, but so far had drawn a blank. He knew the code must be lying around somewhere. Les had a very unreliable memory, and often wrote things down so that he wouldn't forget them. The code for the alarm system; the code for the front door, even the code to his office – Les had them all jotted down somewhere in a notebook. Tommy had seen the fucking thing, here in Les' apartment, but now he couldn't find it anywhere.

Tommy pulled out the kitchen drawers and tipped the contents onto the floor. That notebook had to be here somewhere. It just had to be! Rummaging through invoices, bills and leaflets he couldn't see it. He opened the larder unit and, reaching in to the back of the shelves, he swept the entire contents of each one out onto the kitchen floor. Cans and bottles crashed onto the marble tiles, some of them breaking as they made contact with the floor. The strong aroma of tabasco sauce, the contents of one of the bottles that had smashed, filled Tommy's nostrils and he kicked the offending bottle towards the far wall.

"Shit!" he yelled at the top of his lungs "Where the FUCK is it, you fuckin' ponce?" Tommy could feel his blood pressure beginning to rise now as the frustration of his fruitless search took hold. Scrambling unsteadily in his bare feet over jars of pitted olives and bottles of exotic cooking oil, Tommy almost hit his head as he slipped in an oily patch that had formed in the middle of the floor. Groping for the door handle, he grabbed a tea towel and wiped the soles of his feet roughly. Throwing the tea towel into the sink, Tommy surveyed the mess all around him. It was no good, he realised. The bastard had obviously taken the notebook with him.

Bending down, he began to clear the bottles and jars off the floor and dropped each one in the bin. One jar in particular caught his eye and, even in his frustrated state of mind, Tommy couldn't help but grin. Les was a bugger for his curries and must have had every curry powder known to mankind in his kitchen cupboards. As he looked down at the label on the jar, Tommy recalled the first time he had met Les Bryce, that night outside the club where he had been working as a bouncer. Les had offered him a job on the spot, and they had gone for a couple of pints to celebrate their new alliance.

As the two men had sat, drinking at the bar, Tommy had listened as Les told him about his business ventures, his failed marriage and his only daughter, Ruby. Tommy remembered Les had thrown back his head and laughed until he cried as he told him about how his daughter had come to be called Ruby.

"I named her after me favourite grub, didn't I?" Les chuckled as Tommy looked at him, bewildered.

"Sorry, mate, you've lost me"

"Ruby, son...RUBY!!" he went on "After the old Ruby Murray" Les looked at Tommy expectantly but, seeing that the penny hadn't dropped he figured he'd have to spell it out for him.

"Fuckin' hell, Tommy, it's bleedin' obvious that you ain't from round 'ere. A ruby, son, is cockney rhyming slang, innit? Ruby Murray – curry. Get it? I named my one and only daughter after my other passion in life, Tommy"

Tommy had felt like an idiot once he cottoned on to what Les meant. Of course, being from Ireland, Tommy was not familiar with cockney rhyming slang. Sure, he'd heard a few – apples and pears, stairs; whistle and flute, suit. Ruby Murray was a new one on him though, and he had laughed good-naturedly as Les proceeded to take the piss.

Suddenly, Tommy began to chuckle to himself as he stared at the jar of curry powder in his hand. Of course! It was obvious. It had been staring him right in the face all along. How the hell had he missed it?

Tommy pushed open the door to the master bedroom and, doing his best to ignore the ever-increasing odour that was now emanating from the floor space at the side of Les' bed, made his way over to the large mirror which hung on the opposite wall. Reaching behind the mirror, he located a small lever which he pushed upward. He heard a satisfying 'click' as the lever released the mirror from its mounting and he was able to swing it away from the wall, revealing the safe hidden behind it.

Grinning from ear to ear, Tommy McLaughlin entered the four numbers of Ruby Bryce's birthdate – 4-7-80 – into the electronic keypad. The light on the console changed colour from red to green, and Tommy pulled down the lever and opened the safe door.

Inside were bundles upon bundles of fifty pound banknotes, stacked one on top of the other. Tommy couldn't believe his luck. It was just sitting there in front of him and it was his for the taking!

Opening one of the mirrored, sliding wardrobes Tommy located a large sports holdall at the back of the top shelf and took it down. Placing it on the bed, he pulled open the zipper, took out the tracksuit bottoms and tee shirt and proceeded to fill the bag to the brim with bundles of money. His hands couldn't get the money into the bag fast enough. As soon as he had crammed in as much as the bag would hold he stuffed more bundles into his jacket pockets and a couple down the front of his jeans. He was going to take as much money as he could carry, because this was one opportunity that wouldn't come along again.

As he carried the heavy sports bag into the lounge, placing it on the floor by the lift, Tommy McLaughlin couldn't possibly have known that Les Bryce was flying back to the U.K., five days earlier than expected.

CHAPTER FIFTY FIVE

Max opened his eyes and, for a split second, everything felt like it used to. For a split second he felt happy, content and looking forward to the future. Then, in that split second, it all changed and the horror of the past thirty-six hours hit his conscious mind like a freight train. The truth wrapped itself around his heart like a leaden, black cloak and threatened to overcome him. Gasping for air, Max sat bolt upright in his empty bed and gave way to his emotions. The tears streamed down his face as the terrible finality of his situation once again filled his every waking thought. There was no escape from it – this was his life from now on, empty and guilt-ridden; devoid of any happiness or hope.

He had lain awake most of the night, at the lowest point of his life, and contemplated ending it. He thought of his parents and how they might feel were they to receive a phone call telling them that their only son had committed suicide. He tempered any thought of the pain they would feel with his own reasoning: they would understand; they would know why he had chosen to take the easy way out. They'd know that he couldn't bear to live without his wife and child. Yes, he told himself, his parents would understand perfectly.

He thought of his friends. He was sure that none of them would blame him for taking his own life. They would gather at the wake and shake their heads sadly. They would all nod in agreement when somebody suggested that 'it was the only thing he could do, *after what had happened*'. Of course, no-one would actually come out and say it, but they'd all be thinking it, every last one of them: 'It was his fault she died. *He could have saved her but he didn't'.*

'Yes' Max had told himself over and over again as the darkest night of his life gave way to the raw, early-morning light and the inevitable pain of a new day without his wife, 'everybody would understand why I had to do it. In fact, they'd probably say that I couldn't have done anything else *in the circumstances'.*

Somewhere in the back of his subconscious mind, Max now had another thought, this one very different to the rest. It was lost amongst the grief and the self-torture, the blame and the self-loathing, but it was there nonetheless. As he lay hugging his wife's pillow to his face, breathing in the scent of her, it came to him like a bolt from the blue.

If he died, if he were no longer around, who would get the bastards that killed Jenna and his unborn child; who was there left if he took his own life to seek retribution for the senseless murder of the woman he loved and the child he had longed for?

Who was going to make someone pay for their deaths, if not him?

Once the thought had taken hold it became a definite plan and Max began to pull himself together. He *had* to go on living, *had* to have his revenge. Suddenly, Max Reid had a purpose for staying alive - pure, unadulterated hatred.

Dragging himself out of bed, he showered and dressed. He knew he looked like shit, and he felt like it too, but someone had to pay for this.

Someone had to be held accountable, and he was going to find the cunts responsible for this if it took him until the end of his days.

Walking into the lounge, Max saw that Rob and Eileen were already up and dressed. Rob turned to greet him with a half-hearted smile, but Eileen stared straight ahead, stony-faced and silent. Max didn't blame her for the way she felt, he even understood it, but right now he had more important things on his mind.

Eileen could hate him as much as she wanted to, but he didn't plan on wasting any more time on self-pity or self-recrimination. Today, he was going to start looking for the murdering scum who had put a bullet into her daughter.

*

Les Bryce had driven his daughter home to Brighton on Monday evening and had slept overnight in the spare room. Carol, thankfully, hadn't yet come home so, after making Ruby and himself some hot chocolate, he had put her to bed and settled down to sleep for the night, totally worn out from the flight and the long drive.

Carol had turned up at ten o'clock the following morning, hungover and foul-tempered. Les was in no mood for a slanging match. He made a pot of coffee for himself and Carol, and poured out a bowl of cereal for Ruby. The sooner he could get out of the place, the better as far as he was concerned. Les felt the chill in the air every time he was in the same room as his ex-wife. He kissed his daughter on the top of her head as she noisily crunched her breakfast.

288

"Daddy's got to be goin' soon, Munchkin, you be a good girl for your Mum, okay?" he smiled now as she wrinkled up her nose at her mother's back. Shaking her head, a mischievous look in her eyes, she said "I want to come with you, Mummy's got a headache" to which her mother responded with "Yeah, I 'ave, so shut up the pair of ya, will ya?" Les and Ruby grinned silently at each other. Carol's moods were legendary.

"Can I Daddy? Can I come with you? Oh, pleeeeeese!" Ruby grinned at her father now, knowing full well that he wouldn't be able to resist. "Just for a few days, Daddy - Mummy doesn't mind, do you Mummy?" she persisted.

"NO! I DON'T MIND! NOW WILL YOU PLEASE SHUT – THE – FUCK – UP?!" Carol Bryce poured herself a second cup of percolated coffee and turned to Les. "Look, make your fuckin' mind up, alright? If you're takin' 'er then get on with it, I'm goin' back to bed. My 'ead's fuckin' bangin'"

With that, Les winked at Ruby and told her to go and pack a couple of day's clothes in her overnight case. "You can stop until Friday, alright Rubes? I'll bring you back Friday afternoon and we can spend the weekend together as per"

Ruby Bryce was over the moon. She loved her Daddy more than anything in the world. Now she was going to stay at his apartment in London until Friday! She skipped upstairs to fetch her case, kissing Les on the cheek as she passed him. Les smiled to himself. 'Gawd, she's got me right where she wants me' he thought to himself.

Half an hour later, Les and Ruby buckled themselves into Les' BMW and started on the journey back to London. Les was looking forward to a few cold beers and a bit of Sky Sports on the television. Ruby had brought her hand-held games console with her for the journey and she sat now, engrossed, playing a game of Pokemon.

"Alright, Rubes?" he ruffled his daughter's hair now as they stopped at traffic lights. "Soon be 'ome, girl. Get you a pizza on the way if you like, eh?" Ruby nodded enthusiastically. She loved pizza. "Can we have ham and pineapple, and pepperoni, Daddy?" she asked him, one eye still on her game. "Sure thing, sweetheart, you can 'ave whatever you want, girl". Les knew that once they got to the pizza takeaway, Ruby would probably have changed her mind and would ask for something else completely. It never ceased to amaze him how his only child had turned out to be such a darling, considering who she had for a mother. Les prided himself on being a positive influence on his daughter, and credited himself on having taught her right from wrong. Not to mention proper manners. Les was big on proper manners – he hated anyone who didn't use 'please' and 'thank you' when spoken to.

As he reached the M23, Les Bryce was feeling good about life. He had a lucrative business deal in the offing, and his daughter was coming to stay. As he joined the steady flow of the Tuesday lunch-time traffic, he turned on the radio and tapped his fingers on the wheel as Bruce Springsteen's 'Dancing in the Dark' blared out of the speakers, singing along to the chorus. "..this gun's for hire, even if we're jus' dancin' in the dark".

He could not possibly have imagined the horror of what lay in wait for him back at his apartment. He couldn't, in his worst nightmares, have foreseen the catastrophic sequence of events that would begin to unfold once he reached home.

Turning to his daughter, Les Bryce smiled and said cheerily "You lookin' forward to bein' tucked up in bed tonight with your new, pink duvet then?"

Ruby Bryce nodded happily. She loved staying at her Daddy's place.

CHAPTER FIFTY SIX

Tuesday Afternoon

It was now four days since Tommy McLaughlin had accidentally shot and killed his pregnant lover Jenna Reid. He knew that the longer he hung around, the more chance there was of him being caught. The way he saw it, he could be on a flight out of London as early as Wednesday morning, and once he was on that plane he'd be home and dry. There was no way that Max Reid and his cronies would ever look for him because they didn't know he existed. Nobody knew his name, so nobody would come looking. No, Max Reid hadn't got a clue about who Tommy was, and whilst he conceded that perhaps, right now, that was a good thing it galled him at the same time.

One day, though, Max Reid would know who Tommy McLaughlin was. One day in the not-so-distant future, when all this had died down, he would come back to find the bastard who had caused him so much heartache and put him out of his misery. His would be the last face that Max Reid ever saw.

All Tommy needed to do now was to get rid of the body and he was safe as houses. To do that, though, would take careful planning. It wasn't as though he could just walk out of here with a dead body thrown over his shoulder. No, he'd need to think of something smart, something clever. Tommy smiled to himself. Yeah, he could do smart, he could do clever. He had Les' money, and he had a way out. Life was starting to look rosy.

Picking up Jenna's car keys, Tommy decided to pop back to his own place, pick up his passport and a few items of clothing to see him through until he could shop in Spain. He figured he might as well use Jenna's car. After all, she wasn't going to need it any longer. Whistling softly to himself, he walked over to the lift where he had placed the sports bag full of banknotes and zipped it up. It wouldn't do for anyone to get an eyeful of what he had going on in that bag!

Ten minutes later, Tommy let himself into his flat. There was the usual pile of mail – unpaid bills, junk mail, a special offer leaflet from Dominos. Tommy threw them all into the bin. He had no intention of paying any of those bills. Come to think of it, he realised, hc was four weeks behind with his rent too. 'Oh, well, fuck it' he thought wryly. 'Not like the landlord's goin' to be comin' round to break my balls over it, anyhow'. With that, he went to the fridge, took out a can of Fosters and popped the tab.

Tommy savoured the ice-cold liquid as it slid down his throat. Boy, it sure did taste good. There was going to be plenty of drinking once he got to Spain, he decided. Tommy loved the local beer, and the laid-back Mediterranean life-style. In addition, he loved the Latino looks of some of the local women. Tommy couldn't wait to get his first taste of Spanish pussy, and promised himself that as soon as he'd found a place to stay, he'd go out on the prowl for a new, willing bed-mate.

Jenna Reid never once entered his thoughts.

*

Les Bryce pulled into the underground car-park and found his allotted parking space. Unclipping his daughter's seat belt, he reached onto the back seat for his briefcase before opening the driver's door. Ruby sat, patiently waiting.

Les had instilled it into his daughter that a gentleman always walked around and opened a lady's door, helping her out if so required. It became a game between the two of them. Les would climb out of the car, button up his coat, adjust his tie and pretend to be looking for something in his wallet, all the while keeping a watchful eye on Ruby to see whether she would try to open the passenger door herself. Over the years she had learned that her father expected her to wait until he opened the door and she sat now watching him, a broad grin on her face.

"I KNOW WHAT YOU'RE DOING, DADDY!" she mouthed through the window at her father. Les chuckled. She was her Dad's daughter alright. Walking swiftly around to the passenger side, Les stood to attention and saluted before opening the door in a grandiose manner. "Good afternoon, Mi'Lady" he said, in an affected voice. Ruby fell about laughing as he held out his arm to her. "Oh, Daddy, you're so funny" she giggled.

Once she had alighted from the car, they walked hand in hand to the apartment lifts. Inside, Ruby pressed the button for the Penthouse Suite, checking her appearance in the mirror. She wasn't old enough to wear make-up as far as Les was concerned, but she did like to use flavoured lip-balm. Strawberry was her current favourite and she stood, her mouth forming a perfect 'O', and applied two liberal coats.

"There! What do you think, Daddy, do I look nice?" she beamed at her father.

Les couldn't have been more proud of his little girl, and his heart ached as he realised just how quickly she was growing up.

"You'll do for me, darlin'" he said with a smile.

The lift 'pinged' its arrival at the top floor and Les picked up his daughter's overnight bag and his briefcase. He'd go back downstairs at some point this evening to fetch his suitcase up. Right now, he needed a hot shower, a cold beer and a nice, relaxing afternoon watching the football.

The lift doors opened. Les stepped into his apartment lounge and his nostrils immediately picked up a strange, acrid smell tinged with something else – a kind of sickly sweetness. He stood for a few moments trying to ascertain what the odour was and exactly where it was coming from. After a few seconds the smell seemed to get stronger. It was pungent, foul-smelling, like rotting meat. Les wrinkled his nose up in disgust. What the fuck had Tommy been cooking for fuck's sake? The place was boiling hot too. Tommy had clearly not bothered to turn the heating off before he left. Les made a mental note to take a hefty wedge out of Tommy's pay to cover the cost of his gas bill.

"Ewww....Daddy, what's that horrible smell?" Ruby covered her mouth with her hand, the sticky strawberry lip-balm a welcome relief from the gut-churning stench.

"It's okay, Rubes, I'll just open a couple of windows, love. Probably me mate, Tommy, left something on the stove - stupid bugger he is!"

CHAPTER FIFTY SEVEN

Striding across to the large, central window Les pulled back the curtains and flung both side windows wide-open. He then switched off the thermostat, which had been set to thirty degrees. 'Jesus, he must be one nesh bastard' Les couldn't believe how hot the place was, and the smell – instead of disappearing - was getting worse!

Ushering his daughter towards the huge, leather sofas Les said "'Ere, you sit down on the sofa near the window, Rubes, an' I'll go and fetch you a drink, alright?"

Making his way into the kitchen Les Bryce couldn't believe the sight that met his eyes. There were bottles and jars everywhere, covering half the floor and filling the bin. What the hell did Tommy think he was playing at?! He must have had a party or something in Les' absence. Well, this would be the last fucking party he ever went to when Les got his hands on him. The cheeky bastard hadn't even bothered to tidy the fucking place up, to say nothing of running up a ruddy great gas bill. At that point, Les could have cheerfully throttled Tommy McLaughlin.

Tip-toeing across to the sink, Les filled the kettle and opened the fridge to see whether Tommy had, at least, bothered to leave him some milk to make a drink. Seeing none, Les slammed the fridge door shut and bellowed to Ruby.

"There's no milk, darlin', and no juice either. Daddy will have to pop out to the supermarket in a minute, love"

Ruby was sitting with her knees up to her chin and both hands covering her mouth. The stench in her father's apartment was making her feel decidedly queasy. It was all she could do not to throw up all over the leather sofa.

"Daddy...." she was trying not to breathe in too deeply "Daddy, I think I'm going to be sick" she said, dolefully.

Les, upon returning to the lounge to attend to his daughter, realised that the foul aroma he had first smelt on arriving at the apartment was now a lot stronger than before. Whatever it was, whatever was causing it, it was in this flat somewhere. He had to find out where it was coming from. First though, he needed to sort out some food shopping and clean up the mess in his kitchen.

Beckoning his daughter to follow him, Les picked up his wallet and pressed the button to call the lift. Once inside it, Ruby felt able to breathe again without covering her nose. Les grinned down at his only child now. She was fast becoming a young woman, and her little ways made him love her all the more.

"Tell you what, Ruby, why don't we grab a takeout on the way back from the supermarket eh? Daddy don't feel like cookin' tonight, let's 'ave a Chinese, eh, what d'you say?" Les loved his Chinese takeaways almost as much as he loved his curries. "I'll get some stuff for the fridge and some bloody bin-bags while I'm at it, clean up that shit-hole of a kitchen once we've eaten. By the time we get back, that awful smell will have gone" he reassured her.

Forty minutes later, armed with two bags of groceries and a couple of takeaway meals, Les and Ruby opened the lift door to the apartment only to find, much to their dismay, that the earlier stench had not disappeared as they had hoped. In fact, now that the air had had chance to circulate around the room, it was a lot stronger. It seemed to permeate everything around them, and Les found it difficult to inhale without wanting to vomit.

Putting the bags of shopping and the Chinese takeaway meals on the dining table, Les decided to follow his nose. Wherever the smell was coming from, he certainly would not be able to eat a mouthful until he had gotten rid of it.

Grabbing the roll of bin-bags, he made his way over to the open window and breathed in a good few lungfuls of air. Les realised that the stench was coming from one of the bedrooms. Gesturing for Ruby to stay put, he covered his nose with one hand and made his way towards the master bedroom. Whatever was causing the stink it needed to be gotten rid of fast, before he threw up all over his polished, parquet flooring.

Ruby sat quietly on the dining chair, her head out of the window, trying to ignore the disgusting odour that threatened to spoil their take-out. She had been looking forward to eating with her Daddy, and now it would be cold!

Suddenly, Ruby felt something against her foot. Looking down, she saw to her amazement that there was a gun lying underneath the window, against the skirting board. Jumping down from her seat, she bent down to take a better look at it. She wondered why her Daddy had a gun in his apartment. Did he use it to shoot people? Was it a real one or just a pretend one? Reaching down, she carefully picked up the weapon, feeling the weight of it in her tiny hands. It looked very shiny and new. Ruby decided that it must be a real one, being as it was so heavy. Placing it carefully onto the glass dining table she wandered over to where her father had just disappeared into his bedroom.

"Daddy, why have you got a gun in your apartment?" she asked, innocently.

Hearing no response, Ruby skipped over to the bedroom door and pushed it open. The sight that met her eyes caused her to stop dead in her tracks. For there on the floor, next to her father's bed, was a woman who was covered in blood, and her Daddy was crouching over the woman muttering something under his breath, which Ruby could not quite make out.

"D..Daddy, who is that lady on the floor" she whispered. "Is she asleep?"

Les, realising that his beloved daughter had now seen Jenna Reid's body on his bedroom floor, was suddenly snapped out of his stupor. Jumping to his feet, he scooped Ruby into his arms and told her not to worry.

"She's just had a bit of an accident, darlin', that's all.....you don't need to worry, Rubes, everything is alright"

Ruby felt reassured by her father's calm demeanour. Outwardly, Les appeared to be the epitome of control, stroking his daughter's hair and hugging her tightly. Inwardly, however, he was a nervous wreck. There was a dead body lying on his bedroom floor, stinking to high heaven.

Clearly, it had been there for a few days and the stench that had assailed his nostrils when he had first arrived home could now be easily explained.

What could not be explained, however, was what the hell Max Reid's wife was doing in his apartment in the first place! Les had recognised her from the moment he had laid eyes on her face, although God knows she hadn't looked anything like that when she was alive!

CHAPTER FIFTY EIGHT

Turning on the bedroom light, he had first lifted his daughter's pink duvet and thrown it onto the bed, angry that it had been used to cover up a dead body – because he reckoned he could bet his last pound on it being a body under there, judging by the smell.

Les had seen a few dead bodies in his time. Some of them had died by his own hand, but never in all his born years had he seen anything like the sight that lay before him now. Crouching down, Les had retched violently before peeling back the corner of his king-sized quilt, which was covered in dried blood. The pungent, metallic smell of the blood filled his nostrils and he had to cover his mouth to prevent himself from throwing up all over the body.

"Oh fuckin' Jesus!" Les had exclaimed upon seeing the face of Jenna Reid, her lifeless, emerald green eyes staring up at the ceiling. "Tommy, what the hell have you done, son? What the fuckin' hell have you done?"

Jenna's face was pale and bloated; small deposits of blood-soaked foam had dried around her nostrils and open mouth. It was very clear to Les that she had been dead for some time. Pulling the duvet down, Les could clearly see the gaping bullet wound in Jenna's chest. She had been shot and killed in this room, that much was obvious – but why? What had she been doing in his apartment in the first place?

Les' thoughts were whirring around now as his brain struggled to accept what his eyes were telling him: Jenna Reid was lying dead on his bedroom floor, and Tommy McLaughlin was undoubtedly her killer. What possible reason could Max Reid's little wife have for being here with Tommy in the first place?

Almost as soon as his mind had set the question, it also gave him the answer. Jenna Reid had been having an affair with Tommy. She had to have been! What other possible explanation could there be, unless they had been doing a spot of business together. Almost as soon as he thought of it, Les immediately dismissed the notion that Jenna and Tommy could have been involved in any kind of business venture. For one, Jenna Reid had moved in very different circles to the ones that Tommy moved in. Hers had been a world of fast cars, high fashion and bags of money; she and Max had wealthy friends and business associates, well-heeled clientele who would have turned up their nose at the likes of Tommy McLaughlin. They'd have seen him for exactly what he was – a rough diamond from across the water, a gopher, a bit of muscle whenever things got out of hand. For another, Max Reid wouldn't have allowed it. There was no way he'd have had his wife associating with the likes of Tommy. Men are usually very good at spotting a philanderer, especially when that philanderer is hanging around their own wife. Les felt sure that Max would have nipped any potential venture in the bud, before it had any possible chance to go anywhere.

Which left only one, undeniable truth – they'd been shagging behind Max Reid's back!

At that moment, Les was startled back to reality by the sound of his young daughter in the doorway of the bedroom. She was staring down at

303

the body, her eyes wide like saucers, unable to comprehend what she was seeing. Les knew he'd need to get her out of the apartment before he could deal with any of this.

Gently scooping her up into his arms, Les was about to carry her out of the room when he happened to glance across at the large, ornate mirror which was usually positioned flat against the wall at the foot of the bed. Now, though, it was hanging away from the wall on its fittings. Les instinctively knew that the safe would be empty without even bothering to look and it sickened him to realise how naïve he had been to trust Tommy McLaughlin.

Tommy had cleaned him out, taken every last bundle of cash. Les had great difficulty holding his temper in check at that point. He felt like committing murder himself such was his rage, but he was also acutely aware that his little girl was frightened so venting his anger was not an option right now. That would come later, when he caught up with that thieving little toe-rag, Tommy McLaughlin. Les inwardly cursed and promised himself that if he got to Tommy first, Max Reid would have to make do with what was left – which wouldn't be much!

Carrying his daughter into the lift, Les pressed for the eighth floor. He knew a nice woman who lived in number eighty four and he knew that, if he asked her to, she would gladly look after Ruby for a little while until he figured out what to do.

As they stepped out of the lift, Les bent down and looked his daughter in the eye. "Listen, Rubes, it might be just as well if we don't tell Mrs Harris about the lady in Daddy's bedroom. We don't want to upset her, do we love?" Les knew that his daughter, although still only a child, would do as he asked and keep the grim discovery to herself, simply because her Daddy had asked it of her.

 "Okay, Daddy, I won't tell Mrs Harris..." Ruby whispered, conspiratorially. Throwing her arms around his neck, she hugged her father and then asked him "...but, Daddy, why have you got a gun?"

CHAPTER FIFTY NINE

Max and Rob were in the office at The Starlight Club, poring over the list of members on the office computer system. There was close to five hundred names in all, and the two men sat together now, their eyes skimming the screen for anyone who might be a potential suspect.

Rob was convinced that the ring-leader must be someone who was close to the Reids. He had known where Jenna had her shop, and that she was looking to sell up. Therefore, it made perfect sense to Rob that the bastard who had master-minded the kidnap was somebody who was right under their noses; someone who knew them personally.

They had both agreed that Roy Richards was in no way involved, even peripherally, which left them scratching their heads. Most of the clientele at the club were either personal friends of Max's or fell under the heading of 'a friend of a friend'. Try as they might, neither man could pick out any one name from the hundreds who paid their annual membership fees to the club as a likely suspect. They had already gone over the membership list for 'Annabel's' but had drawn a blank. The majority of members were well known businessmen, and Max could vouch for them all.

"The way I see it, Rob, it's got to be someone who isn't on this list. Nobody in their right mind would fuck with me, certainly not any of this lot, so it's got to be someone we haven't thought of yet"

Rob nodded in agreement, relieved to see that his boss was now concentrating all his efforts on finding Jenna's killer, rather than sitting around feeling guilty and blaming himself. He felt sure that would come later, and he knew that Max would need his help and support when that time came. Once this was over, once they had found and punished the people who were responsible for the murder of Jenna Reid and her unborn child, Max would undoubtedly fall apart. Rob sensed that the only thing that was getting his best mate out of bed, and into the real world, right now was the desire for revenge.

Rob knew that Max was planning to torture, and then murder, the men who had killed Jenna. He knew that once Max found the man who had pulled the trigger, the one who had taken his wife and unborn child away from him forever, he would exact the worst possible pain on him. It was all Max Reid thought about; all he talked about, and Rob had already mentally committed himself to helping his mate achieve it, no matter what.

"Look, mate, why don't we take a break eh? Go and grab something to eat. We've been at this for hours and..well, I dunno about you but I could certainly do with a drink right now" Rob smiled at Max, unsure of how he would react. Rob knew that Max was finding it difficult to focus on anything right now other than finding the murdering scum who had killed Jenna, and he half expected to get a mouthful from his boss for even thinking about food. He'd take it on the chin, though, if that turned out to be the case.

Surprisingly though, instead of voicing any objection, Max seemed to slump in his seat at the mention of taking a break. The lines of worry were clearly visible around his eyes now, and Rob felt for the man. "Up to you, boss. We can carry on here if you like, I could order a takeaway – have it delivered if you don't fancy going anywhere else"

Max reached across and grabbed hold of Rob's forearm. "Thanks, Rob. I could do with a break myself" he admitted. With that, Max and Rob picked up their jackets and, locking the office door, made their way downstairs to the bar.

Ordering two double scotches, Rob made his way over to the corner booth that Max had decided on. It was tucked away from prying eyes and Rob had made it clear to the barman that his boss was not to be disturbed under any circumstances. The young barman, sensing that something was amiss, nodded his understanding to Rob and assured him that he would make sure that nobody bothered them.

The two men sat, locked in deep conversation, for half an hour. Rob signalled for two more drinks and the barman brought them over on a tray, placing the drinks on the table and picking up the empties before making a swift and discreet exit.

Martin Dean had been head barman at The Starlight Club for almost eight months. During that time he had gotten to know his boss reasonably well and, on a number of occasions, had welcomed Max and his wife at the bar whenever they dropped in for an evening with friends. He liked working for Max Reid, found him to be a very fair and pleasant man. However, something was most definitely up and Martin sensed that all was not well between Max and Jenna Reid.

Mrs Reid had not been coming in quite as often over the past couple of months, and not at all over the past five days. Martin saw this as unusual, since his boss' wife liked to frequent the place and flaunt the fact that she was married to the club's owner.

If he were being honest, Martin didn't care for Jenna Reid. He fancied the arse off her, yes, but he didn't necessarily like her. She could come across as a right snooty bitch at times, although Martin had to concede that the very thing which turned him completely off her was perhaps also the thing that turned him on about her, too.

The bar telephone rang and Martin picked it up. "Good afternoon, The Starlight Club, Martin speaking" he spoke eloquently into the receiver, ready with a notepad and pen to jot down any message. His cut-glass, Home Counties accent had proved to be a real asset in his line of work and Martin had never had any problem attracting the opposite sex. They seemed to hang onto his every word, fascinated by his public-school demeanour and boyish good looks.

"'Ello, son, is Mister Max Reid in the buildin'?" the caller asked, his Cockney twang evident.

"May I ask who's calling, Sir?" Martin prided himself on his ability to screen his boss' calls, separate the wheat from the chaff. This particular caller, in Martin's book, sounded like a drayman, or a grocery delivery driver.

"No, son, you can't fuckin' ask, just put Max on the phone, alright?" Les Bryce's impatience was beginning to show.

"I'm sorry, Sir, I'm afraid that won't be possible, Mister Reid is currently in a meeting and has left strict instructions that he does not wish to be disturbed *'for any reason whatsoever'*" Martin stated firmly, quoted Rob Marsden's instructions. "Would you like to leave a message, Sir?" he asked, pen at the ready.

"NO! I FUCKIN' WOULDN'T!" Les bawled. "Get him on the blower, my son. Tell 'im.....just tell 'im it's a matter of life and death!

Martin placed the receiver on the top of the counter and walked over to where Max and Rob were sitting.

"Excuse me, Mister Reid, but there's a man on the telephone who says he needs to speak to you. In fact, he says it's a matter of life and death, Sir" Martin felt distinctly uncomfortable at having interrupted his boss – particularly as he was under strict instructions not to do so. Max looked up at him now, a glazed expression in his eyes.

"Alright, Martin, tell him I'm coming will you?" He didn't need this aggravation right now. He didn't want to speak to anyone, least of all some fucking punter with an attitude problem. "It's probably a merchant trying to get hold of me" he explained to Rob "I've been off the radar for a few days, probably thinks I don't want to do business with him anymore" With a half-hearted smile he made his way across to the bar where Martin passed him the phone.

"Yes, this is Max Reid" he spoke quietly, his voice heavy with lack of sleep. "'Ello, Max, Les Bryce here, mate. I dunno if you remember me, we did a spot of business back in the day when you was on the buildin'"

"Yeah, yes I remember you Les. What can I do for you, only it's a bit difficult at the moment...."

"That's why I'm ringin' ya, son. I think you'd best get round to mine, sharpish!"

CHAPTER SIXTY

Les poured himself a brandy and paced the floor of his apartment. Max Reid would be here in less than fifteen minutes and he was going to want answers. Right now, though, all that Les could think of was how the hell he was going to explain to Max that his wife must have been shagging one of his employees. It was the only reason he could think of that could explain why she'd be in his apartment in the first place. He was dreading having that particular conversation, and threw his drink back in one for a bit of Dutch courage.

Les was no coward, and when it came to confrontation – one on one – he was never shy about starting the fight. Right now, though, he felt agitated and anxious because, although he had nothing to do with Jenna Reid's death, it was still going to be down to him to explain to the grieving widower just what his darling wife had been up to.

There was no other explanation. Max Reid's pretty, little wife had been playing away from home - and with a loser like Tommy McLaughlin too. Jesus, Max would have a fit of epic proportions when he heard that one!

*

Max and Rob jumped into Max's BMW and the car took off like a bat out of hell. Max floored the accelerator, flying through two red lights and narrowly missed hitting a parked car. Rob wanted to urge him to slow down but he knew that it wouldn't do any good. Max was like a man possessed, and telling him to slow down was like telling him to stop caring about finding out who had killed his wife. It was pointless even to try, so Rob just gritted his teeth and prayed that they'd get to Les Bryce's place in one piece.

They raced through the streets of London at over a hundred miles per hour, weaving in and out of busy lanes of traffic, and Rob closed his eyes more than once as a vehicle pulled out of a side street only to be halted by the blare of Max's car-horn. He wasn't slowing down for anyone, not now that his wife's body had turned up. Now, finally, he would get the answers he'd been praying for; now at last he would find out just who was responsible for Jenna's death.

Rob pointed out the turning up ahead which led to Les' apartment block. Max took the corner on two wheels, his car hurtling its way down the ramp into the underground car-park before it came skidding to a halt. Jumping out of the driver's seat, Max was heading for the lift before Rob had time to undo his own seat-belt. "Max, hang on a minute, mate" he called after him, but Max was already in the lift. Rob barely made it before the lift doors began to close and as he arrived, out of breath, Max pressed the button for the Penthouse Apartment.

"Max, listen mate – keep a cool head here. We don't know what has happened yet so don't go in all guns blazing, alright?" Rob was the voice of reason now as Max's adrenaline started to kick in. He was breathing heavily, his nostrils flaring as he prepared himself mentally for what lay ahead. He was about to come face to face with the body of his dead wife, and nothing – nothing – had ever prepared him for this moment.

He thought of her now, as the lift wound its way upward. He thought of her beautiful face; her bright, emerald eyes and her auburn hair, shining in the sunlight. His heart ached as he pictured what he would find – her lifeless body, gunned down in cold blood, whilst still carrying their unborn child. At that moment, Max Reid was ready to kill.

CHAPTER SIXTY ONE

The lift doors opened silently and Max Reid stepped out and into Les Bryce's apartment, with Rob Marsden following closely behind. As soon as he entered the room Max could smell death. It seemed to permeate every last drop of air around him and he felt his stomach lurch as he realised that what he could smell was the body of his own wife.

Les motioned for Max to follow and led him towards the master bedroom. "I found 'er in 'ere, Max" he began. Then he added "I'm sorry, mate, it's not a pretty sight in there; looks like she's been dead a while, if you ask me".

Max closed his eyes for a few seconds and then, pushing Les aside, he pushed open the door to the bedroom. As he stepped over the threshold the acrid stench filled his nostrils and he had to fight the urge to turn and run. He had seen death in his time, knew the metallic smell of fresh blood, but this was a whole new ball game for Max and he struggled to breathe as he neared the body lying on the bedroom floor.

"Jesus Christ!" Rob exclaimed, covering his mouth with his hand as he reached the doorway. He stood just outside, giving his boss some moments of privacy in which to view the body of his wife. He knew from the stench that was emanating from the corner of the bedroom that Jenna Reid was not going to look too pretty.

Max was crouched down beside Jenna, and he lifted back the duvet which had been covering her. The sight that met his eyes was the most horrendous thing he had ever witnessed, an image which would stay with him for the rest of his days. Gone was the beautiful, pale skin; the emerald eyes; the mischievous smile. In their place was a hideous, bloated mask with staring, glassy eyes and grey, transparent skin. Around the nose and mouth were deposits of dried blood. Max thought how his wife looked like a wax-work dummy; that she had died whilst still in her youth but that her remains had decayed almost beyond recognition.

He reached down and placed a hand across her belly, still swollen with the promise of life. That life had been snuffed out in an instant, though, by a maniac with a gun. The little child inside Jenna's womb would not know of the glorious world outside. He would never take his first breath, nor feel the sun on his face, or know the wonder of his first Christmas. He was forever sleeping in his cocoon, the promise of life snatched away in an instant.

As Max reached across to smooth a stray hair from her forehead, Rob and Les heard a strange, guttural sound like a howling wolf in the forest, crying out for its mate. It seemed to fill the whole apartment, and tore at the hearts of the two men. Max Reid's pain was palpable, and it stirred their very souls to hear his anguished cries.

It took several minutes before Max Reid realised that the animal wailing he was hearing was, in fact, coming from himself. Rob stepped forward and took hold of his friend's arm, gently pulling him to his feet.

"Max. Max, come on. There's nothing you can do for her now, mate. We need to find that bastard before he has chance to skip the country" Rob urged his boss to start thinking now, as time was of the essence if they were going to catch up with Tommy before he jumped on a plane. "We'll see to this, later. Alright, Max?"

"Yeah, you're right, Rob. Nothing I can do for her now". With that, Max covered over Jenna' body and, wiping away tears, pulled himself together. "Time to go find the bastard who did this Rob, and put him out of his misery".

CHAPTER SIXTY TWO

"So you're telling me that this no-mark, this bloke you had working for you – he's the cunt who kidnapped my wife and put a bullet in her?" Max was trying to make sense of it all. Why would this Tommy McLaughlin want to harm him or his loved ones? Max had never heard of the man. It just didn't make any sense.

Les looked bewildered for a few moments. Then he said "Kidnapped? I..I don't understand, Max. You're saying that Tommy *kidnapped* your wife?" Things had just taken on a whole new twist in Les' eyes. So, perhaps Jenna Reid hadn't been playing away from home. Maybe she had been completely innocent, after all. At that moment, Les Bryce felt a wave of relief wash over him. The bloke's wife was dead, yes, but at least she hadn't been unfaithful.

"That's right. I got a telephone call on Sunday morning, demanding a half a million in ransom money. I refused to pay up until I'd spoken to my wife, and the bastard put a bullet in her. She....she was pregnant with our first child" he faltered, fighting back tears now as Les and Rob looked on. "I...I didn't think....I just wanted to hear her voice, to know that she was alright. He shot her. He fucking shot her....." Max's shoulders heaved with emotion now as he recalled the terrible moment when he had heard the gun go off; a moment he felt entirely responsible for.

Les was utterly at a loss. He hadn't thought for a moment that Tommy would be capable of such a thing. Kidnap? Why the hell would he want to do such a thing? He paid the bloke a decent wedge, for fuck's sake. It wasn't as though he needed the money, so it seemed beyond belief that he could pull a stunt like this one.

"You know where this fucker lives, I take it?" Max was pacing the room now, having knocked back a large brandy for the shock. Now he wanted to get his hands on the bastard who had killed his wife and child.

"Yeah, I know where he lives, Max. The thing is – we need to plan this carefully. If you want to put the fucker away, it needs to be thought out properly. The last thing you need is to end up doing a stretch for murder, mate"

Rob agreed with Les "We need to work out a plan, Max. We need to figure out how and where we're going to finish this cunt, but we need to make sure there are no come-backs"

"I've got to figure out what to do about Jenna's body, too, Rob. I can't involve the police, because they'll arrest McLaughlin and take the cunt into custody. Any chance I might have had for revenge will be gone, and I want to look that bastard in the eye when I finish him. I deserve that much"

"I agree, we can't involve the police, but if we go down that route then what the hell do we do about Jenna? Eileen will have to be told, so whatever we decide to do we have to consider her feelings. She was her mother after all"

"Leave Eileen to me, Rob, I'll sort things out with her. Right now, I'm more interested in how to get my hands on the murdering fucker who did this. One thing's for sure, he won't be seeing another sunrise" Max stared at the two men in front of him, the bitterness and hatred in his eyes clearly evident, as he planned Tommy's downfall.

"Who is this bloke, Max? Do you know him?" Rob was puzzled as to why Tommy McLaughlin would choose his boss as a target. "D'you reckon he is someone we overlooked at the club earlier?"

Max shook his head. He hadn't ever heard of the bloke, and he never forgot a name. No, Tommy McLaughlin wasn't someone who had ever come into his orbit. He was certain of it. He had wracked his brains for the last ten minutes or so, trying to place the name, but drew a blank. Whatever the motive behind this, it wasn't personal.

Les suddenly had a thought. "Tommy doesn't know I'm back in the country. He thinks I'm still in Florida with Ruby, therefore, gentlemen, we 'ave the element of surprise! If we 'ead over to his place tonight, chances are he 'asn't left the country yet. The gun he used to kill Mrs Reid was still under the table, so I reckon he must be plannin' on callin' back 'ere to wipe it before he takes off. He's cleaned me out, taken every penny out of my safe, so he 'as the funds to disappear, yes, but not before he gets rid of any incriminating evidence" Les smiled at Max now. "We 'ave got the bastard where we want him, all we gotta do is go pick him up"

As the three men stood up to leave the apartment, the red warning light above the lift doors suddenly lit up. Max looked at Les, and saw that the bloke was grinning like the proverbial Cheshire cat. Turning to the others he said

"I 'ad that light installed in-case any unwelcome visitors decided to pay me a visit, unexpected like. Anyone presses the button for the Pent'ouse suite, it lights up like a fuckin' traffic light. Well gents, it seems that Mister McLaughlin has saved us the bother. If I'm not mistaken, 'e's on his way up here right now!"

Max and Rob pulled out their weapons and positioned themselves at either side of the lift doors. This was too easy! The fucker had decided to come back to the apartment after all, just as Les had predicted, to wipe his prints off the gun. He obviously didn't realise that there would be a welcoming committee waiting for him.

Well, it would be the last journey he ever made if Max had anything to do with it. He'd be meeting his maker this evening and Max intended to make his final hours on earth the most painful he had ever spent.

CHAPTER SIXTY THREE

Tommy had woken with a hangover. It was almost eight thirty in the evening and he still hadn't booked a flight to Spain. Before he could do that, though, he had the small matter of a gun covered in his fingerprints to take care of. Shit! Why the hell hadn't he brought it with him when he'd left the apartment this afternoon? He could have been on that plane tonight, and all of this would be behind him.

Things hadn't worked out the way he'd wanted, if he was honest with himself. He hadn't wanted to kill Jenna - that had been a pure accident. If only she had called out his name when she'd walked into Les' apartment on Saturday afternoon. If only she had let him know that it was her, and not some gun wielding maniac, who was about to step into the bedroom then she'd still be alive today.

Tommy had been convinced that it was Max Reid and his heavies who were creeping towards the door. He'd smoked so much weed it had made him paranoid, and when Jenna hadn't shown up on time he'd put two and two together and come up with five. Now, though, it was much too late for regrets. She was dead and he had to sort this mess out before he could safely leave the country.

He thought of Jenna now – and he felt a pang of guilt about the game he had been playing. He had lied to her, told her that he loved her, when all the while he had been planning on leaving her once he got his hands on Max's money. He reminded himself that Jenna Reid was not the innocent party in all of this, though. It had been her who had devised the kidnap plan; her who had insisted that her husband would pay any amount to get her back alive. It had been her who had been ready to lie to Max Reid and let him believe that it was his child she was carrying. So why should he feel bad, when she had been the instrument of her own downfall? It wasn't as though he had loved her, after all said and done. She had just been the means to an end.

Tommy had learned from an early age not to get too close to anyone. He had learned that when you love someone, really love them, you make yourself vulnerable to heartbreak. His heart had been broken many years ago, and he had vowed then never to allow anyone under his skin in the future.

When Jenna Reid had told him that night that she was pregnant with his child, he had fallen for it hook, line and sinker. However, as the weeks had gone on and he had realised just how manipulative and devious she was, he had questioned whether the child was really his. Perhaps Max Reid was the real father of Jenna's baby. Perhaps Jenna had seen in him a chance to get away and start a new life. Either way, he would never know for sure now. The child would never be born, and Tommy felt genuinely sad about it.

If the truth be told, Tommy had never really had a concrete plan for getting his revenge on Max Reid. The opportunity had presented itself when he had been offered the chance to attend Jenna Reid's twenty-first birthday party by one of the many invited guests. He had taken one look at the lovely, young wife of the man he despised and seen her for what she was – trapped and miserable. Oh, she had the money and the lifestyle but she wasn't happy. Clearly her husband thought more of his business interests than he did of her, or at least that's the way it looked to Tommy.

He had seen her disappear into the ladies' with a bottle of Cristal and come out some ten minutes later as high as a kite on coke. He had then watched as she had berated her husband of four years in public for neglecting her. If ever there was a woman who needed some loving it was Jenna Reid, and Tommy had made up his mind there and then that he would make her acquaintance before very long and give her some of his own brand of loving.

Jenna Reid had been easy, desperate for some attention, and she couldn't get enough of him between the sheets. If she happened to fall in love with him then that was hardly his fault, was it? Most of the women that Tommy had fucked had declared their undying devotion for him, only to find themselves dumped when the novelty wore off.

Jenna Reid had been different. He hadn't been in love with her, but there had been something different, something that told Tommy she was the same as him in some way. She was just out for what she could get, and that made them very suitable bed-mates - very suitable indeed, in Tommy's eyes.

The fact remained, though, that Tommy had had no intentions of shacking up with the lovely Jenna. As far as he was concerned she would have outlived her usefulness once the cash was in the bank. Tommy acknowledged that he would have preferred to put a bullet in Max Reid's brain, but he also recognised that losing half a million, with the possibility that his wife was carrying another man's child, was punishment enough - for now.

If he couldn't screw Max Reid one way, he'd screw him another, and if he got to screw the bloke's wife at the same time well – so much the better!

Now, though, she lay dead on Les Bryce's bedroom floor, and he had the unenviable task of getting rid of her body. He hadn't really figured out just how he was going to achieve that, he just knew that he had to get it sorted sooner rather than later if he wanted to get out of the country before Les got back from Florida. It was now Tuesday evening, which meant that Tommy would have a three day head-start on Les once he discovered that his money was missing from the safe.

What Tommy didn't need, however, was the police chasing him to Spain, therefore it was important that he got rid of any and all evidence of his involvement with Jenna Reid. He intended to wipe his prints off Les' gun and put it back into the bedside drawer. Les would be none the wiser. He'd never know that anything untoward had taken place in his apartment, provided that Tommy cleaned up properly. As for the duvets, he wouldn't bother to replace them. Les would assume that his house-guest had been sick on them and had just thrown them out. The truth was, Tommy didn't give a fuck what Les thought. From now on, he was in the past.

Finishing his can of beer, Tommy picked up the keys to Jenna Reid's Mercedes and whistled as he locked the flat door for the last time. He posted the keys back through the letterbox, with an I.O.U. for four weeks rent, addressed to the landlord. Tommy laughed aloud as he pictured the look on his landlord's face when he read the note.

He was feeling good, excited about the new life that was waiting for him in Spain. He figured he would spend a few weeks getting to know the place, suss out the lie of the land, then invest in a little bar somewhere along the coast. He fancied himself as a bar-owner, with lots of pretty girls coming in every night and plenty of cash in the tills. As he started the engine he pictured himself in shorts and flip-flops, sipping cocktails at the waterfront bar with a new girl on his arm every night. Yes, that was the life for him alright!

Pulling away from his flat, Tommy put in a Guns and Roses cd and turned up the volume. He felt in the mood to party and, once he had dealt with the matter in hand, he thought he might treat himself to a few lines of coke and a pretty girl for the evening before leaving the U.K. for good.

Ten minutes later, Tommy swung the Mercedes down the ramp and into the underground car park, parking in a secluded spot behind a tall, concrete pillar. He was so preoccupied that he didn't see the dark blue BMW parked in Les' designated spot. Had he done so, he might have thought twice about getting out of the car and, instead, would have turned it around and gotten the hell out of there as fast as he could.

Tommy was blissfully unaware of the fact there were currently three men awaiting his arrival in the apartment on the top floor, two of them armed with very powerful weapons.

Whistling to himself, he pressed the fob which locked the car and sauntered over to the lift. As he waited for its arrival, he sang to himself 'kind woman take it slow and things will work out fine. All we need is just a little patience'.

Stepping into the lift Tommy pressed the button for the Penthouse and leaned back against the mirror-tiled wall. He was sorry in a way to be leaving. He'd had a good time working for Les and he'd miss the boozers and the humour that could often be found in a typical London pub. Yes, he thought, it was good while it lasted. Now, though, he was about to start a brand new adventure and his mind was filled with ideas and plans for his future.

As the lift arrived at the top floor, Tommy pulled out a pack of cigarettes and lit one. Drawing deeply on it, he felt optimistic as the doors swished open. Les would kill him if he knew he'd been smoking in his apartment. Les hated smoking, and he was also extremely house-proud so he'd have a fit when he came back to the stink of cigarette smoke in his place. Tommy didn't care. He wouldn't be here to take the flak anyhow.

Stepping out of the lift, he suddenly felt something hard being pressed against his temple. Shit, Les must have come back early. Tommy took a deep breath, throwing the cigarette into the lift behind him. Clearly Les had found Jenna's body, and the empty safe.

"Les, I can explain..." he began. Suddenly, a blow caught him at the side of his head, smashing into his skull, and he dropped to his knees before looking up to see the face of someone that he hadn't been expecting to see at all.

"Hello, Tommy, surprise, surprise" Max Reid pulled the safety back on his gun and pointed it straight at Tommy.

"I think you and me need to have a little talk, my old son, don't you?"

CHAPTER SIXTY FOUR

Rob Marsden gripped Tommy by the scruff of his neck and dragged him across the polished, parquet floor before booting him hard in the ribs. Tommy doubled up in pain, his arms instinctively wrapping around himself to ward off further attacks. He knew that he was in serious trouble, that the chances of him getting out of this alive were very slim indeed, and he mentally kicked himself for not getting rid of the gun earlier in the day. He wouldn't have needed to come back to the apartment. He could have been free and clear. Instead, Max Reid would have his revenge, and there was absolutely nothing he could do about it.

Les, sensing that things were about to get very messy indeed all over his nice, polished floor turned to Max and pleaded. "Max, not here – please. I've got Ruby to think of. She's gonna be comin' back 'ere in the mornin' an' the last thing I need is to 'ave the place covered in this fucker's brains"

"What the fuck do you suggest, Les. You want me to take the cunt out of here, you need to come up with a place to take him, because right now I just want to cause the bastard as much pain as possible" Max spat angrily.

Tommy groaned as Max grabbed a handful of his hair, yanking his head back in the process. "You are not going to see another fucking sunrise, son. You can bet on it. In fact, by the time I'm through with you, you'll be begging to fucking die!"

"I know of a place, Max, not too far from here. In fact, it's at the back of my office. It's a breaker's yard, to be exact, and the bloke who owns it is a diamond geezer. I could arrange for this fucker to disappear – no questions asked – for a couple of hundred grand"

"Sounds like a plan, Les. Get on the blower will you? Tell him we'll be over within the hour. Rob, give me a hand here will you?"

Rob Marsden thanked his lucky stars that he wasn't in Tommy McLaughlin's shoes right now. The bloke was going to die a horrible death, and it would be no more than he deserved.

"Do you want me to call Eileen, Max? She'll want to know that we've found Jenna's killer"

"Not just now, Rob. Maybe later, okay? Right now I want this fucker out of here. Do me a favour, mate, will you? In the boot of my car is a length of rope. It'll be in a black bag. Fetch it will you? In the meantime, give me your tie"

Rob took off his tie and handed it to his boss, who then used it to gag Tommy. "Be back in a jiffy, mate" he said.

Les phoned the owner of the breaker's yard, a giant of a man named Jack Baines. He had earned the nickname 'Crusher' because of his penchant for crushing alive anyone who crossed him in one of his motors. The doomed man would be bundled into the boot of a car and the vehicle would then be reduced to a four by four feet cube of metal. It was the perfect way to get rid of the evidence. There was nothing left of the man save a pool of blood at the bottom of the pile of cars. Crusher also provided the same service to anyone who found themselves with a dead body to dispose of, no questions asked, for the right price. He could be trusted to keep his mouth shut, and Les had used him more than once in the past.

At one point, he had even toyed with the idea of having his ex-wife, Carol, crushed to death but in the end he had decided better of it. For all her faults, she was still the mother of his child, and Les knew that he wouldn't be able to reconcile himself to it afterwards, once his daughter started asking the inevitable questions.

Five minutes later, Rob returned with a six foot length of rope and the two men bound Tommy McLaughlin's arms behind his back. He eyed Max and Rob as they pushed him into an armchair, clearly terrified about what was going to happen to him. He was going to die a long, slow painful death and he knew it.

"Crusher's expectin' ya, lads. Says ya can sort 'im out later with the cash"

"We need to move Jenna's body, too, Max" Rob said gently. "Have you thought about what you want to do?"

"Yeah, we can take her in the boot of my car. We'll need something to wrap her in first" Looking around, Max spotted Les' carved Chinese rug. "Maybe that will do" he said. Les rolled his eyes upwards. "Fuckin' 'ell, lads, does it 'ave to be that rug? It's me pride an' joy that rug is" Realising that he was being in-sensitive, Les shrugged his shoulders and said "Alright, alright.....you can use the fuckin' thing. D'you need a hand...y'know ....with the body?"

Rob nodded at Les and, turning to Max, said "Leave it to us, Max. We'll move her."

"No, I want to do it. Give me a hand, Rob." The two men made their way over to Les' bedroom, with the rug thrown over Rob's shoulder. It was large and very heavy, but they would need to cover Jenna's body completely. The underground car-park had CCTV cameras everywhere and the last thing they needed was to find themselves coming face to face with a nosey security guard and having to explain what they were doing moving a dead body in the middle of the night.

"Take my gun, Les, and keep an eye on this cunt. He moves shoot him!" Les took Max's gun and positioned himself opposite Tommy McLaughlin. He would be glad when this was all over, when the three men were out of his apartment and he could begin cleaning up the bedroom. He would have to go out and buy new bedding for himself and Ruby, since Tommy had used the duvets to cover up Jenna's body.

Ten minutes later, Max and Rob emerged from the bedroom with Jenna's body rolled inside the Chinese rug, and they indicated to Les that he needed to summon the lift. They told him that they would take Jenna's body down to the car, then come back up for Tommy.

Max's face was ashen as he and Rob bundled the rolled up carpet into the boot of his BMW. Slamming it shut, they looked at one another for a few moments, each aware of the task ahead of them, each complicit in their intentions.

"Come on, let's do this" Max strode purposefully towards the lift and pressed the button for the Penthouse. It was time to get to the bottom of all this. *It was time to find out just who Tommy McLaughlin was and – more importantly – why he had targeted him in the first place!*

CHAPTER SIXTY FIVE

Crusher Baines was waiting at the entrance gates as Max and Rob pulled up. Tommy was lying face down on the back seat of Max's car, his hands and feet tied together behind him to ensure that he had no possible means of escape. Rob had driven over in Jenna's Mercedes.

"The place is all yours, lads. I've switched off the security cameras. Take all the time you need, no-one will disturb you. Once you're done, give me a bell on this number and I'll come over and sort out the machine" he smiled now, displaying broken, black teeth and handed Max a slip of paper. "Don't matter how long it takes, just give me a bell and I'll be straight over. Oh – and there's a bottle of whiskey in the desk drawer, just in-case you fancy it"

Untying Tommy's hands and feet, Rob dragged him out of the car and pushed him into the breaker's yard, throwing the rope over his shoulder as he did so. Max locked the car and followed them.

There was a portakabin straight ahead and to the left was a large storage shed which housed old oil drums, spare tyres and other second-hand car parts. Behind the shed was a large breaker's yard with pile upon pile of cars stacked one on top of the other. Rob had always marvelled at how anyone managed to stack the vehicles on top without toppling the pile. Clearly, there was a real knack to it.

Just as he was pondering on it, Tommy stopped dead and Rob walked straight into him.

"Oi, you fucking arsehole, just keep going or I'll shoot you in the back of the legs and drag you there myself, alright?" he yelled. Tommy began walking slowly towards the storage shed, totally aware of the fact that this would be where he spent his last hours on earth. This was where he would die tonight, of that he was certain.

Max pulled open the big, wooden doors to the storage shed and, grabbing hold of him by the arm, dragged Tommy inside. The place was dimly lit and it took a few moments before their eyes adjusted to their surroundings. The whole place smelled strongly of diesel and damp. Pushing Tommy further inward, they found a wooden chair in the far corner of the shed and positioned it in the centre of the floor. Dragging Tommy over to the chair, Rob ordered him at gunpoint to take a seat. Tommy sat down and Max proceeded to tie his hands to the back of the chair with the rope.

It was time to begin.

CHAPTER SIXTY SIX

The two men had been interrogating Tommy McLaughlin for over an hour and still he wouldn't answer their questions. He had so far steadfastly refused to utter a word. He just continued to stare at Max Reid, his face a mass of bruises where the two men had repeatedly punched him.

"Who are you? Why did you target me and my wife? FUCKING ANSWER ME!" Max was almost at the end of his tether now as he paced the floor in front of Tommy. Taking his gun, he smashed it into the side of Tommy's head, opening up a large, gaping wound which began spurting blood down the front of Tommy's shirt.

Tommy looked up at the man he despised, his eyes filled with hate and anger, but still he said nothing.

Max aimed his gun at Tommy's foot and fired. Tommy screamed in pain as the bullet tore through flesh and bone.

"I'll shoot you in every fucking part of your body if you don't answer me, you low-life piece of shit! You murdered my fucking wife and child and you think you can just sit there and say fuck all to me?"

Tommy spat the blood from his mouth. He had lost two of his teeth and his lips were cut and bleeding. He glared at Max Reid. Maybe it was time to tell the bloke the truth about his lovely, fucking wife.

"It was an accident" he said, quietly. "I hadn't intended to kill her"

"Hadn't intended to kill her? I HEARD YOU SHOOT HER!" Max screamed in Tommy's face now.

"No, you heard me fire a gun, Max. Jenna was already dead"

Max suddenly remembered the feeling that he had had at the time of the 'shooting'. He had sensed that something was amiss and now he knew what it was. His wife had already been killed, which was why this fucker couldn't bring her to the phone.

"But you let me think.....you let me think that it was my fault. That it was because I wouldn't pay...." Max's voice was low now as he took in the enormity of what had happened. It hadn't been his fault that Jenna had died. She hadn't been shot because of his refusal to pay – she was already dead!

"So, let me get this straight. You demanded a ransom for my wife, and she was already dead?"

"That's right, yes"

"Why? Why the fuck would you want to harm my wife? She was pregnant for fuck's sake. We were expecting our first child"

Tommy sneered now, his contempt for the man in front of him evident. He was going to enjoy this!

"That what she told you is it? That it was *your* child she was carrying? Ha! That's a fucking good one, that is"

Rob and Max looked at one another now, both of them aware of the implications of Tommy's statement.

"She told me I was the father, *Maxie boy* – it was *my child* she was having, not yours" he grinned now, despite the pain he was in. Clearly, Max Reid had no idea that his wife had been cheating on him for months.

"YOU'RE A FUCKING LIAR!" Max yelled now at the top of his lungs "You're trying to tell me that you and my wife...my Jenna...that you were....."

"That's about the size of it, yeah. We were seeing each other for a while as it happens. She wanted to leave you, start a new life with me and our child. She was in love with me, Max. It was me she wanted, not you"

Max could hardly believe his ears. This no-mark, this low-life piece of shit was sitting there and telling him that he and Jenna had been shagging for months behind his back. No way! He'd have known! He'd have sensed something was going on, wouldn't he? Right at that moment, Max realised just how little he had really known about his wife's daily routine. He had been so wrapped up in his work, always at the office or the club. He had neglected his duty as a husband, and now it was too late. Jenna was gone, and he would never get the chance to make it up to her.

"But why for god's sake? Why would you demand a ransom for her if the two of you were running away together? None of this is making any sense. You demanded money for her even though she was dead, and now you're telling me her death was an accident?" Max looked totally bewildered as he struggled to absorb the information.

338

"The ransom wasn't my idea. It was your wife's. She planned the whole thing. We were going to stage a kidnap, and demand half a million in ransom money so that we could run away and start a new life together. She said you'd pay up once you thought that she was carrying your child; that there was nothing you wouldn't do to get her back Fact it, Max, neither of us will ever know who the real father of her baby was. For all I know, she could have been lying to me. After all, she was one devious little bitch, and no mistake. I wasn't planning on sticking around if I'm honest. Once the money was paid, I was going to take off. She wasn't part of the plan, I'm afraid"

Max sat down on the desk and opened the bottle of whiskey. Taking a long swig from the bottle, he eyed Tommy McLaughlin through his tears. His Jenna, and this toe-rag, had been cavorting in the sack for months? She had led him to believe that she was carrying his child so that he would pay the ransom money, no questions asked? It was all too incredible to believe and yet, deep down inside, Max Reid knew that this man was speaking the truth.

"So you say her death was an accident. How did she die?" he needed to know everything now, no matter how much it might hurt. "Tell me everything, from the beginning" he said.

Tommy began by telling him how he had first had the idea of making Jenna's acquaintance on Christmas Night at her birthday party. He confessed that he had formed a plan to seduce her and then had set about meeting her at the opening of her shop. Max listened intently as Tommy regaled him with every sordid detail of the affair. How he had first had Jenna on the kitchen table in the back of the shop, and how she had been so eager for it to continue afterwards.

Rob could barely look at Max, such was the pity he felt for the man. It must have been humiliating beyond belief for Max to have his wife's affair laid bare in front of his best friend in that way.

"She died because I thought it was you coming to kill me. When she didn't show at the apartment, I figured you'd found out about us. I saw that someone was on their way up in the lift and I thought it was you and a couple of heavies. I hid in the bedroom, and when the door opened I fired. That's the truth, I swear"

"Did she die straight away?" Rob interrupted.

Tommy shook his head. There was little point in lying now, he was going to die whatever he said.

"Why the hell didn't you ring for an ambulance, if she was still alive?" Rob demanded.

"I figured it was more trouble than it was worth. I'd have had to tell them who I was and why she had been in the apartment in the first place. I couldn't take the chance that I'd be charged with her murder. It was an accident, but no-one was going to believe me, were they? They'd never believe that we were involved with each other. There would have been too many awkward questions. I ....I had to let her die" Tommy admitted.

"So you then demanded the ransom money anyway, even though she was already dead? You fucking piece of shit!" Rob bellowed. "What kind of low-life does something like that, eh?"

Taking another long swig of whiskey, Max stood now and walked over to the chair where Tommy was sitting, covered in his own blood, his head hanging down.

"Why, Tommy? Why did you set your sights on my wife? What the fuck have I ever done to you?"

CHAPTER SIXTY SEVEN

Tommy knew that his moment had come. At last, he would get the chance to tell Max Reid why he hated him so much. First, though, he wanted to be able to look the man in the eyes.

"Untie me. Let me stand and I'll tell you exactly why I hate your fucking guts" he spat "I want to look you in the eye when I tell you who I am. Oh, I know I'm a dead man, Max, but at least give me that much"

Max considered this for a moment and, sensing that the final piece of the jigsaw was about to be laid down, he nodded to Rob to untie Tommy and took a seat on the edge of the desk.

Free of his constraints, Tommy McLaughlin stood up slowly. The pain in his foot from where Max had put a bullet in it was excruciating. He eyed the bottle of whiskey, wondering whether it would be worth asking for a drink of it.

Max, seeing the look in his eyes, held out the bottle to Tommy. He figured that if the man was going to die, he might as well get a drink inside him first. From what the bloke had told him, his wife had not been the sweet, loving girl that he had believed her to be. Oh, he had known she was fiery, that she could cause a war in an empty room if the fancy took her, but this? He would never have thought her capable of this in a million years. She had betrayed him in the worst possible way. She had lied and she had cheated, but the worst thing of all was that she had been prepared to let him believe that he was going to be a father for the first time. Just so that she could screw him out of his money. Max Reid's heart was broken. He would never recover from the shock of finding out about Jenna, he felt certain of it.

*

Taking the bottle from Max, Tommy took two long mouthfuls from it before handing back to him. Taking out a pack of cigarettes and a lighter from his back pocket, he took one and lit it, taking a few drags on it before speaking.

"My name" he began "isn't Tommy McLaughlin, it's Thomas Siddall, and my parents were Michael and Catherine Siddall"

Max stared at the young man in front of him, unable to take in what he was hearing. "You - You're Thomas Siddall? But....I....I didn't realise..."

"What, that I'd come looking for you, Max? Because of you I was orphaned, left without a mother or father, at the age of eleven. You killed them both. You killed them both and I wanted my revenge"

Max looked at Tommy now with a look of incredulity on his face. "It was an accident, you must know that! It was raining, I..."

"YOU WERE SPEEDING, MAX!" Tommy shouted now, tears running down his face as twenty eight years of anguish and sorrow came pouring out. "You were doing over a hundred and twenty miles an hour when you ploughed into their car. They were killed instantly. They were so badly mangled that they couldn't have an open casket for the funeral, you fucking bastard!" he lunged at Max now, his rage and torment spewing out.

"Why couldn't it have been you that died that night, instead of my parents? They were such lovely people. Why did you have to get in the car that night, eh? You'd been drinking too from what they said in the papers"

"No! I'd had a couple of whiskeys, that's all, but I wasn't drunk. I was trying to get to the hospital for god's sake. My Father had just suffered a heart attack. I was terrified I'd lose him, that's why I was driving so fast. I was trying to get to the hospital in-case he died. My....my Mother....she was alone at the hospital"

"I don't give a shit about your fucking Mother" Tommy sneered "As far as I'm concerned, you robbed me of my proper up-bringing that night. I was sent to live with my mother's sister and her husband, in Ireland. They adopted me and changed my name to McLaughlin. They did their best to help me forget, but I never forgot what you did. You wrecked my life, Max. Thanks to you I grew up in a strange country, without any of the friends I'd made at school. I had to leave everything behind. When I was older I looked up the story in the local library, and there it was. 'Death by dangerous driving' the headline read. Dangerous driving, Max! Ten years was all you got for killing my parents. You were out in less than seven, and you think that's enough do you? You think it makes up for what you did? I have wished you dead so many times, *Max fucking Reid;* I've dreamt of it, for years. So when the chance came along to do you damage, I took it. What's more, I'd do it again given half a chance"

Max had heard enough. "You sick fuck! You chose to seduce my wife in an attempt to get back at me? Why couldn't you have just faced me, brought a fucking gun with you and faced me like a man, eh? You shagged my wife, probably got her pregnant and then planned to screw me out of half a million, and you think that the fact I killed your parents in a car accident can possibly justify that? Well, you're sadly mistaken, son. I served my time for the accident! I paid my debt to society. Do you honestly think I just walked away from it unscathed? It has haunted me for years – *years!* I've lain awake at nights, tormenting myself over the decision I made that night. I couldn't have known that my car would skid on the wet road. I did everything I could to control it, but the road was just too slippery. All I could think of was getting to the hospital to be at my mother's side. My father could have died that night..."

Rob Marsden had heard enough. "Max, this fucker targeted you. He knew who you were and he set out to destroy you. He let you think that you were responsible for Jenna's death, mate"

"I know" Max spoke quietly now "And it ends here" Turning to face Tommy McLaughlin, or Thomas Siddall as he now knew he was, Max held the gun to the man's head and pulled the trigger. Thomas Siddall dropped to the floor, his legs shaking in an uncontrollable spasm, before he finally drew his last breath.

"Let's get him into Jenna's car, Rob. I'll give Crusher a bell, he can do the rest"

"What about Jenna" Rob asked.

"Yes, what about Jenna, eh, Rob? It's been a real eye-opener tonight, I can tell you! She can join her lover in the fucking crusher for all I care" and with that Max took out his mobile and, pulling the piece of paper from his jacket pocket, dialled Crusher Baines' number.

"Ready when you are, mate" he said quietly. "Ready when you are".

EPILOGUE

Max had felt no remorse as he'd watched the jaws of the baling press compress the Mercedes down until it could go no further. He had learned the terrible truth that night about his wife, about how she had cheated and lied, and he truly believed now that he was in no way responsible for her death.

Once it was done, he shook Crusher's meaty hand and promised him that someone would be calling round the next day with the five grand for the job. Crusher had assured Max that he was the soul of discretion and that the night's activities would be forgotten as soon as they closed the yard. Max knew he would be true to his word.

Rob telephoned Les Bryce and told him that a sports bag, containing just over nine hundred and fifty grand, had been found in the foot-well of Jenna's Mercedes. Les was overjoyed to know that he would be getting his cash back and had immediately telephoned his ex-wife and offered her the lot if he could have full custody of Ruby. Carol, upon hearing the amount involved, had readily agreed. Ruby Bryce never returned to Brighton.

Max had gone back to his apartment that night and told Eileen everything. At first, she had refused to believe it. She couldn't accept the things he was telling her about her daughter, but eventually – with Rob's help – Max managed to convince her that Jenna had, indeed, cooked up the whole thing and that she had been sleeping with Tommy McLaughlin for months behind his back. It had been a painful night for them all, and by the time dawn broke they were mentally and emotionally drained.

The following morning the three of them had sat, quietly contemplating the events of the night before, when Eileen suddenly broke the silence.

"I never told you about Jenna's real father, did I, Max?" she said. Her eyes were filled with tears now as she prepared to open up to her son-in-law for the first time about the terrible thing that had happened to her on that Easter Saturday night all those years ago.

"I thought you said he was lost at sea, Eileen" Max answered her, gently.

"No, love, he wasn't lost at sea. 'is name wasn't George Smedley either. That was just a name I conjured up out of thin air for Jenna's sake. I wanted 'er to think she 'ad been wanted, see? No, her real father was a bloke called Jimmy Wilson, and....." her voice broke now as she recalled the awful thing that Wilson had done to her.

Max leaned across and placed a hand on Eileen's arm. "Take your time, Eileen, it's alright" he said.

Rob saw this as his cue to leave. He had learned enough secrets about Max's family business over the past 24 hours. He felt it would be inappropriate for him to listen to any more. Beside which, he wanted to get back home and call Lucy – he had a very important question that he needed to ask her. He bade Max and Eileen goodbye and promised to call his friend later in the week, once they'd all had time to come to terms with things.

Max stood and shook the hand of his Manager and long-time friend. He had needed his support over the past four days more than he had ever thought possible, and Rob hadn't let him down. Max knew that Rob intended to propose to Lucy Adams, and he had decided to offer Rob a partnership in the club, as wedding gift to them both. He felt it was the least he could do after the way the man had come through for him.

Once Rob had left, Eileen took a few moments before continuing with her story.

"The truth is, Max, I was raped that night that my Jenna was conceived. 'e took me round the back o' the pub because I'd 'ad too much to drink. Probably buyin' me doubles, 'e was, only I was naïve and didn't realise. Anyway, the thing is....I didn't want 'im to, Max, I mean – I'd never...you know...been with a boy"

Max's heart went out to the broken woman who now sat in front of him, re-living the nightmare of her ordeal.

"Eileen, it wasn't your fault, love. You weren't to blame for what he did, you must know that"

"I never told no-one, about the baby I mean. 'id it from me family until I was due, I did. 'Course, once the baby came, me father wouldn't 'ave nowt to do with me afterwards - kicked me out, 'e did, there and then. God knows what I'd 'ave done if it 'adn't been for Mary Evans, God bless her. She took us both in and gave us an 'ome"

"And you've carried that secret with you all these years" Max looked at his mother-in-law now and he could see the years of anguish and worry etched on her face. She had suffered appallingly at the hands of Jenna's real father, and then had to suffer the shame of bringing a child into the world as an unmarried mother, to say nothing of losing her family through no fault of her own.

Eileen nodded, tears of shame and embarrassment streaming down her face. She knew that there had been something amiss with her daughter. That day in her house, when she had first discovered that Jenna was expecting, there had been something not quite right. Now, Eileen knew what that something was and it grieved her to know it.

Taking Max's hand in hers, Eileen looked into his blue eyes, the pain and heartbreak clear to see. She needed to tell him she was sorry, for all the wicked things that she had said on the night that Tommy had called. She had wished him dead, and now she wanted him to know that she was heart-sorry for it.

Sensing that she was carrying the burden of guilt, Max smiled at her and said "It's alright, Eileen, I know you didn't mean any of it, love. It was grief talking, that's all. I'd have probably said the same if I'd been in your shoes"

Eileen sniffed and said "The thing is, Max, she looked so much like 'im, Jimmy Wilson I mean. I could see it every time I looked at 'er. But I never thought she 'ad any real bad in 'er, not until now. Maybe she 'ad more of that bastard in 'er than either of us thought, eh? What's the old sayin' - blood will out?"

Max hugged Eileen tightly. "Tell you what, Eileen, why don't I go make us both a nice cup of tea, eh?" he offered.

"Aye, go on then, son, only....put a drop of whiskey in mine, will ya?"

Max winked at her "How about I put a couple of drops in, just to be going on with?"

Eileen Kelly smiled warmly at her son-in-law.

God was good. Hadn't she always said so?

ENJOYED THIS BOOK?

Please visit Amazon and leave a review.

Thank You

Printed in Poland
by Amazon Fulfillment
Poland Sp. z o.o., Wrocław